CALLING
of LIGHT

CALLING of LIGHT

Lori M. Lee

PAGE STREET YA

PAGE STREET YA

Copyright © 2024 Lori M. Lee

First published in 2024 by
Page Street Publishing Co.
27 Congress Street, Suite 1511
Salem, MA 01970
www.pagestreetpublishing.com

Distributed by Macmillan, sales in Canada by The Canadian Manda Group.

28   27   26   25   24   1   2   3   4   5

ISBN-13: 9781645676201
ISBN-10: 164567620X

Library of Congress Control Number: 2023942734

Cover and book design by Laura Benton for Page Street Publishing Co.
Cover illustration © Charlie Bowater

Printed and bound in the United States

For the ones who kept fighting.
And for the ones who couldn't.

ONE

The last time we climbed this rise, I was a prisoner and Prince Meilek was my captor. Now, he is to be king and I his Shadow. It's curious how much can change even as we tread the same paths again and again.

Sunlight dapples the forest path like golden cobbles. The path turns, and what had once been a prison unfurls below.

The Valley of Cranes has been split open. The shamanborn have smashed through the prison's enclosure. The heavy bars lie discarded in the debris, casualties of war. The guardhouse where I'd been imprisoned has been reduced to rubble, although I'm not certain when that occurred. In the past few months, the Valley has seen a prison revolt, a battle between the queen's soldiers and Prince Meilek's allies, and liberation after the queen's death.

It's been barely two months since Prince Meilek returned

to Vos Talwyn, and the prison is unrecognizable. The cabins where the shamanborn had slept, crammed onto cots nearly piled atop one another, are gone. All that remain are fragments of wooden beams, frayed blankets thick with dust, and the occasional shoe, its matching half lost. Earthwenders, waterwenders, and other shamanborn dig out the banks of the stream, which had once been a much larger riverbed.

Outside the former grounds of the prison, a small army of tents has been erected for soldiers and volunteers. Prince Meilek had left it to the shamanborn to decide what to do with the Valley. Most had chosen to abandon it and the memories that saturated the earth. Others volunteered to restore the river and the grounds, returning the Valley to what it had once been—a mountain refuge.

Now, with shamanborn bonding with familiars, months' worth of work had been completed in weeks. There's talk as well of a monument of some sort, something unobtrusive, and a small shrine to the Sisters, so that future visitors can leave offerings with their prayers.

But for too many, the Valley remains a haunted place. Like Spinner's End, it will house its memories like ghosts.

Since I returned, the Soulless has been worryingly absent from my dreams. As welcome as the reprieve was at first, it didn't take long for dread to settle in its place. His silence can't mean anything good, but the real problem is that I've no idea where he is.

Theyen, the reckless idiot, had opened a gate to Spinner's

End in an attempt to rescue those left behind. He had found only an abandoned ruin, empty of all life.

Even now, weeks later, the question of what happened to the servants and soldiers weighs on us all. I wasn't the only one who'd unwittingly left them there to die, but it still feels like my fault.

Regardless of guilt, the fact remains that the Soulless left Spinner's End. I don't know what that means in terms of his strength. Has he fully recovered? Was Ronin's home no longer a suitable place to hide? Or did he leave for other reasons? If not for my pledge to protect Prince Meilek until his coronation, I would be hunting him through the Empire right now, the price on my head be damned.

As it is, I have to settle for Prince Meilek sending spies in my place to search for him. Thus far, there hasn't been even a whisper of his whereabouts, and I'm not sure how much longer I can remain idle. With every passing day, waiting for him to surface grows harder and harder.

It is both a blessing and a frustration that there's plenty to distract me. I've had to divide my time these past weeks between consulting with the Sanctuary's Scholars about the Dead Wood and ensuring Prince Meilek's safety during his transition to power.

As we descend the path that would have once taken us to the prison gates, soldiers in Evewynian green gather to greet our party. They dust off their hands, brush sweaty hair off grimy foreheads, and smack self-consciously at their uniforms.

Beyond them, many of the shamanborn pause as well. Nearly all of them bow at our arrival.

Clattering behind us, flanked by four Blades, is a laden supply wagon. When we set out from Vos Talwyn with the supplies, it had struck me what a bizarre echo this was to how everything had begun. I'd abandoned a supply run with my fellow wyverns in order to chase an ambition that would upend everything I thought I wanted.

With as tight a leash as I can manage on my craft, I dismount my drake. Yandor shoves at my arm with his large head, thick tongue licking at my braid. Smiling, I poke at his snout, brush my braid over my shoulder, and reach into my saddlebag for a few strips of dried mango.

The soldiers set about emptying the wagon of its goods while the Blades accompany Prince Meilek into the sprawl of tents. He's already deep in conversation with the officits overseeing the Valley's restoration. My presence isn't strictly required, but being seen alongside the prince while he's visiting the former prison has been effective in cultivating goodwill with the shamanborn.

With everyone busy unloading the wagon, I guide Yandor away from the camp and past the remains of the guardhouse. The awareness of souls presses in around me, but I've grown used to it enough that I can ignore the clamoring of my craft, at least to some degree. My boots scrape over dry earth and loose pebbles as we near what might have once been a large shed. Several shamanborn are sifting through the broken boards, evidently trying to salvage whatever might have been stored there.

I leave Yandor to graze near the tree line, where the hard-packed dirt transitions to patchy grass and tufts of weeds, and then join the shamanborn. There are four, all dressed in plain gray tunics with moss green sashes. They pause in their work to stare, and I force my shoulders to relax as I smile in greeting.

"Hello," I say. "Can I join you?"

A woman with eyes like amethysts and short black hair tucked behind overly large ears beams at me. "Of course!"

The others return my smile, cautious but friendly. They've only been free a couple of months, and all of them still wear their time in the prison. Their eyes are tired, their shoulders narrow. As one of them tosses aside a broken board, I see that her fingers and knuckles are crossed with scars.

I flick a fingernail against the hem of my own clothes—dark-gray robes and pants, the sleeves and collar embroidered with green leaves and curling vines. Leather bracers cinch the sleeves at my wrists. My sash is a dark forest green, and the strap of my shoulder belt is snug across my chest, securing my swords at my back. My clothes are simple, sturdy, and functional, yet I am still uncomfortably aware of how starkly different my circumstances have been from theirs, merely because the truth of my magic had been kept secret.

When I reach down to peer beneath a shattered crate, a boy with gray eyes who can't be older than fifteen bows and murmurs, "Soulrender."

The windwender with large ears elbows him. "Her name is Sirscha. She's not some mythical beast."

"She might as well be," another mutters, and I almost laugh.

"They don't mean any disrespect," the fourth shaman, a waterwender, says. She wipes nervously at her hands, and her gaze flits over my shoulder, in the direction of the camp and Prince Meilek.

I shake my head. "Please, call me Sirscha." The last thing I want is to make them uncomfortable. "And what can I call you?"

"Bai," says the windwender eagerly. "I'm a brumys, and I can't wait to be able to use my craft again. It's been so long."

The gray-eyed boy opens his mouth, but someone cuts him off from behind me.

"Sirscha?"

The voice is familiar. Turning, I spot a sapphire-eyed shaman setting down a bucket full of vegetables, her face split into a grin.

As she rushes toward me, I straighten in surprise. "Kudera?"

"I thought it was you," she says, sounding breathless. For a moment, I think she's going to hug me, her body poised to spring forward. But she doesn't, instead gripping her hands at her waist and rocking on her heels.

The last time I saw her was in Vos Gillis. I'd ushered her and two other shamanborn onto a ship, bound for safer shores across the sea. Since then, she appears to have fared well. Her brown skin is warm and healthy, her hair is bound neatly at the nape of her neck, and she's dressed in blue robes. A streak of dirt stains her thigh, like she'd wiped her hand on her pant leg.

"What are you doing here?" I ask.

"News travels fast across the sea. When Morun and I heard that Prince Meilek would be succeeding the throne, we returned at once. We never ventured very far from the coast, in case any news came in about Evewyn." She gestures for me to continue what I was doing.

"What are they saying?" How has the story of what happened outside the Dead Wood been distorted beyond Evewyn's borders? Even within Evewyn, I've heard a dozen different versions passed around, usually behind my back but not always.

Together, we grab hold of either end of a large beam and move it from atop the pile of debris. We toss it onto the growing mound of wood meant for burning later.

"The courier claimed a powerful soulrender had murdered the queen, and Prince Meilek had taken her place," Kudera says. "It sounded a bit exaggerated, but everyone seemed to agree that Queen Meilyr was dead. So we came back to see for ourselves."

The others unearth large sacks of what must be rice. Hopefully, they can be salvaged. At the mention of the queen, they pause, casting me furtive glances. Many of the shamanborn volunteers are like Kudera—refugees who'd hidden in the Empire or across the sea, returning only now that the shamanborn are free.

"I never imagined that the part about the soulrender was

real or that it was you," Kudera continues, waving away a cloud of dust from her face. "But once I heard your name, I knew it had to be."

Although they don't speak, the other shamanborn are clearly keen to know how much of what they've heard is true. While I've kept certain details to only myself and Prince Meilek, I don't mind dispelling some of the more outrageous claims, like that I was a spy for the Soulless who was sent to assassinate the queen or that I'd tied her up and fed her to the Dead Wood. Not that she wouldn't have deserved it, but it does cast me in a rather bloodthirsty light.

Useful when it comes to Prince Meilek's enemies, but less so to his subjects, who are meant to trust me with their future king.

"I didn't murder the queen," I offer, although I might have if not for Prince Meilek. "She pursued me to the Dead Wood and got too close to the trees. It was an accident. Prince Meilek only ever wanted a peaceful transition of power."

"There would have been no version of peace with her," Bai says without meeting anyone's eyes. The others grunt in agreement.

Since it'd be unwise to say much more, I smile at Kudera and ask, "Where are Morun and Maiya?"

I help her haul a broken crate onto the woodpile for burning as she replies, "Morun is outside Vos Talwyn." Her smile falters. "Maiya chose not to return. I think she'd rather forget everything that happened here."

"It's no wonder," Bai says, bolder now that I hadn't objected to her remark about the queen. "Most everyone I knew before we were locked up here is either dead or missing, and the house I lived in was given to another family."

In the time since Queen Meilyr's death, many of the shamanborn who had been released from the Valley or had returned from abroad have reunited with their nonmagical kin. But just as many have no family or home to return to, everything they'd owned seized by the crown. Prince Meilek and his advisors spend a significant amount of time sorting through paperwork, trying to identify who had owned what. Thank the Sisters the queen's accountants had kept records.

The work has been immense and has taken a mental toll that Prince Meilek refuses to speak about, especially as he is still grieving his sister. But he does it without complaint, despite that I sometimes wish he would.

The gray-eyed boy mutters, "Serves the queen right. The Dead Wood was created by shamans, and we got her in the end." He casts a nervous glance at a few people passing by. They're not soldiers, just civilian volunteers, but they don't pay us any attention. They're busy hauling a pulley of some kind toward the heavy bars that had once enclosed the prison.

According to Prince Meilek, every person here is a volunteer, even the soldiers. He would have gladly assigned soldiers to the work, but luckily, that hadn't been necessary. The civilians are either those who lost shamanborn family or who sympathized when they were wrongly imprisoned.

I'm too cynical to not be wary of soldiers working alongside former prisoners, but so far, what conflicts have arisen have been peacefully resolved. That hasn't stopped me noticing the flash of hatred, though, in the eyes of some shamanborn when they're in the company of soldiers.

"The Dead Wood is just as much an enemy to us, idiot," Bai says, giving him a light shove.

"Anyway, a shamanborn now stands beside our future king," the waterwender says. "It's only fitting."

The others readily agree, including Kudera. Given that I *have* been seen at Prince Meilek's side more often recently, anything I say could be construed as the word of the future king. So I keep my thoughts to myself. It's enough that they're hopeful.

Shortly after his return to Vos Talwyn, Prince Meilek offered me the position of Shadow. At finally achieving what I'd sought for so many years, I'd felt . . . hollow. It had not been the triumph I once expected because I'd given up on that ambition. I wasn't even sure whether I ought to accept the offer.

But Prince Meilek insisted that I was the best person for the job, having been trained by the previous Shadow. In truth, I haven't thought about what sort of occupation I might pursue once all of this is over. Provided I survive. So I'd agreed on the condition that I could walk away from the post at any time.

Only to Saengo could I admit that, possibly, my acceptance might also have stemmed from guilt, even though the queen's death wasn't technically my fault. Prince Meilek had meant to challenge her for the throne or force her to abdicate with the support of the northern reiwyn lords and the Evewynian navy. He would have taken it by force if needed, but he'd never intended for her to die.

In truth, had she survived, she would have always been a threat to Prince Meilek's power. He knew that, of course, but it was a threat he'd been willing to endure if it meant keeping his only family left alive.

But she'd been murdered by the Dead Wood. Although her death benefitted Evewyn, although I wished her dead more than once, Prince Meilek mourns her. It pains me to see him hurt.

If being his Shadow can, in some small measure, make amends for my part in her death, then it's nothing I can't do. I didn't tell him this, though. He would have been offended that I agreed to be his spy out of guilt, even if only in part, and would have probably rescinded the offer.

Regardless of my reasons, for Evewyn's shamanborn, seeing one of their own—regardless of certain bloodthirsty rumors—in a position as high as the King's Shadow is a promise of healing and better days to come. I desperately hope they're right.

But the gnawing worry in my gut reminds me again of the Soulless. Not only that, but there's also the mounting tension among the kingdoms. War is coming, and these people have been touched enough by death and violence.

As Kudera makes a face at the discovery of rotting apples, her gaze lifts to mine and then to something to the left of me. Her eyes go wide before she scrambles to straighten out her clothing and brush off her hands. Then she drops into a bow. When the others begin mimicking her, I turn and find exactly who I expect.

Prince Meilek smiles as he approaches, trailed as always by his Blades, among them a man named Kou. He is one of Prince Meilek's closest friends and most loyal supporters. Prince Meilek holds the reins of his dragule in one gloved hand but releases them as he stops before me and nods to the shamanborn.

He's dressed plainly, in riding pants and a dark tunic. Green sashes circle his waist, the leather belt of his sword slung around his hips. A golden hair clasp ornaments his half knot, the lower half of his hair loose around his shoulders, windblown from spending all morning in a saddle. He looks at ease out here, far from a council room and his ever-present chattering advisors.

He once told me that he had no desire to be king. But then, I had no desire to be a soulrender, tasked with defeating one of the most dangerous shamans in Thiy's history. Sometimes, we don't get to decide where our paths are set down.

TWO

This is the first time Prince Meilek has returned to the Valley since delivering the orders to restore it. He hasn't exactly had the time. Strictly speaking, he still doesn't, but he'd needed to get away from the palace and spend a few hours in the open air.

"Your Highness," I say.

"I'm heading back," he says, and I suspect I'm one of only a few people who can hear his disappointment. But his advisors really will begin sending falcons if he doesn't return soon. "Will you be coming?"

With a glance at Kudera, who is still staring wide-eyed at the prince, I say, "I think I'll stay a bit. I won't be long."

Being surrounded by so many other shamanborn is somehow comforting. They've welcomed me in a way those in Vos Talwyn have not.

He smiles, his brown eyes warm. "Find me later. The stars will be visible tonight."

I bow and try not to laugh at the quiet gasps from the shamanborn. Prince Meilek wants to push the narrative that we are friends, not simply prince and servant. It's the truth, of course, but he hopes it'll help soften the people's view of soulrenders in general and me in particular.

I wave to Kou and the other Blades as Prince Meilek mounts. Once they've turned away, Kudera grips my shoulders and forcibly swings me around to face her. The other shamanborn are staring at me, and half of them are blushing.

"Did he just suggest that you go *stargazing* with him?" Kudera asks, voice hushed.

This has been a common misunderstanding. Pasting on an amused smile, I say, "It's not like that. We're only friends."

Three of them seem content with this response and return to their work. The gray-eyed boy makes a face when he finds a pair of rusty shackles.

Kudera and Bai, though, shuffle closer, eyes lit with curiosity.

"You do keep interesting company, Sirscha," Kudera says. "People are saying the most fascinating things about you."

I know. I've heard a number of them—I'm a seductress, I've ensorcelled Prince Meilek, I murdered Queen Meilyr, I'm the Soulless disguised, I crawled out from the depths of the Dead Wood, I'm a long-lost Yalaeng, and on and on, each growing in absurdity.

"Don't believe the gossip, especially if it's to do with me and Prince Meilek."

He is my prince and soon to be my king. After the role I played in his sister's death, that I can still call him a friend is nothing short of a miracle.

"So it's not true you're also close friends with a Kazan prince *and* the Phang heir?" she asks, eyebrows raised. Bai's eyes go, if possible, even wider.

It does sound peculiar when she puts it that way. Me, a girl of no means nor family, friends with royalty and reiwyn? Those like Saengo's parents would bristle at my insolence, daring to keep company so high above my station. But it was pure coincidence and perhaps a nudge from the Bright Twin that my path had crossed with theirs.

"Only friends," I repeat. Family even. But that's a truth still too new and precious to lay bare. Then, because she looks disappointed, I add, "I count you among them."

Kudera's warm skin flushes, and she wipes her dusty palm on her thigh, adding to the stain already there. I laugh, pointing it out.

"But truly," she continues, brushing ineffectually at the dirt. She only makes it worse. "It's not every person who can say they go stargazing with the prince."

I shrug one shoulder, but I don't explain. Prince Meilek and I do sometimes steal an hour to watch the stars from the palace's tallest tower, but only when Saengo isn't around to keep me company.

The reminder sends a pang between my ribs. I've been trying not to think about her absence. Currently, she's in the Nuvalyn Empire, the last place I want her to be. But my wants aren't a factor when it comes to her decisions.

That doesn't mean I'm not worried sick, though. She's only been gone a day, and while I know she's as safe as possible— she took Falcons Ridge soldiers as escorts, and a few humans in the Empire isn't unusual enough to be suspicious—it's little comfort. Theyen had assisted in getting her party to Luam. From there, she and her guards would have ventured northeast to the lonely peak known as the Spirit of the Mountain.

She hadn't explained why she needed to go. It was . . . peculiar. Not that I'm entitled to an explanation. Her decisions are her own, but still . . . I couldn't help feeling a little hurt.

The only reason she'd been willing to give was that the Mountain had been calling to her from the first moment she'd set eyes on it and she could no longer ignore the lure. Of course, I'd warned her that lures often led to traps, but she'd been adamant it had nothing to do with House Yalaeng.

The entire thing left an uncomfortable knot in my chest that wasn't worry alone. The discomfort pushed at the back of my throat, tasting a little too much like fear. Specifically, that flavor of fear I've come to associate with the Soulless and the ugly seed of a thought he'd tended in my mind.

"Maybe not today, maybe not tomorrow, maybe not even a year from now, but someday, she will leave you.

"Make no mistake, Sirscha. Your friend's love will turn to hate."

Saengo has spent much of the last few weeks with her father. She'd made him a promise. If Prince Meilek sat on the throne, then she would return to him as the heir of Falcons Ridge. While it isn't the path she wanted for herself, I know she'll take to it as naturally as she wields a bow. She was born to lead. She's loyal, brave, and shines far too brightly. She isn't meant for shadows, not like me.

I shove down those dark thoughts. Saengo will be back soon, if for no other reason than to tend to her rot.

For the next two hours, Kudera and I steadily increase the pile for burning while the other shamanborn heave rice sacks and other salvageable items onto a cart. Then I reluctantly say my goodbyes and track down Yandor. I find him not far into the trees, digging up roots and worms with the massive claws on his hind feet.

"You're a menace," I tell him fondly before grasping his reins and tugging him away from the mess.

As much as I'd like to spend the rest of my day here, I'm needed in Vos Talwyn, and I'd told Prince Meilek that I wouldn't be long. While his Blades are more than capable of protecting him, I'd still like to catch up before they reach the capital.

For over a week now, a steady stream of foreign dignitaries, representatives, and reiwyn have been arriving in Vos Talwyn for Prince Meilek's coronation in two days. Planning a parade, coronation dinner, and ball and housing so many guests with barely two months to prepare has left the palace in a state of constant frenzied activity. Fortunately, Prince Meilek's staff have been intimidatingly competent.

For the sake of diplomacy, House Yalaeng was also sent an invitation. To my surprise, they accepted. They're sending the Emperor's fifth cousin twice removed or some such nonsense. For the coronation of a king, it's customary for a direct member of the imperial family to attend, such as the Sun's Heir, one of his siblings, or even the Emperor himself. Anything less would be an insult.

For Queen Meilyr's coronation, the former Ember Princess had attended, but her entourage had almost been stopped at the northern border. The Queen had fought with her advisors about allowing foreign shamans into the kingdom. She'd relented only because insulting a country as vast and powerful as the Nuvalyn Empire would've been a poor way to begin her reign.

Given current circumstances, the fact that House Yalaeng is sending anyone at all might be considered encouraging. They know I'm under Prince Meilek's protection, seeing that I'm still wanted in the Empire.

But it's for that same reason that I'm wary. Like the Soulless, the Empire has been worryingly quiet. A part of me has spent the last several weeks in anticipation of . . . I don't even know what. *Something* that will disturb the veneer of calm, the inevitable rock flung into a still pond.

But it's the waiting, the breath held against the unknown, that's maddening.

Traveling swiftly, Yandor and I spot the spires of the Grand Palace within hours, their gold and jade finials stretching for the clouds. Not long after that, the marble domes of the Sanctuary of the Sisters and each of their statues peer over the city walls. When I was in the Queen's Company—soon to be the king's once Prince Meilek is crowned—a supply delivery to the Valley would have taken two days. First years usually accompanied those deliveries, and they always made the trek on foot.

The city gates become visible soon after. With the queen gone, I can come and go as I please, the same as any Evewynian.

I'm home, I tell myself, as I've been telling myself every time I pass through those gates.

However, Prince Meilek wouldn't have returned to the palace yet, so I tug Yandor off the main road and head east of the city walls.

Prince Meilek set up a temporary community there for shamanborn who haven't yet been returned to their homes. Most of them have taken up residence in tents or portable huts of wood and thatch. Many of Ronin's former soldiers from Sab Hlee are here as well, shaman and shadowblessed alike.

At the outskirts of the community, which the inhabitants have taken to calling Little Talwyn, soldiers in the midst of erecting new tents pause in their work to watch me pass. They neither bow nor call out in greeting. They don't otherwise acknowledge me at all.

But while their gazes follow me, their heads are slightly averted as if afraid to catch my eye. One of them I'm surprised to recognize from my time in the Company—a girl with a thick black braid still adorned with the feathers exclusive to fourth-year wyverns. We hadn't been friends, but she used to laugh when I bested Jonyah in the sparring circle. Now, she frowns at the sight of me, wary.

Thinking only of Prince Meilek, I nod at them and continue on. I never wanted to be a soldier. I only entered the Queen's Company because Kendara had made it a condition of her training—to prove my resolve and what I would endure to win a place at her side. Having Saengo with me had made it bearable, although she hadn't wanted a soldier's life, either. Joining the Royal Army was simply the easiest way to evade the responsibilities her father had been eager to hand her.

Farther into Little Talwyn, shamanborn gather around cooking pots or haul carts of firewood or pails of water, the moving parts of the small but bustling community. Humans from the city rush about as well, helping to wash and hang clothes or handing out rations. While many in Evewyn have welcomed back their shamanborn neighbors, just as many still distrust them, having accepted Queen Meilyr's prejudices. It will be difficult to undo eight years of propaganda, and I don't envy Prince Meilek the challenges ahead.

"Cursed," someone mumbles at my back, the word an accusation, their voice ugly and cutting. I jerk my chin up higher.

Everyone knows what I am. But while the people love

Prince Meilek—or perhaps *because* they love Prince Meilek—most of the human population distrust me. Although the shamanborn see hope in my presence beside our prince, the humans see a threat. They see the person responsible for one Evewynian monarch's death and wonder if I might not cause another.

I've heard the talk. The fearful whispers. They believe I've deceived the prince, that I am not fit to protect him, that I am the greatest threat to their kingdom.

For Prince Meilek's sake and for my own, I catalog their grievances in my head, take note of whose words might be ignorance and whose might be dangerous, and ignore all the rest. I will not entertain their fears. I am Evewynian. This is my home, and I will not be made to feel like an intruder.

I spot Prince Meilek and his Blades between two narrow huts. He's astride his dragule, his party passing leisurely through Little Talwyn. Two additional Blades have joined them. I quietly approve.

This transition period is vitally important, and amidst the reiwyn's promises of fealty, there've also been rumblings of discontent. Queen Meilyr had been an unpopular ruler, but that doesn't mean none of the reiwyn supported her or shared her prejudices. And now, with foreign visitors arriving daily, keeping Prince Meilek safe has been his council's primary goal.

The Blade at the rear of his procession sees me first. She lifts one hand in greeting, alerting the others to my arrival.

Prince Meilek nods as I take position behind him. Soon enough, we pass through Little Talwyn, following the wall until we reach a narrow lane that leads to a private gate for the exclusive use of the two Companies. From there, we pass first the Queen's Company and then the Prince's before arriving on palace grounds.

When we reach the front courtyard, servants are unloading trunks from yet another arrival. This one, however, has me stiffening in my saddle.

A sun with eight golden rays is emblazoned against the door of a white carriage pulled by two pearl-scaled dragokin. Each dragokin boasts four ivory horns painted with golden whorls. Two men stand beside the carriage, one of them speaking briskly to the servants and the other with gloved hands clasped at his back, glowering up at the palace. He wears robes of pale yellow and white, his sash embroidered with golden suns.

I nudge Yandor ahead so that I ride even with Prince Meilek. A moment later, the man speaking to the servants notices our arrival. He's dressed plainly in Yalaeng colors, so he's likely a servant as well. He says something to the Yalaeng representative, who abruptly turns, his scowl easing into something less hostile.

As we reach the bottom of the broad stairs leading into the palace, more servants appear to greet us. One of them takes the reins from Prince Meilek as he dismounts. The Yalaeng representative drops into a bow even before Prince Meilek faces him.

"Your Highness," the man says. "My name is Lord Ge Yalaeng, and I am here on behalf of His Imperial Majesty Emperor Cedral, who sends his deepest regards."

I'll bet he does, I think sourly. I rub Yandor's nose before handing him off to a servant. Lord Ge's gaze flicks to me, his eyebrows twitching, before he returns his attention to Prince Meilek.

The man appears to be in his thirties, his hair not yet gray and his eyes the clear amethyst of a windwender. He's tall and lean beneath his robes, which are slightly wrinkled from hours seated inside a carriage. A spiraling clasp holds his long hair in a low ponytail. His servant hovers at his back, surveying everything with faint disdain.

"It's a pleasure to meet you, Lord Ge," Prince Meilek says as he tugs off his riding gloves. "I hope your journey wasn't too taxing?"

Lord Ge's smile is anything but kind. "Not at all. I've always wanted to see Evewyn's mountains, but the opportunity never presented itself, what with your sister's . . . views."

To his credit, Prince Meilek didn't react other than with a warm, "Then I hope our mountains don't disappoint. Do enjoy your stay in Vos Talwyn. If you need anything, my servants will be happy to provide."

With that, he strides past Lord Ge, whose mouth flaps, startled by the abrupt dismissal. Ignoring him, I follow Prince Meilek up the wide stone steps.

Recovering quickly, the man rushes to catch up to us,

looking harried. "Your Highness, there are pressing matters I'd like to—"

"Certainly, we will discuss whatever you wish after the ceremony," Prince Meilek says, his smile never wavering. "I've much to attend to beforehand. I'm sure you understand."

Lord Ge falters and then, tight-lipped, stops trying to match Prince Meilek's long strides and bows stiffly. I exchange a look with Kou. The King's Guard and I have an understanding: We've known from the moment House Yalaeng accepted the invitation that their representatives would need to be closely observed within Evewyn.

"He's going to be sore about that dismissal," I say under my breath. I can't quite stifle my smile, though, and not for the first time, I'm grateful it isn't my job to counsel Prince Meilek on maintaining good relations with his neighbors. That's for his advisors.

"Let him be," Prince Meilek says. His hand lifts, fingers brushing the back of his head before he catches himself and stills, a flash of discomfort tightening his jaw. He's not used to being cooped up in the castle for long periods of time, and even as a prince, he never dressed in the kind of opulence his sister favored.

"Are you all right?" I ask.

He looks slightly abashed. "I'm putting off ruining what's left of our relationship with the Empire until after the coronation. Is that selfish?"

"Are you so certain a talk will make things worse?" I ask.

He lifts one eyebrow. Aside from the fact that he made a wanted soulrender his Shadow, as Evewyn's leader, he must still answer for his sister's crimes against the other kingdoms. Whatever the Empire asks of Evewyn will likely not be within reason.

"It isn't selfish," I say. "They are set on conflict, but it's a conflict that can wait until after you're crowned."

Guards push open a set of sturdy oak doors, and we pass into a private corridor, leaving behind the bustle of the servants and guests. Two Blades break off to guard the corridor. Only once the doors shut behind us does Prince Meilek release a quiet sigh, rubbing the spot between his eyebrows.

"What is it?" I ask. His Blades fan out through the private wing, doing their usual sweep of the rooms and windows.

Prince Meilek drops onto a green settee, its wooden feet carved into curling leaves. "Some among the reiwyn don't believe I am fit to be king. Frankly, I don't disagree with them."

"Prince Meilek—" I begin.

"But I must make right my sister's crimes against our people. I have to restore their faith in Evewyn's leaders. To do that, I cannot give the reiwyn a reason to stand against me. If I enflame tensions with the Empire before I'm even crowned, they will embrace the excuse to organize. I must ensure the coronation proceeds as planned before I make any decisions regarding Evewyn's future peace."

While his words only deepen the sense of foreboding that shadows my steps, I smile fondly. "You don't have to explain making a pretentious Nuvali royal wait a couple days to voice his emperor's demands."

He releases a small laugh. He hasn't laughed much lately, and judging by the way Kou turns in his direction, I'm not the only person who has missed it.

THREE

As the King's Shadow, I take up residence in Kendara's old tower. Every time I walk inside, I'm struck anew by the strangeness.

All of the weapons she'd mounted on her wall, the books crammed onto her shelves, and the miscellaneous keepsakes stuffed into the backs of cabinets were stripped from the tower when Kendara abandoned Queen Meilyr. However, her belongings hadn't been destroyed, only shoved into a cellar. Prince Meilek had allowed me the decision of what to do with them.

So I had her things returned to her former rooms. They currently sit in disorganized piles and crates all around the tower. Swords, daggers, and even an axe are propped against the walls or heaped on shelves. Books are stacked across two tables, and two boxes overflowing with everything else are shoved into a corner. I haven't yet had the time, nor the heart, to sort through it all.

The first thing I did upon moving in was remove the half dozen locks on the door. A single one would do for me. In truth, a single one would have sufficed as well for Kendara, who is impossible to take unawares, but the excess had only been for emphasis. She *really* did not enjoy being disturbed without reason.

The second thing I did was walk through each of the rooms I'd never been allowed in before. There aren't many. There's a separate bedroom, with sheets and blankets I deposit outside my door every few days in exchange for fresh ones. No one is allowed within the tower without my permission.

A window sits high on one wall, too high to provide any sort of view, but not too high for a trained Shadow to use as an escape should the occasion ever arise. A wardrobe stands beneath it, along with a small writing desk. The only other room is the washroom.

I've only lived here a little over a month, and seeing as I don't possess many belongings other than my clothes, the tower doesn't bear much of my mark yet. Everything I once owned was seized by Queen Meilyr when I awakened my craft, and since Prince Meilek hasn't been able to uncover what happened to my things, I can only assume they were destroyed.

I was a little heartsick at the thought of how easily all trace of my existence could be erased. But then Saengo had taken my hand, and I'd been reminded that it isn't our belongings that hold the memory of us—it is the people we love.

In any case, although the tower isn't especially large, it still seems strange to have so much space to myself. For as long as I can remember, the sum of my belongings have always fit within a single trunk. I wouldn't know what to do if I had an entire house.

Sisters willing, I might even live long enough to decide if I want a house or not.

Prince Meilek had ensured I was fully furnished with a new wardrobe—practical clothing only, I'd insisted—along with new weapons and full access to nearly every part of the palace. It's still a bit surreal. By rights, I should have had Kendara here to guide me, to soften the transition. But that's a bruise best left alone.

I wash quickly and then change out of my travel-worn clothes into dark pants and an embroidered tunic, forgoing a sash for now. I'm at the balcony, pulling a comb through my hair and watching the rush of carriages, pedestrians, and drakes on the city streets far below when a series of knocks sound at my door.

"Come in," I call.

I'd sensed his soul minutes ago as he was climbing the stairs to the tower. Servants don't come up here unless I call for them, and Prince Meilek summons me via falcon, so only guests arrive unannounced. Even had I not recognized his soul, my tower has seen no more than two guests aside from the prince, and since Saengo is away, it can only be Theyen.

Theyen closes the door behind him, his gaze quickly finding me at the balcony. As ever, he looks immaculate. A circlet of braided silver rests against his snowy hair, and he's dressed in a turquoise tunic with white accents at the cuffs and collar. A broad silver sash cinches his waist along with a metal belt inlaid with pale blue stones.

"Did you just arrive?" I ask. Aside from taking Saengo to Luam, I've barely seen him these past weeks. There's been too much to do with the Nuvali at the Kazan border, attacking anyone without a travel permit and deliberately provoking shadowblessed scouts to determine which of the border clans are the weakest.

"Yes. Prince Meilek asks if you'll be present for dinner."

I sigh, shaking out my hair, which is now mostly dry. "For the first time in my life, I'm invited to royal dinners, and I can't even wear pretty gowns."

"No one's stopping you from putting on a gown," he says with only a slight roll of his eyes. He leans one hip against the threshold to the balcony, his arms crossed. Even though he remains just shy of standing in direct sunlight, he still squints a little as he gazes skyward.

His eyes, which are bright blue rimmed in lavender, sometimes glimmer strangely when they catch the sun. Presumably something to do with how most shadowblessed prefer to live underground.

"Don't encourage me," I say, setting the comb on the stone rail of the balcony. If necessary, I could fight in flowing robes and slippers, but why chance losing the advantage of closer fitting, more practical clothing?

Still, I'm tempted. Prince Meilek *had* offered to send me to a dressmaker any time I wanted. And who says I can't have practical clothing that isn't also pretty?

"You don't need my help with making poor decisions."

I direct an unamused look in his direction. "And yet you still go along with them, so what does that say about you?"

Theyen replies in a perfect monotone. "That I am a bleeding heart, willing to sacrifice my well-being for the whims of my foolish friends."

I throw my head back and laugh, harder and longer than is warranted, just to press my point. Theyen lifts one white eyebrow and straightens off the wall.

"If you don't stop behaving like you left all your sense in the Dead Wood, we'll never make it to dinner. And I hear they're serving layered tapioca cakes."

"Why didn't you say so from the start?" I hurriedly braid my hair. My fingers move through the motions as I step past Theyen to check my reflection in the mirror above the mantel.

"It's crooked," he points out.

"Saengo usually does this for me."

"You're going to embarrass your prince in front of half the continent because you can't braid your own hair."

"I'm a soulrender and a wanted criminal in the Empire. No one is going to care that my braid is a little crooked."

"It's for those reasons that you need to present the best

possible version of yourself. Would you have them think Prince Meilek a fool for putting his trust in you?" He makes an exasperated sound before saying, "Here."

I stiffen, tamping down the reflexive impulse to elbow him in the face when his fingers brush the nape of my neck. He swats away my own hands and then quickly unravels my hair.

Bemused, I watch through the mirror as he separates the long black strands into three equal parts. His deft fingers work quickly and neatly. His expression is closed, his pale lashes lowered.

"How did you learn to braid hair?" I ask.

"My hair wasn't always short. Besides, I have two older sisters."

I assumed Theyen had siblings, given he was to marry into House Yalaeng, but I'd never asked. We've never had much opportunity to simply . . . talk. It's foreign territory, and I'm not sure how to proceed, so I say nothing.

Instead, I hand him a leather string, and he skillfully knots off the braid. When his hands fall away, I pull the tightly woven length over my shoulder. It's as impeccable as any time Saengo has done this for me.

"Thank you," I say, and if my smile in the mirror looks a little confused, neither of us acknowledge it.

Theyen gives me a flat look and says, "Cake."

I beam at the reminder. He waits by the door as I put on my sash. It's a simple green length of cloth, with swirling embroidery in a lighter shade. I wrap it around my waist, over the long black tunic with billowing sleeves. Tying the ends hastily at my back, I locate my dual swords and shoulder belt on a table next to a stack of books. It might be a little much for dinner, so I opt for a single sword instead, which I buckle just beneath the sash.

"If you're quite finished," Theyen says.

I smile sweetly as I pass him and step out into the hallway. "Please, you probably took twice as long to pick out your belt."

He doesn't argue my point as I lock the door. He does look far too amused, though, so I elbow him on our way down the stairs.

In the great hall, tables stretch down either side of an aisle leading to the head table. Green and silver banners hang from the ceiling, and the walls are dressed in vibrant tapestries depicting Evewynian kings and queens of old. Stone columns carved into the likeness of trees run the length of the room.

Nearly every seat is already occupied. Servants fill the plates of guests or set out heaping platters of fresh fruit and sliced meats swimming in savory juices. I spot Saengo's father, Lord Phang, and immediately avert my face before our gazes can connect and we're trapped in the awkward dance of whether to acknowledge one another. We've never gotten along—even now the veneer of civility is thin at best—and there's little doubt that he is among those who feel I've no right to climb above my station.

But as Shadow, I now claim one of the highest positions in the kingdom, and not greeting me would be a slight to the prince. House Phang is one of the oldest families on the continent, dating back to when the northern half of the kingdom was not yet a part of Evewyn, and Lord Phang was crucial in helping Prince Meilek stop the queen from massacring the shamanborn at the Valley of Cranes. My not greeting him would also be a slight.

So really, it's best to simply avoid the awkwardness and pretend we didn't see each other.

I usually attend these dinners with Saengo. As she is reiwyn, she always takes the lead in terms of etiquette, and I'm happy to follow her example. But with Saengo preparing to take her place at Falcons Ridge, I suppose I should get used to being alone. I resolutely ignore the bitter flavor trying to climb up my throat.

"When . . . when do you expect to retrieve Saengo?" I ask Theyen.

"In a couple days at most, but I'll check on her later this evening if I've the time. Are you worried already? It's barely been more than a day."

"I know, I know. It's just . . . the rot hasn't been as responsive to my treatments lately. Ever since the queen's death, it's as if . . . This will sound absurd."

"You always sound absurd," Theyen says easily. "Might as well keep at it."

With a reluctant smile, I say, "It's as if the rot is fighting back. Against me. Specifically." I wince at how that sounds. "Like . . . it contains the will of the Soulless."

Instead of laughing at me, Theyen is silent a moment before saying, "It could be possible."

"What do you mean?"

"If we think of the rot as an extension of the Soulless's tainted magic, then wouldn't that mean a part of him lies within every infected familiar?"

It makes sense, and my stomach sinks further. The impatience nudging at my heels, the urge to do more than run around a palace while the Soulless roams free, grows stronger.

Prince Meilek catches my eye, and I smooth away the concern from my expression. He is seated at the center of the head table, two Blades stationed at either end. I nod to him, and he returns the gesture with a small smile.

"So it's true," a voice says from behind me.

Theyen and I pause as we near our table. The voice belongs to the Yalaeng diplomat, Lord Ge.

He cocks his head, and the look he gives me could be either curiosity or criticism. I'm betting it's the latter. One bejeweled hand rests on the hilt of his sword. He wears a hair ornament at his temple in the shape of a small sun. Those Yalaengs do love their sun imagery.

"You *are* the King's Shadow," he continues before his lips settle into a slight purse.

"Lord Ge," I say. It doesn't surprise me that news of my appointment has spread to the Empire.

If I wasn't Shadow, I might ask him how the Emperor is doing and whether they've spotted the Soulless in Mirrim yet.

Instead, I smile serenely and gesture to Theyen before making quick introductions. The man looks surprised and is a little too slow to hide his disgust. He isn't as practiced in diplomacy as his more prominent Yalaeng relatives.

"Ah, yes," he says, fussing at the sleeves of his robes. "You were recently engaged to . . . yes. Well. I'd heard that the Fireborn Queens had formed an understanding with Evewyn."

The way his eyes pass over the great hall isn't flattering. Is he implying the Fireborn Queens gave up an alliance with the Empire for a much smaller kingdom? He would be wrong. Theyen had wanted to end his engagement regardless, but not at the cost of inciting the Empire. With Queen Meilyr, the Soulless, and my masquerade as a soulguide, things had fallen apart without any assistance from the Fireborn Queens.

"I hope you enjoy your stay," I say mildly. "The palace staff has prepared traditional Evewynian fare for the evening. Do let us know if it's to your taste."

I nod curtly and turn on my heel. The man hadn't bothered to greet me properly, so I don't feel bad about my rudeness. Fortunately, my curtness will be blamed on my upbringing—he has no such excuse.

"They sent someone who's barely a Yalaeng to represent the Empire," Theyen says as we find our seats.

"It's an insult," I agree, "but that they sent someone at all is something." Even if that "something" is only to deliver the Emperor's demands. Or to act as a spy. Either way, it's insight into the Empire's motives.

Without being obvious, I watch the unpleasant man settle at another table, beside a shadowblessed woman dressed in scarlet robes. I'm not familiar with the clan symbol hanging on a pendant from her neck, but she isn't an ally of Theyen's if the way her eyes narrow in our direction is any indication.

I nod in thanks to a servant who sets a small bowl of white rice before me alongside a variety of other dishes, such as tender bamboo shoots, seared bitter melon, and roasted peppers. The servant bobs her head with a bright smile. The air within the palace these past months has been unusually festive despite that Evewyn is still technically in mourning.

Traditionally, after the death of a monarch, the next in line would wait a requisite six months for mourning and preparations. However, given Evewyn's tenuous position with the Empire and the recent conflicts with the shamanborn in the Valley of Cranes, even Prince Meilek's advisors agreed it best not to tarry overlong without a leader on the throne.

He was always the favored sibling among the people, human and shamanborn alike. There's a measure of satisfaction in knowing that should his enemies attempt to usurp him, they would face no small task in earning the people's favor.

"This is the coronation of a king," Theyen continues as he selects a few pickled vegetables and a thick slice of roast, glistening in a brown sauce. "There has been no formal declaration of war, and the conflicts between your countries have been due to his sister, who is now gone. Any animosity should be set aside for the occasion. A direct member of House Yalaeng would have been perfectly safe here."

"Well, that's stupid," I mutter. "Specific times and places they're not supposed to kill each other?"

"It's called diplomacy," he says wryly.

"It's called accepting an invitation to your execution. Not," I add quickly, "that Prince Meilek would have broken that understanding. The Emperor himself would have been safe here, at least from Evewynians, but not everyone plays by the same rules."

I don't fault House Yalaeng for not sending a more prominent member. Although Prince Meilek had safely traveled the Empire a few months ago, that was under different circumstances. That was when he'd been an ally to their supposed soulguide.

Now, he's protecting a soulrender who'd tricked her way into the heart of the Nuvalyn Empire to gain information about the Soulless. To defeat him, yes, but the truth is whatever they say it is.

Theyen makes a small sound of agreement. "All of our systems would fall apart if nobody cared about the rules, arbitrary as they may sometimes seem," he says, although I'm not sure if he thinks this is a good or bad thing.

Lord Ge turns away from the shadowblessed woman to speak with a reiwyn lord at his other side. Eyes narrowed, I murmur to Theyen, "His retinue is surprisingly small for the occasion. I don't suppose you know anything about this Ge Yalaeng?"

Theyen is one of the most well-informed people I've ever met, aside from Kendara. As a shadow gate, he can travel enormous distances in an instant, and although he's never said as much, I suspect he's placed spies all over the continent. I wouldn't be surprised if his duties as a prince of the Fireborn Queens aren't so different from those of a Shadow.

"Very little," he says, which is surprising. Something of the feeling must show on my face, because he clarifies. "As far as politics go, he's insignificant. Perhaps that's why he was chosen, but I haven't been able to confirm anything with Mirrim under lockdown."

"Lockdown?" I echo softly.

"The Emperor is having the entire city searched. Any lightwender who wishes to enter the capital is being stopped and forced to verify their craft. Everyone else is required to provide proof of their need to travel. It's been difficult getting any news in or out of the city."

I consider all this as I shovel rice into my mouth and then wash it down with a tart plum wine. They're taking every precaution against the Soulless getting near the Emperor. It's no wonder they didn't send a direct member of the imperial family. The palace is likely the safest place for them. And unless someone's been holding onto a portrait of him for the last seven centuries, no one knows what the Soulless looks like except me.

At least everyone now knows he's alive. While recovering at Sab Hlee, even before sharing the news of his sister's death,

Prince Meilek sent falcons across the continent to alert Thiy's leaders of the Soulless's return. He hadn't mentioned the Empire's role in keeping his existence at Spinner's End a secret, only that Ronin had deceived them all and paid for it with his life.

While the purpose had been to avoid retaliation from the Empire, I still bristled at allowing House Yalaeng to escape the consequences of their lies. But for now, to face this threat, the kingdoms would need to set aside their grievances and work together.

Naturally, there are many who don't believe the claims, but enough do that the prince's contacts in Luam report pockets of unrest across the Empire.

There's little doubt that House Yalaeng fears the Soulless—they would be stupid not to—but they'd known about his return for some time and had done nothing. Well, aside from burdening me with defeating him. Acting on those fears would have made them look weak or tipped off their enemies that something was awry.

But then why take all these precautions now? Even if locking down the capital was a smart move, they risked looking like cowards, hiding within their golden halls. The Soulless was only one shaman after all.

"Why do you think he left Spinner's End?" Theyen asks. His hand rests on the table beside his bowl, fingers tapping lightly against the polished wood. He doesn't seem to have much of an appetite despite our earlier teasing about cake.

I shake my head. "I've some guesses, but I suppose now that everyone's aware he's alive, he wants to remain ahead of any plots." Especially if he's regained enough of his strength to travel. My window of opportunity to defeat him while he was still recovering has passed.

"But no one can reach him there," Theyen says.

"He's the Soulless. He isn't worried about his enemies reaching him." I take another sip of wine and suppress a grimace.

I don't drink if I can help it. I dislike any loss of control over my mind or body, but a sip or two does help to settle my nerves.

"Fair enough," Theyen says. "So then he'll be targeting House Yalaeng."

"Yes," I agree. "He'll make his move before they can truly go to ground. Without Queen Meilyr creating a distraction, he'll likely travel alone to avoid attention. He'll slip into Mirrim and take out the Emperor quietly."

Theyen turns to face me, eyes sharp. "Why are you so certain of this?"

I shrug one shoulder. "Because that's what I would do."

FOUR

That evening, well after dinner when the palace has gone quiet and the lights have been dimmed, I find Prince Meilek in the Grand Palace's tallest tower.

The top of the tower is open to the skies, a wall with wide crenellations enclosing the circular, flat space. It's meant to be a watchtower, but it also provides a breathtaking view of Vos Talwyn and Needle Bay. When I find the prince, he is seated on a plain wooden bench, his head tilted back to watch the stars. A torch bracket above the winding staircase provides the only source of light, but it's enough to accentuate the tired planes of his face.

His arms rest on the edge of a crenellation, fingers lightly laced. He doesn't look like a man about to be made king. But then, this isn't how he wanted to take the throne. I settle onto the bench at his side and look up as well.

The night is clear, countless pinpricks of light spilled across the dark. A quarter moon sits like the crown jewel on a bed of gems.

When the silence stretches on, I ask, "Are you all right?"

He takes his time replying, which I hope means he's genuinely considering the question. When he finally speaks, his voice is subdued. It's not the voice he uses in public, surrounded by subjects, servants, and advisors.

"Is it foolish of me to miss her? I shouldn't, I know. She hurt . . . *killed* so many people. Broke apart families." He releases a single breath like a humorless laugh. "Our own included."

"Even kings are only human," I say. In any other context, such words would sound like a threat. "You can't help the way you feel." It's how one reacts to their feelings that matters. Queen Meilyr had used her grief at her parents' deaths to punish the shamanborn, and it's uncertain whether the kingdom will ever recover from that.

Again, he doesn't respond for a long while. The silence isn't uncomfortable, and I'm constantly bewildered that he allows himself to be vulnerable in front of me. Very few people hold that honor.

"Maybe it's not her I miss," he says. "Just the person she used to be. I've been mourning her for years now. I ought to be used to it. Does that make me a terrible brother?"

"I'm sorry," I say. It's not Queen Meilyr's death I'm apologizing for. In truth, I'm glad she's gone. I would never say so to

Prince Meilek, but he knows it well enough on his own. His sister was a tyrant. Evewyn is better off without her.

Even so, I'm still sorry he lost the only family left to him. I know what it is to be without anyone to call your own, someone bound by blood and bonds rather than obligation.

"But you're not alone," I continue. "You helped me to see that when I'd always believed I only had myself to rely on. I hope you'll allow yourself the same grace."

He smiles then, and it's like the stars shine a little brighter. "I should make you an advisor instead of Shadow."

"Please don't," I say at once, and he laughs.

We remain there for a time, neither of us speaking, the moon and stars ample company. After a while, footsteps echo up from the stairwell, disturbing the quiet.

We both turn. Theyen steps onto the landing. When he sees us, he stills, his expression unreadable in the torchlight. For long seconds, he says nothing.

I lift one eyebrow. "Care for a bit of stargazing or are you planning to lurk on the stairs?"

The question draws him back into movement. Wordlessly, he joins us on the bench. I shift closer to Prince Meilek so that Theyen can sit at my other side, but it's a tight fit. I almost laugh at the sight we must make, especially if Saengo were here as well, and then suddenly, I'm missing her so dearly that my breath catches.

Aside from the requirements of our shaman-and-familiar bond, I know Saengo can't stay with me for much longer.

Since our return to Vos Talwyn, I've been prodding at the notion, hoping every time that it will hurt less. But ultimately, my feelings don't matter. I can't allow Saengo to feel guilty for wanting to take her own path, even if that path leads away from me and the shackles I placed on her.

"You two do this often?" Theyen asks. His gaze sweeps first over the city spread out below, at the spots of light from distant windows and streetlamps and then up at the sky.

"Only recently," I say.

"Only when needed," Prince Meilek adds. He sighs and briefly closes his eyes, the torchlight at our backs gilding the edges of his hair. Then he pushes to his feet, his hands smoothing down his clothes. "I suppose I should return to my rooms before my Blades grow restless. They're taking my safety before the coronation very seriously."

"As they should," I say.

He smiles. "I'm perfectly safe. I'm with you."

My lips press together as I dip my head in a bow. The sound of his retreating steps lingers in the still night. His words should warm me. Instead, they terrify me.

How can I be trusted with the life of my future king when I couldn't even keep Saengo safe? When I couldn't protect Phaut? But the emotion is fleeting before I take control of my thoughts. I'm not a child, shying away from shadowy corners. I was trained to be a Shadow, and I rather like the dark. If it came to it, I would die for Prince Meilek—not necessarily because he is my prince and the future of our kingdom, but because he is my friend.

Whatever disruption might be coming, in whatever form it might take, I must be ready.

I tilt my head to look at Theyen. He's in the same clothes he wore to dinner, but he's removed the jeweled belt. "So what brings you all the way up here?"

"No reason," he says. He leans his palms flat against the stone and tips his head back to expose the long line of his neck. "You and Prince Meilek are simply the only people in this city I can tolerate for more than a few minutes."

I laugh and mirror his pose. The whole of the sky consumes my vision. "What a compliment. Although you should really acquaint yourself with Prince Meilek's advisors now that the Fireborn Queens are an ally."

"Tomorrow," he says, a hint of weariness bleeding into the word. "There's far too much speaking involved. It's exhausting."

I bite back a retort about his fondness for hearing himself talk. There's no need to disturb the peace with our squabbling. So I nod, my eyes searching for patterns among the stars.

After a moment, Theyen says, "When I'm in Penumbria, sometimes I don't see the sky for days at a time. There are caverns in the mountains, though, with crystal formations that glitter, not unlike stars."

It sounds lovely. "Do you miss it?"

"I'm never away long enough to miss it, and I can come and go as I please. I do sometimes miss the sky, though, when I'm away from Wyrst for any great length of time."

The memory of salty wind in my hair and the clouds near

enough to touch tugs a smile from me. Watching the world fall away beneath us had been like nothing else, and even if I were a shadow gate with the ability to travel from one end of the continent to the other in an instant, I might still prefer a wyvern.

Not that Yandor isn't the very best companion in the world, but he does have his limitations. Besides, with a wyvern, Saengo could go anywhere she wanted on Thiy and not worry about always being tethered to my location.

With a sigh, I glance at Theyen and find him watching me. My mouth twists into a smile and I point skyward. "The stars are up there."

He doesn't answer immediately. His expression is unreadable, still as stone in the dark. Then he looks away and asks, "Worried about Saengo?"

When did he become able to read me?

"I've been to see her. She requested more time at the Mountain," he says.

My throat feels suddenly too dry, and I struggle to swallow. Somehow, I manage to choke out, "The rot?"

"Unchanged," he says, gazing upward again. "She'll be back before the coronation, and she'll be fine. I wouldn't have left her if I didn't think it was safe, and anyway, your friend is a capable fighter."

"Isn't it time you admit she's your friend, too?"

"We haven't reached that milestone yet."

A laugh escapes me. "Thank you. Truly."

His profile is all shadows and sharp angles as he shrugs one shoulder. "It's not like I'm a prince with my own responsibilities, endless meetings to attend, plans to enact, and proposals to turn down."

I lean my weight on one arm and elbow him with the other. He avoids it easily, but he's smiling.

Pointing to a collection of five bright stars in the west, I say, "That's the Demon Crone's pouch. She held within it the seeds of life. But the Twins, being a mischievous pair, stole the pouch and spilled the seeds by accident. Or on purpose, depending on who you ask. Where the seeds scattered across the earth, the first sparks of human life began." I pause, my fingertips running over cool, rough stone. "In the Empire, they tell of the Fall of Suryal."

"I know the tale. I studied Nuvali culture to prepare for my marriage."

I wince, wishing I hadn't mentioned the Empire. Now, darker, grimmer thoughts taint the evening. Any such marriage between him and Princess Kyshia is unlikely, given that even peripheral members of House Yalaeng like Lord Ge are aware their union has been indefinitely postponed.

The Fireborn Queens have a number of allies, but not all the Kazan clans are so fortunate. With the conflict on the verge of open war, many of the larger clans have closed their borders, hoarding their resources and compromising trade, both across the country and abroad. As a fractured kingdom, many of the smaller clans rely on access to those traded goods to survive.

I frown as my thoughts turn to war. With House Yalaeng so intent on guarding themselves from the Soulless, why refuse to make peace with their neighbors? Doing so would free up resources that would be better served hunting down the Soulless. But perhaps such a concession would only make them look even weaker.

Whatever the reason, House Yalaeng is planning something. I need to figure out what that is before they bring all the kingdoms down with them.

Working alongside the King's Guard, I'm kept apprised of every guest in the castle and where they've been placed for their stay. Lord Ge's rooms are on the second level of the guest wing, at the farthest point from the entrance hall. The windows of his rooms are visible from one of the guard towers.

The following morning, he joins Prince Meilek and some of the other guests for a tour of the city. Once they've left the palace, it's a simple matter to avoid the other guests' servants whose tongues can't be trusted and slip inside Lord Ge's rooms.

The space is tastefully furnished with polished floors beneath a vibrant, patterned rug. Tall twin windows dressed in green curtains frame a marble fireplace. A door leading to an adjacent room for Lord Ge's manservant sits to the right. Fortunately, he'd accompanied his master into the city.

I do a cursory sweep through the servant's chamber, but

except for a valise and a pitcher of water beside the bed, the room bears little evidence of its occupant. I enter Lord Ge's chambers next. The bedsheets are meticulous, not a wrinkle in sight. A large trunk is pushed against the wall beside an armoire. Inside, a full wardrobe has been hung or tidily folded, and it doesn't take long to confirm there's nothing of note aside from the Nuvali's obsession with the color yellow.

I open the trunk next, the lock posing little challenge. Tucked beneath more stacks of folded clothes, not even hidden, is Lord Ge's travel permit. Months ago, when Saengo and I had journeyed through the Empire, the Nuvali lord leading our party had displayed a travel permit at each checkpoint on our way to Mirrim.

Although I'd only gotten a glimpse of that one, I recognized the Nuvali sun printed in gleaming gold leaf. Deciding the permit isn't of interest, I rummage through the rest of the trunk's contents. When that turns up nothing, I run my fingers along the seams of the trunk, first down to the bottom and then along the heavy lid.

Something pricks the pad of my forefinger. Digging harder into the satin lining, my nails snag on a small metal latch. With a tug, it falls open.

I can't help the small smile tugging at my lips. The compartment isn't large, and it contains a single folded slip of paper. When I slide it out, my breath catches at the wax seal, which bears the crest of the Temple of Light. Lord Ge isn't a lightwender.

There isn't a name on the letter to indicate who it's for. With the assistance of a candle flame and the knife tucked inside my bracer, I remove the seal without damaging the wax.

The last thing I expect to find when I unfold the letter is my name written at the top. Frowning, I scan the contents and the signature at the bottom. It's from the Ember Princess.

My pulse quickens. It's not long, reminiscent of Kyshia's penchant for getting straight to the point. She wants to meet to discuss plans for how to destroy the Soulless. She lists a place and time—a teahouse outside Luam in a fortnight. I grudgingly respect her boldness.

"You and I both know that you're the only shaman with any hope of victory." The entire letter is suspect, but those words in particular spark my anger. Was she seriously, even now, still trying to foist the responsibility of the Soulless's defeat onto my shoulders?

The fact that I have every intention of facing him anyway is beside the point. I allow myself a moment of pettiness before a voice of reason—which always sounds like Saengo in my head—tells me to move past my emotional response.

Assuming Lord Ge is meant to give me this letter at some point during his stay, why wouldn't the Ember Princess simply send the letter by falcon? Unless she wrote this without her father's permission. She sealed her letter with the Light Temple's crest, not House Yalaeng's.

Thoughts swirling, I secure the wax again to the paper

with the heat from a candle flame and return everything to its proper place.

I need to know what the Ember Princess is up to, and simply sending a falcon to Mirrim is out of the question. Now that I am Shadow, Prince Meilek has given me control over his various contacts across the continent. Had Kendara been here to properly pass on the title, I would have access to her network as well. As it is, I am not completely without resources.

FIVE

The morning of the coronation dawns clear and bright. Blades and soldiers are stationed at every corridor and entryway within both the Grand Palace and the Sanctuary of the Sisters, where the coronation is to take place.

I perform a sweep of the Grand Palace from the rooftops to ensure no one's lurking beyond what's visible from the ground. Although I find nothing suspicious, I can't dispel the notion that I'm missing something. Disgruntled, I ride ahead of Prince Meilek's procession to the Sanctuary. Guests already fill the Hall of the Demon Crone, and the abbess leads a prayer from the dais.

I remain out of sight, high on a gallery that overlooks the main chamber. My gaze passes slowly over the crowd. I spot Theyen first, standing alongside a Kazan diplomat from one of his clan's allies. Not far from them are Lord Phang and Saengo, just left of the aisle. She returned the previous evening, but with all the preparations for today, we haven't had much time to talk.

The hair at her right temple is swept back with a silver hair ornament in the shape of a swooping falcon. She's dressed in flowing blue robes with plumes of gray falcon feathers around the collar and a silver sash wrapped tight around her waist, fastened into an elaborate knot fitting of her station. Standing among other reiwyn, diplomats, and foreign leaders, she looks every inch the highborn lady she is.

I roll my shoulders to ease the ache attempting to form beneath my ribs and resume my task. Today of all days, I must be thorough and vigilant. Kou had the catacombs beneath the Sanctuary thoroughly explored and guarded, and I ensured there would be no easy routes an assassin might take to reach the domed roof. The Sanctuary is as secure as it could possibly be.

On the dais, the abbess has fallen silent. A moment later, the large oak doors open, announcing Prince Meilek's arrival.

With the blessing of the Sisters, the coronation proceeds without incident. But somehow, I can't yet breathe easy. Maybe it's just my anxiety over the Soulless's absence or the fact that Lord Ge hasn't given me the princess's letter or tonight's meeting with Evewyn's potential allies, but the sinking sensation in my gut remains.

When the doors to the Hall of the Demon Crone open once again, an immense cheer from what seems like the entire city, human and shamanborn alike, welcomes their new king.

A parade through the streets follows the coronation. King Meilek is surrounded by Blades, and handpicked soldiers are stationed at every rooftop along the route. One can never be too careful, and neither I nor the King's Guard are willing to take any chances.

Once the procession returns to the Grand Palace, a feast is held within the great hall as the celebration continues throughout the city. The entire market has been transformed into a festival, with food and flowing wine, while kites in the forms of falcons, wyverns, and drakes are freely distributed. Music fills the streets, rising high on the wind and carrying even to the roofs of the palace.

I don't participate in either celebration. Instead, I perch on one of the ceiling beams in the great hall and watch the merriment.

Everything is going so well. Have I become so accustomed to disappointment and tragedy that I expect every joyful occasion to end in disaster? Sisters, how depressing.

Still, I remain watchful. When the feast is cleared away and the guests begin to filter into the ballroom, I don't follow. Instead, I return to my tower, where, as I hoped, a falcon awaits me at the balcony.

What I don't expect is to find Saengo there as well, brushing one finger down the falcon's neck.

"You're going to make Millie jealous," I say when Saengo

looks up at my arrival. "Also, this doesn't look like an emergency?"

Still dressed in layers of fine robes, she tilts her head in confusion. The silver hairpin catches the waning sunlight. Then her cheeks flush as she realizes what I mean. She and King Meilek both possess keys to my rooms, the latter because he's king and the former in case of an emergency.

"I didn't want to lurk outside your door," she says, apologetic.

"You're missing the party." Crossing the short distance to the balcony, I gently remove the message from the falcon's foot.

The bird ruffles its feathers once before spreading its wings and taking flight. Saengo watches it fly away with a fond smile. "It'll still be there in ten minutes. I imagine it'll still be there at dawn given the atmosphere."

I laugh and close my fingers around the small, rolled message. Then I nod at her clothing. "Lady Phang, you wear the title well. Your father must be pleased."

"Ah yes, the secret behind every reiwyn—an excellent stylist." She brushes her hair behind her ear with a sly smile before breaking down in laughter. "Sirscha, stop distracting me. I wanted to ask if you'd join me the next time I visit the falconers. We haven't had much time to talk lately, and I thought it'd be nice."

Warmth fills my chest, carrying through our connection from her to me. "Of course. I would love that."

She beams. "Good. I'll let you get back to your duties then. I know you've a lot to do yet." Her gaze flicks to the rolled bit of paper in my hand before she steps forward to wrap her arms around my shoulders. "Let me know if you need anything."

"Same," I say softly as I hug her back.

With one last fond smile, Saengo leaves, shutting the door behind her train of embroidered silks.

Once the latch clicks, I shift my attention to the message. I'd sent a falcon to one of Prince Meilek's contacts in Luam, a shamanborn merchant who often traveled to and from Mirrim.

I unfurl the correspondence and then go still, fingers tightening around the thin paper. The words are written in Kendara's hand.

All at once, the weeks of anticipation and inevitability converge within me, knocking the breath from my lungs. A tremor races through my limbs, settling in my hands as Kendara's words become a blur.

I close my eyes, focus on my breathing to calm my quickening heartbeat, and then force myself to read the note.

Mirrim has been locked down. The Ember Princess requested that Lord Ge Yalaeng attend the coronation in her stead, and he readily agreed as it would allow him an escape. As of writing this, there are four dead Yalaengs, none of significance, although any such news is being kept silent. Victims and all within their vicinity were found dead with no visible wounds or signs of struggle.

I turn over the scrap of paper as if there might be something hidden on the back, but there is nothing else. For a moment, I allow myself to indulge in my bewildered anger at the complete lack of personalization. Then I wrestle back control of my feelings and tuck the note into my sash.

My gut tells me that this is what I'd been waiting for, that unknown certainty at last taking shape. Thank the Sisters it didn't come in the form of a disrupted coronation, but the sense of impending disaster remains the same. After her last message, in which she all but washed her hands of me, Kendara would not have written again unless the situation were truly dire.

I've been on edge for months wondering when and in what manner the Soulless would resurface—a perpetual state of unease he no doubt intended with his absence from my dreams. But this explains why House Yalaeng is now taking the precautions they'd blithely avoided before—the Soulless is in Mirrim.

If House Yalaeng is desperate to capture him while he's still within Mirrim's walls—and presumably before he kills anyone of "significance"—why would the Ember Princess still need to reach out to me in secret? Wouldn't requesting the help of another soulrender be worth the Emperor's pride if it means saving his own skin?

With Kendara's revelation and what that meant alongside Kyshia's message rattling in my skull, I lock my tower door and make my way through the palace to the council room to await the king and his guests. It wouldn't do for his Shadow to miss his first meeting as king.

A circular table stands at its center. Various maps cover three walls, while an enormous window takes up the fourth.

A wooden lattice constructed in the image of Vos Talwyn, complete with swooping rooftops, the spires of the Grand Palace, and the domes of the Sanctuary, covers the window glass.

I find my seat against the wall beneath a map of Evewyn's southern coast and wait. Within minutes, the door opens again.

Standing, I bow deeply at the waist and say, "King Meilek."

His smile is fleeting as he enters, followed by two Blades and then a host of foreign dignitaries, including Theyen. Returning to my seat, I watch in silence as Lord Ge takes the chair closest to the window. His gaze flicks to mine, brows narrowing in distaste. He doesn't behave like a man whose family is being hunted, but maybe that's because he believes he's safe here in Evewyn, far away from the Soulless.

King Meilek sits across from him, with Theyen to his left. Predictably, Lord Ge insists on speaking first. He stands, fingertips digging into the tabletop as he leans forward.

"Your Majesty, it is long past time to discuss reparations for Queen Meilyr's attack in the north. If you will permit?" he says, in a way that makes it clear he isn't asking. I want to punch that condescending smile off his face.

King Meilek only nods, his expression far too magnanimous. At his side, Theyen's eyes are hard and flat. The others present watch with interest, like spectators at a play.

Lord Ge begins to rattle off things about safe sea travel, individual compensation for Nuvali soldiers killed in the attack, and merchant routes through the grasslands, and then, as I expected, he looks directly at me and says, "Emperor Cedral requires the return of this criminal for impersonating a soulguide and infiltrating the Temple of Light."

I meet his glare with steady and determined blankness. I doubt he has any idea what it is the Ember Princess asked him to deliver, although it amuses me that he came here carrying both his Emperor's demands and the princess's opposing request for my help. When exactly is he planning to give me that letter?

After I revealed what I'd found to King Meilek, the first words out of his mouth were to forbid me from meeting with Kyshia. I wisely didn't mention how forbidding me from doing something only makes me want to do that thing more, but I'm not an idiot, and I don't trust her.

King Meilek remains pleasant and placid as he says, "Sirscha is an Evewynian citizen and under my protection. She will not be returning with you to the Empire."

Part of me wants to object that he can't protect me and risk the entire country's safety. If he gave me into Lord Ge's keeping it would be easy enough to escape during the long journey back to Mirrim without jeopardizing the peace. But that will have to wait for later. I can't challenge his authority in his own council room in front of other leaders.

Lord Ge's lips thin, but he continues. "Emperor Cedral also requires Evewyn remain neutral in any future conflicts between the Nuvalyn Empire and Kazahyn."

Theyen, openly glaring, says nothing. There are other shadowblessed leaders in the room as well, potential allies and enemies both, but they all wait for King Meilek's response to this demand.

He's doing an excellent job of keeping whatever he's thinking to himself. I quietly applaud Kendara's training.

Her note remains tucked in my sash like a searing ember. I have so many questions. I sent the falcon to King Meilek's contact. How did Kendara come to be the one to respond? She was supposed to leave all of this behind—wasn't that the point of abandoning me in Mirrim?

I'd made my peace with never seeing her again, and now, here she is, dangling before me the temptation of contact with her.

Of course, Kendara wouldn't think of it that way. She isn't sentimental, and the nature of her message is purely business. Still, I can't help the flame of hope flickering in my chest. It infuriates me. I don't *need* her. But I want her in my life, ornery mood and sharp tongue and all.

At last, King Meilek says, "Evewyn has already established treaties with several Kazan clans. We will not break peace with one party to make peace with another."

For the part Theyen and the Fireborn Queens played in assisting King Meilek with regaining Evewyn's navy, Evewyn agreed to provide aid to them and their allies if it came to war with the Empire. While the Fireborn Queens mean to face the conflict, other clans of equal size have chosen to hole up within their mountain homes and wait out the war.

I'm not sure how I feel about that, as a united Kazahyn has proven in the past capable of withstanding the Empire. But that was centuries ago, when the clans grew desperate and wrung out after decades of war. According to Theyen, the clans uniting against a common enemy would be impossible now.

"Then you've decided there will be no peace between our kingdoms," Lord Ge says, lip curling.

Evewyn's resources are already stretched thin trying to provide what they can for the newly freed shamanborn. I don't know how Evewyn will manage to meet the reparations the Empire is demanding. We've allies across the sea, and in Kazahyn, of course, but it's a precarious position.

"On these two points, Evewyn cannot concede. Please inform Emperor Cedral that I will gladly negotiate alternate terms."

The tension in the room is palpable. Lord Ge, however, must realize that to continue arguing would be useless, so he sinks back in his chair, spine rigid.

King Meilek was right to hold off this conversation until after he was crowned. He promised peace, and certain reiwyn will not be pleased. Hopefully, Emperor Cedral won't want a war with both his neighbors *and* the Soulless.

At least until a solution is presented for how to destroy it, the Dead Wood stands as a barrier between Evewyn and the Empire. The only passage by land between our kingdoms is through the northern grasslands, where the Dead Wood has yet to reach. No shaman would bring their familiar within a day's ride of the trees, and without their familiars, their shaman craft would be limited.

By ship, the northern waters are too icy for a fleet to pass safely, and the southern waters are guarded by the Kazahyn.

There are certainly ways around each obstacle, and King Meilek will see that they're addressed. But for now, I can only hope that Evewyn isn't at risk of an attack from the Empire.

This is a delicate time for the kingdom. King Meilek is trying to piece together a people that his sister tore apart. Shamanborn and humans, distrust and betrayal, fear and resentment. Even with the help of the Kazan, Evewyn might not be able to withstand a war with the Empire.

The rest of the discussion passes with far less tension, although the way Lord Ge watches King Meilek makes my fingers tighten around the edges of my seat. I'm relieved when everyone rises, bows, and files out to rejoin the celebrations. I catch King Meilek's eye, and he lingers until we're the last ones left. The guards close the door again to give us privacy.

I rise from my seat and tug Kendara's message from my sash, handing it over wordlessly. As he reads it, a line appears between his brows.

"It's the Soulless," I say. No one else could kill the way Kendara described—whole rooms of guards and attendants, all dead without a single drop of blood.

"Kendara wrote this," he murmurs, and I nod, although he doesn't see it. The mask he'd worn throughout the day slides off, leaving bare his exhaustion and uncertainty. "Why is the Soulless going after minor members of House Yalaeng?"

Even if his victims have no influence over the decisions House Yalaeng makes, if Lord Ge is anything to go by, they've still profited from the prominence of their House. They don't deserve to die, but perhaps they do deserve to be removed from power.

My jaw tightens as I recall the Soulless's quiet demeanor at Spinner's End and that brief but bright vein of rage hidden beneath. I think of his last words to me through Queen Meilyr's broken voice, of his promise for vengeance. He has waited centuries for his revenge—nurtured it, crooned to it in the dark of the Dead Wood and the silence of his own thoughts.

"I know why," I say, not certain whether I should be disturbed by how well I can understand the Soulless's motivations. "He's going after them to torture the Emperor and the imperial family. He wants them to know what's it's like to wait for death."

SIX

Saengo always looks at ease surrounded by falcons.

We've accompanied the palace's falconers outside the city walls. Perches and cages have been set up throughout an open stretch of grass near the surrounding forest. I feed slivers of fresh red meat to a few falcons as Saengo and the palace's Scholar of Falconry release several more to allow them to hunt. Her family is renowned for producing the best messenger birds on the continent, and it's clear by how comfortable she is around them that she's been handling falcons her entire life.

Once I've finished my task, I retire to the shade, content to watch the experts at work. Millie, Saengo's pet falcon, is perched on a nearby branch, cleaning her silver-tipped feathers. Saengo catches my eye across the field as she releases a brown falcon, her smile bright.

I don't know much about this part of her life. She's told me, certainly, but I've rarely had the opportunity to see her at it. Back in the Company, nearly all my spare hours were spent training with Kendara or running off on various impossible tasks she'd given me.

Saengo looks happy surrounded by birds and falconers and blue skies, at home with a task so far removed from what a Shadow must do. The distance between us stretches a little farther.

Raised voices carry across the field from somewhere south of us. They seem to be coming from Little Talwyn, which isn't far. I stand, brushing off the seat of my pants. When Saengo looks in my direction again, I point toward the source of the noise to indicate where I'm headed. With a nod, she hands off the falcon on her gauntlet and then removes the leather.

Today, she's dressed plainly in a long, sleeveless tunic over dark-green underrobes. The layers are cinched at the waist with a green sash and then hang loose to frame sturdy gray pants and black boots. Her hair falls loose around her face. It's grown long enough to reach her shoulders now.

I wait, feeling somewhat guilty for pulling her away from the falcons. She doesn't need to come with me, but I won't reject her company, either. Even though she'd invited me along with the intent to talk, we haven't done much of that yet. The awkwardness is unusual between us.

"What do you think is happening?" Saengo asks as we follow the city wall toward the broad sprawl of temporary homes.

"Nothing good," I say.

Before long, we reach the outermost edges of Little Talwyn. It's easy to spot the source of the disturbance. A large group of people are gathered outside a hut. Others try to push through the crush of eager spectators to glimpse what's happening, and I can't make much out over the shouting and cursing.

A few of those on the fringes of the commotion notice me and Saengo. They break away from the crowd, bowing hastily.

"What's going on?" I ask.

One of them bows again, lower this time, and stammers, "Th-the soldiers. They insulted us first."

With a curse, I push forward, unmindful of those I elbow aside in order to cut through to the center. At last, I find two people in the dirt, grappling and shouting, fists flying. At the sight of me, everyone surging around them falls silent, flashes of guilt and defiance in the way they lower their arms and avoid my eyes.

"Sisters save me," I hiss. Dodging a foot, I haul off the person currently on top of the other, about to deliver another punch.

He's a soldier, dressed in Evewynian green. His sword lies discarded in the dirt. Thank the Warrior that neither of them had drawn a weapon.

"Get off—" he snarls before he sees who's taken hold of the back of his uniform. Then his mouth snaps shut. He pales beneath the dust streaking his face and the fresh bruises swelling around his eye and jaw. "Sh-Shadow."

Without a word, I reach down and help up the water-wender he'd been fighting. The man doesn't look much better, a bruise darkening the corner of his mouth and hair sticking out at all angles, gray with dust. His knuckles are bleeding.

The waterwender doesn't even look at me. He glares at the soldier, hatred flaring his nostrils as he spits into the dirt. "Before your queen locked me up, I was a soldier, too. It's clear what Evewyn's military has become under the rule of a tyrant."

The soldier's fists clench, and it's only my presence that prevents him from tackling the waterwender again.

Still, his words are thick with venom. "After everything King Meilek has done for your lot, you should show some respect for those of us who serve him."

"Just because the orders you're obeying no longer include subjugation and murder doesn't make you a saint," the water-wender growls back.

"Okay, enough," I say, stepping between them, my hands outstretched. I turn to the soldier first. "If you've got a prob-lem, take it up with your superior." I nod toward two officits finally approaching, visible above the crowd on their drakes.

The soldier stalks away without a word. Shamanborn spit at his back, snarling words like "traitors" and "Queen's dogs." Saengo makes a shooing gesture at the crowd, which is slow to disperse.

I approach the waterwender. He's young, midtwenties probably. He would have been serving his six years in the army when Queen Meilyr ordered the shamanborn imprisoned. He doesn't hold my gaze, instead looking down at his feet, jaw clenched tight.

"You're not wrong to be wary of them," I say, which makes his head jerk up in surprise. "But King Meilek is trying to make things right. Every person here"—I gesture to the community at large—"wants a better way forward. They *need* a better way forward, and starting a fight a week after he was crowned is a poor way to help."

"I don't need to be told how to help by a child too green to have seen a real fight," he says, although he doesn't look me in the eye. Instead, his gaze flicks to the twin swords strapped to my back.

Saengo hovers at my side, frowning slightly. I've never talked to anyone about the night she died, and it isn't common knowledge that I killed Ronin. Everyone assumes the Soulless did it. I'm content to let them. I'm not actually sure who knows that I killed Jonyah, the Shadow who replaced Kendara. Either way, I'm not surprised there are those who think that I've never been tested in a real fight and that my position was awarded to me purely due to my craft.

His words are a challenge, and I've always been notoriously bad at turning them down. I remind myself that my actions reflect on King Meilek now. He wants peace. I need to take my own advice.

Still, I am his Shadow, and if I allow one person to disrespect me, then it won't be long before others follow.

"Respect is earned. I understand that," I say. My voice is quiet, but there's no mistaking the steel in my words. I look around at those who've remained to see this play out. "So if any of you don't believe I deserve my position, you are free to challenge me at any time. I won't even use my craft."

"Sirscha—" Saengo begins, but I touch her wrist. It's probably a bad idea to encourage anyone to challenge the King's Shadow, but if it will put their minds at ease, I can deal with being scolded by the king's advisors.

"He meant no disrespect, soulrender," a bright-eyed earthwender woman says, hurrying forward. She gives the waterwender a strong shove to get moving, but he doesn't budge. "We are grateful for all that King Meilek is doing."

"You don't have to be grateful," I tell her. "None of this should have been necessary from the start. But he's trying to fix things, and the only way that succeeds is by all of us working together. If there's anything King Meilek does that you don't agree with, you take it up with me, and I'll pass it along. Fair?"

She nods, but the waterwender is eyeing me like he's considering taking up my offer of a fight. The earthwender woman gives him another shove, and he finally relents, allowing her to herd him away. The crowd quickly disperses after that.

Saengo grasps my hands. Her gloves are thick but soft.

"Sisters," she says, watching the waterwender's retreating back. "That could have gone so much worse if he'd had the use of his craft."

I take a slow breath and observe the lingering scowls cast in the soldier's direction. One of the officits is shouting at him, which is mildly satisfying, although they're too far off to hear what's being said. I don't know how the rift between the humans and shamanborn can ever be mended. The past eight years have been weighted with too much pain and grief. Too many lives have been lost.

"Come, walk with me," Saengo says, tugging at my elbow. I follow, schooling my expression into something neutral.

She loops our arms together and pats my sleeve. We pass two gray-eyed children playing knucklebones in the grass. One of them waves at us as the other gawks. We wave back, and they duck away, giggling and embarrassed.

It isn't until we've left Little Talwyn and the risk of eaves-droppers when Saengo finally speaks.

Her voice is soft and uncertain. "You've been quiet ever since I got back from the Mountain. I figured it was to do with preparations for the coronation, but then . . . I began thinking about this last month and . . . Sirscha?" She stops in the middle of a broad stretch of grass and clasps my hand in hers. Her head tilts, eyes searching mine. "Did I do something to upset you? Please tell me if I did."

Guilt sweeps over me like a wave. Of course she's noticed how I've been gradually distancing myself, but in my attempt to spare my heart from future pain, I've inadvertently hurt her. I'm an idiot.

Shaking my head, I grip her hands just as tightly. "No. No,

you haven't done anything. I've just . . . been too deep inside my own head. And, well, I didn't want to bring down your mood. You seemed so content."

Her uncertainty shifts to exasperation as her lips purse. "Sirscha, you should and *will* share all news or concerns with me, dire or otherwise, as soon as you're able. I was surprised you looked so somber in your tower given I heard you were stargazing with the king and Hlau Theyen."

I break away from her, throwing up my hands. "Who told you that?" Palace gossips can't possibly know what we were doing so far from prying eyes.

Saengo laughs and catches up to me. "Only Kou."

Oh. My annoyance abates now that I'm reassured my schedule—and whatever I do or don't do with King Meilek—isn't common knowledge or the source of gossip.

"Well?" Saengo prompts. "Stop brooding and tell me what's going on."

"I'm not just brooding. It's Shadow business," I say, relieved that she seems content with my answer. Why do I always somehow end up hurting her? I don't know what to do now except be grateful she's still here.

"If you feel it best to keep such business between yourself and King Meilek, that is, of course, your decision to make," Saengo says. Then she raises her brows and continues loftily, "But I am your familiar, and as I understand it, shaman and familiar come as a set."

"Saengo Phang, are you finding loopholes to snoop into

royal business?" I ask, feigning a scandalized look.

"If I am, it's only because you're a bad influence."

I laugh, loud and unrestrained. It feels wonderful. Sisters, I am *such* an idiot. If my time with her is limited, then why shouldn't I treasure every moment I can?

Saengo grins and pokes me, impatient. Nodding in surrender, I tell her first about Princess Kyshia's letter I found in Lord Ge's trunk and then about Kendara's message.

Saengo's lips pinch to one side as she fingers the necklace in the shape of falcon feathers that curl around her neck. "Do you think Kendara will return to Evewyn now that King Meilek is ruler?"

"I don't know."

"If she did," Saengo says slowly, "would she want to be Shadow again?"

"She's welcome to it."

"After how long you wanted it?" Saengo asks, searching my face for the truth.

I nod. There's nothing to hide. Becoming Shadow was an ambition I'd chased for four years, but that was before . . . everything. I no longer need the acknowledgment or the tangible proof that I am worth something. Now, all I need is to figure out what to do with my future.

Provided I even have one. Despite the uncertainty, the freedom to choose should feel liberating. Instead, I'm simply confused and a little adrift.

"I don't need to be Shadow anymore, but I still want to do

great things. I still want to make something of myself, on my own terms." All my life, I've been plagued by preconceptions based on certain labels—orphan, soldier, soulguide, Suryali, soulrender, traitor, monster. "If I'm to have a reputation, I should at least earn it."

Saengo raises one eyebrow. "Defeating a centuries-old shaman who could transform into a spider and control a dead forest isn't earning a reputation?"

Against my will, my lips twitch into a crooked smile. "Not many people know that. Besides, that's not a reputation, that's just infamy." In truth, there might have been some appeal to infamy if I didn't regret the entire incident. Defeating Ronin had awakened the Soulless, after all.

The shamanborn want peace. They deserve peace, and that will be impossible so long as the Soulless is a threat.

Once Saengo says her goodbyes to the falconers, we head toward the Company gate, which isn't far. The sentinels on the battlements high above have already spotted us and signaled for the soldiers below to begin unlocking the heavy bolts on the outer door and raising the inner portcullis. The soldiers bow as we pass through, and I nod politely.

I wait until we've passed both Companies and entered the palace gardens before I say, "I've spent a lot of time thinking about what to do once the Soulless makes his presence known. I have to find a way to subdue him, at least long enough to buy me more time to figure out how to destroy an entire forest." The enormity of the task will overwhelm me if I let it, so I focus on one step at a time. "Since I'm not strong enough to defeat him with craft, how do I get him to fight me on my terms instead?"

The Soulless wants an end to House Yalaeng. House Yalaeng wants the Soulless dead. More than once, I've considered the merits of simply standing aside and letting them have their way. I wouldn't mourn either side, and whoever emerged the victor, the rest of us would deal with it then.

Unfortunately, that option would endanger too many lives. And while House Yalaeng is responsible for keeping secret the truth of the Soulless's existence, I am the one who released him when I killed Ronin. I also played a part in this nightmare.

"Perhaps a talisman," Saengo says, touching the troll bone at her wrist. It was a gift to me from Kendara and protects the wearer from harmful magic. "Something like this bracelet but bigger. Or stronger. I read once about a talisman that could reflect magic back at the caster, but it was lost at sea when the ship carrying it was attacked by pirates."

"Maybe that's our solution."

"A magic-reflecting talisman?"

"Piracy. We should just steal a ship and run away," I say with a sigh. But her mention of talismans does remind me of something I've been considering for weeks now.

In the Bright Palace in Mirrim is the Hall of Heroes, where dozens of suits of armor are on display. The armor was created from the bones of sunspear wyverns, the only creatures on Thiy whose soul a soulrender couldn't touch.

The Soulless had used a talisman made of sunspear bone to contain his brother's soul. My craft had been useless against it until I'd drawn on the fathomless well of the Soulless's own magic. Before the Dead Wood came into being, the Nuvali had crafted the sunspear armor to face him in battle. Now, with centuries' worth of bound souls to enhance his already considerable power, I'm not sure how effective the armor would be.

I don't think I could actually kill him, either, without destroying the Dead Wood first. I set the greenhouse at Spinner's End on fire, and he came out of it unscathed. But if I'm presented with the opportunity to drive a sword through his heart, I'm not opposed to giving it a try. Even if it doesn't kill him, I might be able to subdue him like Ronin had.

Besides that, though, while all talismans are crafted from the bones of beasts, those suits of armor feel particularly . . . tainted. Wyverns are revered in Evewyn. In Kazahyn, many shadowblessed clans take wyverns as friends and comrades for life. Theyen would balk at the idea of using something made from their bones.

Still, if it works, the sunspear armor might be exactly what I need to face the Soulless. And yet, doing so doesn't just feel disrespectful; it feels like desecration.

I'm also not sure what will happen when a soulrender dons armor meant to shield against their own craft. I've kept the idea to myself for these reasons, but now that we know the Soulless is in Mirrim, we might be out of time and options.

When I admit all this to Saengo, she looks as unsettled as I feel. But she also says, "It does feel wrong. But we must consider . . . What is an ancient suit of wyvern bones worth next to stopping a shaman capable of killing whole rooms of people with only a thought?"

"So you agree this is our best option? Because those suits of armor won't be easy to acquire. I'd have to first get inside Mirrim, which by all accounts is under tight restrictions, and then inside the Bright Palace."

Saengo hesitates, and threads of her emotions weave through our connection. I usually keep a firmly closed window between us, as her emotions can often overwhelm me. But I sense enough to ascertain that she's worried about something and nervous about mentioning it.

"Something else on your mind?" I ask. I don't want to force her to confide in me if she isn't ready. But I also want to remind her that she can, regardless of my poor attempts to put distance between us.

She nods, but her uncertainty remains as we wander past empty plots where there had once been flower beds. They'd been torn up by soldiers during our escape from the palace. The gardeners haven't yet replanted. Landscaping likely hasn't been high on King Meilek's list of priorities.

"There might be another option," she begins, flicking the edge of her sleeve with a fingernail.

She doesn't normally fidget. She's too well-mannered for that. Now, I'm practically brimming with concern and curiosity.

"The Spirit of the Mountain is an ancient elemental," she says. "She's more powerful than any shaman, and she's probably the only living thing left on the continent that's older than the Soulless. If the Mountain helped Suri to create the enchantment around Mirrim, then maybe she would help us as well."

SEVEN

Despite Saengo's joke about us coming as a set, I still wasn't going to ask about her visit to the Mountain. Her being my familiar doesn't entitle me to her time or thoughts. She would tell me if and when she wanted.

I'm not entirely surprised that this is the subject of her uncertainty.

"I've been . . . mulling it over since I got back," Saengo says, her fingers resting against her chest. "When I was there, the rot barely hurt at all. I couldn't speak to her, but I think . . . given time, I might be able to? I know it doesn't make much sense, but I could *feel* her intention. She wants me to be at peace."

The first thing I'd done upon Saengo's return was check the progression of the rot. To my relief, it hadn't been as bad as in recent weeks. I'd been too eager to accept the win and too preoccupied with the coronation to question it. But like I told Theyen, ever since the queen's death, the rot has become more resistant to my treatments and has needed tending more often. Whereas before we were willing to risk a fortnight apart, now I wouldn't chance a single week.

How much longer can I stave off the rot before my craft becomes ineffective? The only real solution is to eliminate the source.

Even if the Mountain did contribute to slowing the rot, the idea of an ancient elemental calling to Saengo unsettles me. The only thing I know about the Spirit of the Mountain is that it awakened when Thiy was still young and shamanic crafts held enough power to breathe life into the very elements. While other elementals faded with the centuries, the Spirit of the Mountain lingered.

Suri, founder of Mirrim, sacrificed her magic to the Mountain at the end of her life to create a barrier around the city so that only those of shaman blood could enter, ensuring that the capital of the Nuvalyn Empire would stand against invaders for a thousand years.

I've only ever seen the Mountain from a distance, and while she'd been breathtaking, a creature that old and that powerful always comes with a catch. Even an elemental has to want something.

"She wants you to be at peace," I repeat carefully, "and so you think she'd help us?"

Saengo pauses on the path and reaches for my hand. "Maybe. We won't know unless we ask. I don't know how Suri managed it, but it's worth a try, isn't it?"

I squeeze Saengo's fingers. "Did you forget that Suri bartered her magic to the Mountain? There's nothing we have that she would want aside from my craft, and that's not an exchange I could ever agree to." Losing my craft would mean losing Saengo.

Saengo's shoulders dip, and she releases my hand. "I haven't forgotten. I simply thought perhaps . . . it would be worth it. To defeat him."

"We've had this talk, Saengo," I say. She'd suggested we perform the same monstrous act as Ronin did, which was so unimaginable that it didn't bear thinking about. Saengo might be willing to give her life to save the kingdoms, but I am not. None of this will mean a thing if I can't save my best friend.

"Sirscha—"

"We'll have to come up with something else. I'm not risking you, so don't ask it of me. Since that option is off the table, I think the sunspear armor is the best bet." Perhaps our *only* bet.

In truth, it's a complete gamble. We've no idea whether the sunspear armor will protect against the Soulless's immense magic as it once did.

A wrinkle appears between Saengo's brows. "I suppose you're right."

"Of course I am, so stop thinking up ways to die. You're making me paranoid."

Saengo's answering smile puts me at ease as we continue through the garden. Since the obvious way to get inside

Mirrim undetected would be through a shadow gate, we seek out Theyen. After questioning his servants, we discover he's hidden himself away in the palace orchard.

The rows of plum trees span acres of green fields northwest of the palace gardens. The plums are nearly ripe, dark clusters heavy on the branches. Technically, only the royal family and certain members of the king's council, like his Shadow, are allowed here. Theyen must have gotten permission from King Meilek.

One of Kendara's earliest tasks for me had been to steal a plum from one of these trees. No easy feat for the untrained given that the orchard lies in full view of the palace walls, where sentinels stand guard day and night.

"What are you doing back here?" I ask Theyen, who we find lounging in the shade, long legs stretched out over the grass. His eyes are closed, and the back of his head rests against the tree trunk.

"I grew weary of being stared at," he says without opening his eyes. "There are few places here to be left alone."

Theyen is a shadow gate, so he can come and go as he pleases—but only at night. Like all shadowblessed, he has no magic so long as there is sunlight. Until night falls, he's as stranded in Evewyn as anyone else.

It's expected that he and his fellow shadowblessed dignitaries have been the subjects of curiosity and attention. With their snowy white hair and gray skin, shadowblessed are more conspicuous than shamanborn, and no shadowblessed had been welcome within Vos Talwyn during Queen Meilyr's reign. She may not have held any personal grudges against the shadowblessed, but she distrusted the magical races in general.

"I know that look on your face," he says, one eye now cracked open. "You want something from me."

As I anticipated, his face tightens with anger when I broach the possibility of using sunspear armor against the Soulless.

His voice is thick with revulsion. "Even were I willing to help you acquire the armor, which I am not, I no longer have access to open gates inside Mirrim."

As far as I'm aware, neither the Fireborn Queens nor House Yalaeng have confirmed the dissolution of their marriage alliance. But if Theyen can no longer enter Mirrim, then that seems fairly conclusive.

"It's just as well," I say. "If we were caught entering by shadow gate, it would implicate the shadowblessed, and you specifically." The last thing Theyen or the Fireborn Queens need is to be accused of stealing into the Bright Palace like thieves.

"You should consider reaching out to Princess Kyshia," he says, tipping his head back to inspect a low-hanging cluster of deep violet fruit. My eyebrow twitches at the suggestion. I hadn't told him about her message, which is still hidden in Lord Ge's trunk. "She doesn't want a war any more than we do, and she has the ear of the Emperor. She's asked me to confirm to her father's court that neither of us knew what your true craft was when you entered Mirrim."

He stands, fingers reaching and closing around one round plum.

I smack his hand away from the fruit. "They're not ripe yet."

He gives me an annoyed look.

"So her loyalty is in doubt," I continue, the loose threads surrounding her message starting to take shape.

Having been thwarted, Theyen returns to lounging in the grass. "Yes, meaning if she's in a tenuous position, she might be open to some sort of deal."

I glance at Saengo, who meets my gaze with the same knowing look. When we were in Mirrim, Kyshia spent most of her time at the Light Temple rather than the Bright Palace. She isn't a favorite within her father's court. If they're now doubting her loyalty, she will be eager to prove herself.

And what better way to do that than to bring down the Soulless?

"Would we be able to trust her?" I ask.

Theyen's lip curls. "So long as she's given you her word. She still believes the word of a Yalaeng carries weight. But if nothing else, you can trust her resolve to defeat the Soulless."

So as long as I am useful, her cooperation can be assured. I could work with that.

Without a shadow gate, if anyone could get us into the Bright Palace without being caught, it would be the Ember Princess. Good thing I know just when and where to reach her.

"Maybe I should do this alone."

I pace the narrow span between the door and the balcony. The sun has just set, a hazy glow fading against the horizon. Saengo watches me from where she's seated at a narrow table, hunched over a crinkled paper bag and a growing pile of discarded melon seed shells.

"Don't try to change our plans, Sirscha." Her fingers disappear into the bag to snag more roasted seeds. She splits one open with her front teeth before neatly sucking out the seed, and I contain a snort of laughter.

Cracking apart a melon seed is a skill no proper reiwyn lady should have, but I taught her the trick one balmy summer in Vos Talwyn's market some years ago. I'd purchased the bag of roasted melon seeds from a woman with a straw hat draped with colorful tassels. Upon witnessing Saengo's hilarious attempt to open them with her fingernails and then with her knife, I'd been delighted to learn that here was knowledge her various tutors had overlooked.

So I sat her down beneath the awning of a bookshop, and we devoured that bag of melon seeds, giggling every time Saengo got a shell stuck between her front teeth.

"We've already agreed that I'm coming with you," Saengo says. She has since mastered the technique. Now, she makes eating seeds look downright refined. "First, because you might need the backup, and second, because we can't guarantee you'll be back before—" She makes a vague gesture at her chest.

And that's the crux of it all, isn't it? My reasons for facing the Soulless aren't only for Evewyn or Thiy. All of this is also for Saengo.

Before I awakened my craft, I'd wanted to be regarded with awe and admiration. It was selfish, but I believed that the only person who would look out for me was me. I've been blessed to learn otherwise since then, but that doesn't mean I'm not still selfish.

The aggressive shift in Saengo's rot has to be related to the Soulless. He is its source after all—a sliver of his magic spreading through her, a blight that I will soon be helpless to stop. Now that we know he is in Mirrim, I can no longer stand still. Saengo's time is running out.

Theyen says Kyshia can be trusted, and although I'm skeptical, I do trust Theyen. If this is my chance to acquire sunspear armor, then I have to take it. With King Meilek's coronation now behind us, there's no need for me to remain in Evewyn. The King's Guard has his safety well in hand.

With the Emperor's demands and the threat of war, King Meilek cannot be implicated if I'm caught sneaking into Mirrim. Even though the hopes of every shamanborn I've met since returning to Vos Talwyn weigh on my mind, I have no choice but to resign as Shadow. King Meilek had promised me when I took this position that I could leave it at any time.

My gaze finds the letter I've already written, waiting on my desk for him to find later. With a sigh, I sink onto the simple wood chair beside the desk. My fingers run along the folded edges, the letter secured with red wax and the king's seal.

I couldn't bear to see him again, even to say goodbye. Fleeing in the night might be a coward's choice, but I can't risk my guilt upsetting my resolve. He's too clever, and he knows me too well. He'd suspect me of planning something.

It pains me to leave so soon after returning home. Every moment we were away, Saengo and I yearned for Vos Talwyn's familiar architecture and raucous streets, the tolling bells and colorful markets. But all the more so, my heart is weary with the idea of losing King Meilek's friendship and his trust.

He's given so much for me, which is why I can't allow him to give any more. He'll be angry but he'll understand. I will pay whatever toll the Sisters require to save Saengo, even if that price is King Meilek's friendship and this city I call home.

Regardless, he will always be included in the family of my heart.

"He'll forgive you," Saengo says, watching the way my fingers flutter restlessly against the letter.

"He shouldn't," I say, finally withdrawing my hand. They're work-roughened hands, calloused and scarred from years of menial chores at the orphanage and then years of wielding a sword at the Academy.

Small white scars crisscross the back of my hand. I can't even recall how I got them, but I do remember the first time anyone had tended my wounds with anything resembling care or gentleness. King Meilek, barely older than I'd been then, had pressed a damp washcloth to my bleeding knuckles and murmured words of regret for how one of the Company officits had chosen to discipline me.

His kindness has always defined him as a leader. While I don't know what he plans to do about the Empire's demands, I won't become a liability for him or Evewyn's peace.

"You're too hard on yourself," Saengo says. "He will understand that you're trying to shield the kingdom."

Probably, but that doesn't mean he won't also be upset. He'd forbidden me from meeting with Kyshia. Once he finds my letter of resignation, he'll know why I left and that I disobeyed him.

"Do you ever get tired of being right?" I ask, squinting resentfully at Saengo.

"I'll be sure to let you know should that happen." She flashes a smile before growing somber again. "Remind me when Theyen said he'd arrive?"

"After sunset."

Because it would be rather difficult to reach Luam in two weeks, Theyen agreed to take us. But after that, we'll be on our own. It's more than enough—certainly more than I deserve, but I'm grateful all the same. His friendship is yet another precious thing I hope not to lose after all of this.

"I don't trust Kyshia, but even if everything goes well, as long as I remain inconspicuous, I can get through Mirrim's ward easily enough, since I'm a shaman. I don't know how she'll get you into the city undetected, though."

Saengo pauses with another melon seed halfway to her mouth. Then she gives me a funny look. "That's not going to be a problem."

Restless, I rise from my seat to inspect our weapons, even though I know they're all cleaned and sharpened. "Because she's the Ember Princess?" I ask.

"Because the ward doesn't keep out familiars."

I go still, my fingers frozen over the stiff fletching of an arrow. The reminder of what she is—or rather, of what she is *not*—slams into me anew. She may look and think and feel as human as she's always been—and perhaps, in all the ways that count, she *is* still human—but her soul is changed. Saengo had died. Now, she is a spirit made corporeal, and my craft is the only thing keeping her tethered to this world.

I turn to her, my hands dropping to my sides. "Sisters, I'm an idiot. I'm sorry."

She lifts one shoulder and finishes her melon seed. "It's fine. Sometimes, I forget, too. It's never for long—a minute or so, when I'm feeding the falcons or when I'm in the archery field. It hurts, but . . . it helps, too."

I shake my head. It's not fine, but I don't know how to say so without apologizing again.

"Is it because I'm a weakness to you?" she asks, brushing off her fingers. "Is that why you want to go alone?"

I suck in a breath at the question. Then I shake my head, lips pinched tight. "Please don't think that. It's only my fear that you'll be hurt."

"But I fear for you, too," she says softly. "Does my concern matter less than yours?"

"Of course not. I shouldn't have made you feel that way."

"I know you don't mean to, and I know that, in your heart, I'm still me. That means a great deal, truly." She stretches her arms over her head, groaning as she arches her back in what I suspect is an attempt to lighten the somber turn of our discussion. "But we both know that every familiar is a weakness to their shaman. It's unavoidable. That doesn't mean I want to be shut away while you face all the danger yourself. You watch my back, remember?"

I nod, trying for a smile and once again calling myself a fool for inadvertently hurting her. "And you watch mine."

With the sunset, it isn't long before Theyen arrives. Saengo and I haven't packed much beyond some basic necessities. We're not sure what sort of deal Kyshia will want to make or how long we'll be in the Empire.

Like the last time Theyen brought us to Luam, we arrive at the Kazahyn Trade Embassy.

As Saengo and I recover from passing through the gate, Theyen says, "I'll follow as far as the teahouse in case it's a trap, but after that, if Princess Kyshia gets the two of you inside Mirrim, you'll be on your own. I won't be able to help, so don't do anything stupid." He pauses, giving me a critical once-over. "I don't know why I'm bothering to tell you that."

Even through a roiling stomach, I manage to give him a sour look. "Which one of us showed up in Vos Talwyn without warning and got himself stabbed and poisoned? I'm trying to stop accumulating life debts, thank you. Actually, that one might count as you owing me, seeing as you passed out a minute into your arrival."

"It was a few minutes at least," he drawls.

"I'm pretty sure no one gets to count that," Saengo mumbles, her palm pressed to her stomach over the layers of her gray sash.

"You do realize the best way to stop accumulating life debts is to stop putting yourself in mortal danger?" he asks.

"It's been months. Should we ask the Soulless if he'll be open to an additional few weeks' reprieve before he murders someone else?"

"If you're both quite finished," Saengo says, before drawing a deep breath and adjusting her sash. "We should get going."

My craft confirms a clear route from our room to the street below. Outside the embassy, light rain has begun to fall. The city is unchanged from what I remember. Boxy wooden buildings sit on thick stilts above the river, while boardwalks and bridges frame waterways choked with boats.

Well, there is one change—the increased presence of soldiers. They stroll the boardwalks in pairs, and their sleek vessels navigate around bulkier fishing boats and merchants hauling their wares home for the day.

As Saengo and I cross a bridge that creaks beneath our boots, I'm grateful for the weather. In Evewyn, the sky was clear, but here the moon and stars are hidden behind thick cloud cover, deepening the shadows beyond the reach of lampposts. The rain isn't more than a gentle mist, but pedestrians walk with hats and hoods pulled low over their faces to shield against the damp. Even with our weapons, Saengo and I don't stand out as we tuck in our chins, eyes shrouded beneath our hoods.

Fortunately, even though daylight has gone, it isn't late enough for people to have found their homes and their beds. People still throng the walkways, with the occasional rickshaw clattering past.

Saengo and I keep our hands loose at our sides, our shoulders and backs relaxed. Everyone walks with purpose, like they have a destination in mind. Anyone who pauses on the boardwalk is rewarded with a glower and a curse to keep the flow of traffic moving.

Getting out of the city becomes a circuitous trek but not impossible. We slip behind a carriage headed toward the governor's home to avoid a patrolling guard and then duck into the sunflowers that grow thick around his manor. Since we're familiar with where the manor guards patrol, we avoid them with ease as we circle the home and escape into the patch of forest beyond.

Even with the weather on our side and my craft to sense other travelers, we avoid the road, keeping it in sight only to ensure we're heading in the right direction. In between the stretches of trees, we cut through fields of sunflowers tall enough to dust our chins.

I've never been inside the teahouse where Kyshia wants to

meet, but our party had passed it the first time we traveled to the capital. I hadn't spared it much thought then. Now, I am acutely reminded of the last roadside teahouse Saengo and I had visited for a clandestine meeting. We'd been ambushed by shamans. It's entirely possible we'll be ambushed again. Kyshia would have the advantage.

At least this time we're better prepared. Theyen has been keeping pace with us as well. I haven't heard or seen him, but I can sense the proximity of his soul. Sometimes it vanishes—likely when he's going through a gate—but it appears again soon after. Shadowblessed can see perfectly in the dark, so he has no trouble moving through the night. I can just imagine him sneering at the careful way Saengo and I have to navigate the deep shadows.

We might not know what we're walking into, but Theyen has spent enough time in the Ember Princess's company that he believes her desire to meet is genuine. I can only hope he's right.

The teahouse is easy to spot in the dark. A single lantern stands outside, hanging from the end of a curved post. The teahouse is small and simple, all clean lines and symmetry. Flickering light warms the window glass from within, and several drakes are hitched to a post beside the entrance. The drakes are plain with dark scales and no distinguishable marks or horns. Kyshia would normally ride dragokin with four curling horns, fully draped in the colors and glamour of her station.

But it seems she does know how to be inconspicuous when it suits her.

Saengo and I pause beneath the cover of trees, the teahouse in sight. The damp mist has come and gone, but the clouds remain thick and dark overhead. It's nearly pitch-black beyond the small sphere of lantern light, and there's little risk of being seen, even without the trees.

"If it's a trap, wait for Theyen before rushing inside," I say softly. I sense Theyen farther off, somewhere to our right and at a higher vantage point. "I can hold them off long enough for the two of you to come in together, but don't take any risks and stay hidden."

If Saengo nods, I can't see it, but she gives my shoulder a squeeze before stepping away. I wince when it sounds like she bumps into a tree, but the noise is too muffled to carry as far as the teahouse.

I tug at the shoulder belt, ensuring my swords are secure, and then start toward that small circle of light. As I draw nearer, my craft picks up on the presence of more souls. There are two souls within the teahouse, which gives me pause. There are three drakes out front. In Kyshia's position, I would have brought plenty of trusted guards and then hidden the number of drakes to make them seem fewer in number.

Warily, I approach the lantern. Droplets of rainwater glint against the metal. The fire trapped within the glass burns by shaman magic, without any noticeable fuel or smoke.

As I pass, one of the drakes snorts and tests its reins by

tugging lightly. I reach out to pat the creature on its snout, smiling briefly when its tongue dashes out to lick my fingers. Then I push open the door to the teahouse.

The moment I step inside, I freeze. Seated at a round table in the center of the room is the Ember Princess. A quick glance confirms four guards, two at either side of the entrance and two more bracketing a door at the other end of the teahouse.

Confusion hurtles through me, the awareness of my craft spreading through the room and beyond. But I can't sense their souls.

And then I recognize the ridges of pale brown sewn into their armor. Sunspear bones.

EIGHT

The leather armor is old but newly oiled. The wyvern bones look brittle, at odds with how difficult talismans are to destroy. With the armor, I can't sense the guards' souls, even as my craft burns beneath my fingertips.

Well, now I've confirmation they still work against soul-render craft. But will they work against the Soulless?

Kyshia, in her own full suit of armor, save the helm, waves me forward. Cautiously, I approach, my gaze sweeping over her guards. None of them move. The two souls I sensed are coming from a back room, possibly the people who run this place. Or more guards.

As I approach the table, I take quick stock of my surroundings. The teahouse is markedly different from the last one I'd been inside. This one, although echoing the simplicity of its exterior, is clearly owned by someone with means. The décor is sparse but deliberately chosen—a series of brush paintings depicting mountains and trees in sweeping lines, simple but elegant. The tables and chairs aren't overcrowded. It feels spacious, despite how small it looks from the outside, and every surface is immaculately clean.

It's a business suitable for serving the Ember Princess.

Kyshia smiles pleasantly, as if we're sharing a meal beneath a courtyard pavilion rather than a secret gathering away from the eyes of the capital. Beneath the leather breastplate and spaulders, her inner robes are plain, without the layers of spidersilk, the glittering jewelry, or the extravagant hair ornaments and gold dust. She wears shades of brown and gray in common fabrics, and her hair is pulled back into a braid.

She's tried hard not to look like a highborn woman, and I don't tell her that she's failed. Despite her efforts, the clothes fit her exactly as they are—a costume. Even covered by armor, I can tell the robes are stiff, neatly creased, without a speck of dirt, a frayed hem, or anything else to indicate they've been previously worn. This wouldn't have been obvious if it was just one piece of clothing, but the newness is evident in every visible thread. I can't see her shoes beneath the table, but I'd wager those are newly acquired as well.

Her face and nails are bare, but her fingers look soft and delicate, the nails perfectly shaped and buffed to a shine. She would stand out in a crowd with painful certainty.

She gestures to the seat across from her. "Please sit."

I sit, but I don't offer a greeting or a bow. She isn't my princess. We are not friends. This isn't a social visit. We're here on business, and she must feel the same because she doesn't waste time on pleasantries.

"It was my job as the High Priestess of the Temple of Light to verify your craft before allowing you into Mirrim," she says. There's a note of annoyance in her voice, which is likely deliberate, knowing how practiced she must be at concealing her emotions. I'm not sure if she's annoyed at me or the situation, though, when she continues. "Never mind that it wasn't possible to verify a craft no one knew much about or that you demonstrated your abilities before the Emperor himself."

"Your father doubts you," I say.

"My father loves me," she says at once, "but his advisors are all spineless imbeciles prone to bribery and ambition. Discrediting me would mean positioning one of my siblings as my replacement."

"You wouldn't trust your siblings in the position?" I ask, curious despite myself.

"Their loyalty is to themselves first and the Empire second," she says without much feeling. I wonder what it must be like to have siblings, parents, cousins, an entire family lineage, and to not love any of them.

"And yours isn't," I say, making it a statement instead of a question, just to test her response. She doesn't take the bait, so I continue. "You asked for my help in defeating the Soulless. I'm assuming this means you have a plan."

"I do, and I confess . . . I'm surprised you came. I know you have no reason to trust me."

I raise one eyebrow and cast a quick glance at her guards. While I can't sense the approach of any new souls, given how many suits of armor had been in the Hall of Heroes, there could be a fair number of soldiers in the surrounding area and I would never know it. That's unsettling—and I am admittedly annoyed with how much I've come to rely on my craft in so short a time.

"You and I both know that the best chance at defeating the Soulless is with another soulrender," she says.

"Yes, but I can't do that without being able to get close to him." I gesture to her armor. "Which you've clearly already figured out."

"The armor was indeed a gift by my predecessors," she says.

Recalling Theyen's disgust, I sneer at the notion of hunting wyverns for their bones as a "gift."

"Don't be so quick to judge," she says. "At least not until you hear my proposal."

"Go on then."

"Return to Mirrim and help me draw out the Soulless. You won't even need to fight him. All we need is to get him out in the open so that my sun warriors can finish him. You'll be rewarded for your help, your name will be cleared, and my father will sign a new treaty with Evewyn, ensuring peace between our peoples."

I scoff, doing little to hide my skepticism. "You invited me here to ask me to be *bait*?"

"It makes sense, doesn't it? My sources confirm it isn't just my family he's after. He wants you as well, and you're the only person he won't kill on sight."

Making a mental note to check into those "sources" once— or rather, *if*—I'm able to return to Evewyn, I consider the offer. If she returns to Mirrim with me in tow, it could potentially restore her reputation with her father's advisors. But if her sun warriors somehow succeed in killing the Soulless, where would that leave me?

Would they allow me to leave, or would my imprisonment become a condition of that peace treaty?

I lean back in my seat, stretching out my legs beneath the table. My gaze moves lazily through the room, settling for long seconds on each sun warrior.

Kyshia smiles wider. "You could try to steal the armor from one of my guards, but you would fail. You may be skilled, but you're not a match for five sun warriors."

One side of my lips quirk even as I wonder, *Five?* Unless she's counting herself, which is unlikely, then the fifth must be outside, lurking in the dark and keeping watch.

In any case, Kyshia is right. Without my craft, I could take one of them for sure. Maybe two. Definitely not five.

"And if I decide I don't like your proposal?" I ask.

"Then you may leave." She leans forward a little, her expression earnest. "You're not a monster, Sirscha. Not like him. The best chance we have of stopping him is to work together. You know that, or you wouldn't have come."

"The Soulless is more powerful now than he was when that armor was first forged. There's no way to be certain they're still effective until he stands before us, and by then, it would be too late to fall back."

"As I said, that's why it needs to be you who draws him out. If the armor should fail, you're assured he won't kill you."

Being killed isn't the worst thing the Soulless could do to me. She does have a point, though. The problem is that regardless of Theyen's belief, I don't know if I can trust her to keep her word.

But if she does, then it would mean a peaceful resolution to the greatest threat to King Meilek's rule. The reiwyn would be appeased, and King Meilek could focus his time and resources on rebuilding Evewyn without the specter of outside forces testing his reign.

She takes a deep breath, perhaps sensing my wavering doubt. "Sirscha, I am asking for your help. The man is a wraith. He won't be found until he wants to be, and we don't have enough armor to protect every Yalaeng relative in Mirrim."

I look meaningfully at the four armored sun warriors just within this room protecting her alone, which she ignores. How unfortunate for those relatives deemed "insignificant."

Lacing my fingers over my stomach, I ask, "If I do this for you, how can I trust that you won't kill me as well once the Soulless is down?"

A faint line appears between her perfect brows. I'd bet she dislikes being questioned, given the scrutiny she's already under. "I guaranteed you a safe meeting, and here we are. My word should be enough."

"A meeting that required me to cross the continent just to attend. Your word isn't enough."

We glare at one another for a few tense seconds before she looks away, her fingers tapping along the edge of the table. Shadows steal across her features as she lowers her face. Although numerous sconces line the walls, they're dim, the flames turned low. Beneath a starless sky, the teahouse is a beacon in the dark for the weary traveler. Perhaps that's where Kyshia's other sun warrior is—outside deterring travelers from stopping for a sturdy seat and warm drink.

"Fine then," she says. "What will convince you? Information? Every suit of sunspear armor has been relocated to the winter wing, specifically the frost chamber. You're free to verify it yourself once we reach the Bright Palace."

I tilt my head. "You said there aren't enough to protect every Yalaeng in Mirrim. Why aren't all of them in use?"

"The Emperor has his reasons."

My lip curls in disgust. Within his own court, within his own *family*, the Emperor has those he favors and those he distrusts. Perhaps he withholds the remaining armor in the hopes the Soulless will busy himself with eliminating those less protected. Appalling but unsurprising.

"You'll have to do better than that," I say. Implying the Emperor would use the lives of his own family members, however distantly related, as shields is hardly reassuring.

Kyshia smiles then and I tense. There's something in that smile I dislike, an edge that will cut if prodded.

"Your mentor was Kendara," she says.

I forcibly relax my jaw. What's her angle? Kendara's response to my message means she's still in the Empire, but does she still work for House Yalaeng?

"What of it?" I snap.

"She's a tough old troll, but a damned good spy. I hated letting her go, but she's done her part for the Empire."

"You let her go?" I repeat, wary. I hadn't considered that Kendara would need to seek permission to leave Mirrim. After the way she'd vanished from Evewyn following the attack at Talon's Teahouse, I'd assumed Kendara simply packed up and abandoned her position again.

It stings a little that she hadn't, but holding onto such feelings doesn't serve me, so I shove them away for now. Just as Kendara would want me to.

"You must have been shocked to discover she's Nuvali," Kyshia says. "I imagine you have questions. It would be expected. As I understand it, Kendara meant a lot to you."

My finger twitches, but I resist the urge to curl my hand into a fist. Had Kendara told Kyshia about me? It would make sense, given her loyalty to the Empire, but even so, it feels like yet another betrayal.

"Fortunately, I have answers," Kyshia continues. "I can tell you whatever you wish to know about her—her true name, her family, where she grew up, how she became a spy. Everything."

The offer is enticing, and I hate that I'm tempted. It gnaws at my desire to know Kendara in the ways that I've never been allowed. As she is the only kind of mother I've ever had, it's always been a raw spot that she refuses me even the smallest measure of trust in who she'd been.

But then, what right do I have to her past? If Kendara wanted to share such details with me, she would have. Even though she's the only person besides Saengo who saw more in me than my station, who taught me how to defend myself, to fight for myself, to survive . . . ? I've no right to her story if she has never chosen to disclose it.

I relax my shoulders and say, "That isn't reassurance you won't kill me."

Her expression doesn't change, but when she speaks again, her voice is cool. "Your familiar is outside. I could have her captured in under a minute."

Fury ignites in my belly. A heartbeat later, I'm out of my chair, the knife in my bracer sliding free. I stab the blade into the table, a hair's breadth from where Kyshia's hand rests. She startles back, rigid with surprise.

Her guards jerk forward, the air thickening with restrained magic. Kyshia raises a hand to stall them. I'm pleased to see her fingers tremble faintly.

"I don't need my craft to kill you," I say, low and clear. "If you even *think* about hurting her, I will make you wish you were facing the Soulless instead of me."

Kyshia is quick to hide the fleeting fear in her eyes. When

she speaks, her voice is admirably steady. "You're loyal. I only wanted to be sure. And you don't need to worry. I would never harm another shaman's familiar."

"She's my friend," I say flatly, jerking the knife from the table. A gash remains in the wood. Tucking away the weapon, I settle once again into my seat. "And don't threaten her again or we're done here. I don't give a damn if the Soulless takes out every last one of you."

At least she doesn't seem to know about Theyen. With his shadow craft, we might still stand a chance if she decides to take me to Mirrim by force.

"I know this is a matter of trust," she says. Slowly, she raises her hands as if expecting me to attack her again, and then she carefully rises to her feet.

I watch, wary, my gaze narrowing on the sword at her waist as she lowers her hands to her belt. She surprises me by gingerly unbuckling it. Piece by piece, she removes the leather armor. First the bracers, then the fauld followed by the spaulders, leg guards, and finally the breastplate. She drops each onto the table between us.

Gradually, her soul becomes more distinct. It begins as a spark, buried beneath layers I can't penetrate. As each layer is peeled away, her soul grows in shape and form. She's close enough that I could grip it without effort. I wouldn't even have to worry about hurting anyone else in the process because her guards are still protected in their armor. They're alert, though, their hostility palpable.

"There," she says, gesturing to the pile. "If you want the sunspear armor, take it and go, but it'll do you little good. The Soulless is in Mirrim, and unless we do things my way, I won't be helping you get inside, nor will I speak on your behalf if you're captured. Then again, you're Kendara's pupil, so I wouldn't put it past you to break into the city undetected. But our kingdoms will remain at odds, and I cannot promise I'll be able to restrain my father and brother if they decide Evewyn is our enemy for its alliance with you and Kazahyn."

My teeth clench, anger simmering in my gut. The peace between our kingdoms shouldn't be a bargaining chip, but she knows as well as I do that a war would favor the Empire. While it's true that their only point of attack by land is through the northern grasslands, which would force them to funnel their troops, the Empire could theoretically draw out the war for years. Maybe even decades. Their army is considerably larger than ours. Even without their crafts due to the proximity of the Dead Wood, they would outlast us.

I scowl and think about Lord Ge making demands in King Meilek's council room and of how King Meilek is willing to protect me, foolishly, at the risk of war with a kingdom vastly larger in size, resources, and troops.

I think of the fight I'd seen between the shamanborn and the soldier, of how many squabbles and skirmishes must happen every day that aren't shared with the king. Evewyn's peace, both within and without, is constantly at risk of tipping toward war, and all of it is King Meilek's burden to bear. It'd be a challenge even for a seasoned ruler, much less one so recently crowned.

My fingers dig into my thighs, my hands aching for the weight of a sword. The sunspear armor lies in a heap on the table. I could just take it. If the sun warriors try to stop me, Kyshia would make an easy hostage until Theyen got us out. But then what?

On the other hand, if I return with her to Mirrim and everything goes according to plan, not only would we remove the Soulless but also the threat of war. It's a dangerous gamble, the stakes too high to quantify.

"I want to speak to the Emperor myself," I say at last. "I want his word in addition to yours. On paper."

Kyshia releases a breath, her entire body relaxing into her seat. "I'll see to it."

"Then I need to speak with Saengo. It's not just my life we're risking."

"Very well, but you should decide quickly. Once you're ready, we can leave immediately and reach Mirrim by tomorrow evening."

I nod and push to my feet. Outside, the moment I slip into the trees, Saengo's voice emerges from the dark.

"How did it go? You look uninjured."

As my eyes adjust, her figure detaches from the blur of trees. Sighing, I tell her I'm fine and then convey Kyshia's offer. Theyen's soul is close by, so he must be listening as well. If not for my craft, though, I wouldn't have known where he is. He remains completely hidden in the shadows.

"You trust her?" Saengo asks. She moves carefully to my side so that our arms brush.

"No. But she did keep her word about this meeting, and she offered to let me take her armor." I rub my temple. "The Soulless is in Mirrim, so we'd have to get into the city anyway. At least this way, we're guaranteed a way in."

"Supposedly."

"Supposedly," I repeat.

"Well . . . I've never liked the idea of you having to face the Soulless alone. If we can avoid it, I think it's a chance worth taking," she says. "All you'd have to do is lure him out of hiding, and then the sun warriors can handle him."

"Kyshia wants the credit for defeating him," I say. "It's the only reason House Yalaeng would be willing to work with me." I trust in that certainty more than I trust Kyshia. If nothing else, being able to claim victory against a man who's haunted Thiy's history for centuries would elevate House Yalaeng's reputation, restore the people's faith in their leaders, and put to rest the doubts about Kyshia's loyalties.

"I'm coming with you," Saengo says.

I bite the inside of my cheeks. I don't want her trapped inside the city with me, but as I'd told Kyshia, it wouldn't simply be my own life I'm risking. If anything happens to me, Saengo would die as well. Besides that, with how aggressive the rot has become, I'm afraid to leave her unattended for more than a few days at a time.

Reluctantly, I nod. "Then you're sure we should do this?"

She releases a small huff of laughter. "Not at all, but I don't see how we have much of a choice. If something goes wrong . . ."

"We'll escape. Like in Vos Gillis." I'd allowed myself to be captured in Vos Gillis, and Phaut had set the queen's ships on fire to allow me the time to escape. With an encouraging smile, I say, "A diversion usually works."

Warm fingers grope for mine in the dark, and I grasp her hand tightly. "We'll watch each other's backs," she says.

Decision made, we enter the teahouse. The moment Kyshia spots Saengo, a satisfied grin stretches her lips. Saengo has to squeeze my fingers to keep me from baring my teeth at the woman.

It doesn't take long for one of Kyshia's guards to retrieve her carriage, which she'd evidently stowed farther down the road. She assures us that so long as Saengo and I remain concealed within her carriage when we reach Mirrim, we'll be safe. With the seal of House Yalaeng and the Temple of Light painted across the door, no one would dare stop us.

Kyshia puts her armor back on, which is just as well. It helps me to relax without the press of nearby souls. I can no longer sense Theyen, although I suspect he hasn't left us yet. Not until dawn, when he'll have no choice but to leave so as not to be stranded until nightfall. I'm quietly grateful.

Although a lantern hangs from a hook beside the driver's seat, the light doesn't quite reach inside the carriage. I can't make out more than Kyshia's general shape across from me and Saengo. Saengo had passed her bow and quiver to one of the guards to be stowed at the rear of the carriage, only holding onto a knife belted at her waist. Although I removed my shoulder belt for comfort, both my swords are propped against the seat within easy reach.

The hour is late, but I'm too anxious to rest, my craft alert for souls outside our carriage. I can sense every creature perched on nearby branches or asleep in burrows beneath fields of sunflowers.

Saengo dozes in fits. She slumps against me every time she nods off before coming awake again with a slight start. If my internal clock is to be trusted, it's well past midnight when she finally gives in and falls asleep.

Kyshia has no trouble drifting off nearly the moment the carriage starts moving. I'm not sure whether to be insulted or amused. Her head rests against a pillow tucked above the back of the seat. Although she doesn't drool or sleep with her mouth open—I sort of hoped she would—she does snore a little. I'm tempted to pinch her nostrils just to see what she'd do.

But I refrain, remembering that I'm not here to amuse myself. She might have a full guard of sun warriors, but it's still dangerous for her to be out here with the Soulless's exact whereabouts unknown.

Then again, were he to materialize in front of our carriage, that would rather expedite this whole process. If I can't take down five sun warriors without my craft, then I don't know how the Soulless would be able to manage it when he's only recently regained his physical strength.

Unfortunately—or fortunately, I haven't quite decided— the Soulless doesn't appear, and we continue on in silence.

NINE

The following evening, we pass the Spirit of the Mountain. Saengo had convinced me to rest, at least for an hour or so before we reach the city. Since I want to have all my wits about me once we're inside, I had conceded.

When I awaken, it's to Saengo's hushed voice and Kyshia's equally soft response.

"When did you realize she's alive?" Saengo asks.

"I've always known. All shamans who live near the Mountain feel her presence, as do our familiars."

My eyes open. Saengo is leaning forward, one hand holding back the window curtain as she peers out. Past her head, a distant peak cuts through a darkening sky. Mist undulates like gauze above a verdant mountainside, and waterfalls split the canopy in silver ribbons. Looking at the Mountain makes me want to rub my eyes, as if I'm not quite seeing right.

The Mountain's presence is indeed palpable, if only in a quiet way. She doesn't call to me—not in the way the Soulless's magic does. And not in the way Saengo seems to be drawn to her.

The waning light spreads a diffuse glow against the slope of Saengo's cheeks and the bridge of her nose. Her gaze remains fixed on the Mountain, steady and intent. She doesn't even blink. My muscles tense, and I have to fight the impulse to tug her away from the window and shove the curtain back into place.

"Have you ever been to the Spirit of the Mountain?" Kyshia asks Saengo.

My eyes narrow, wondering if perhaps she knows about Saengo's recent visit. But her voice is even, and the question seems little more than genuine curiosity.

Saengo shakes her head. "You must have, though. You're still the High Priestess of the Light Temple, I assume?"

"I visit the temple at the base of the Mountain once a year to pay my respects. Many shamans do. She is the oldest spirit on Thiy, after all—the living embodiment of our magic. I could take you after this is all over." Having noticed I'm awake, Kyshia nods to indicate the offer extends to me as well.

Saengo tears her gaze away from the Mountain long enough to glance at Kyshia. "Can you speak to her?"

"It would be impossible. She is wrought of pure magic."

"But then how did Suri do it?" I ask, slowly stretching out my back and neck. I feel groggy. I've gotten far too used to a proper night's rest in a soft bed. I'm going to have to start sleeping on the stone balcony.

"No one knows," she says. "Suri never put it into writing."

Saengo's brows furrow as she returns to gazing out at that hazy peak. She'd said that the Mountain wants her to be at peace.

What if being at peace means putting Saengo's soul to rest? It's only the familiar bond that keeps her here, leashing her life to mine. The worry knots ever tighter in my stomach.

I can't lose her, I think desperately, perhaps selfishly, before I force my thoughts to quiet and my limbs to relax. Wanting Saengo to be at peace could mean anything. Whatever hold the Spirit of the Mountain seems to have on her is a concern for the future, after the Soulless is defeated.

"She's beautiful," Saengo murmurs, "even if she is a spirit."

"The two aren't mutually exclusive. Although some spirits are more beautiful than others," Kyshia says.

I'm amazed to see a red flush rise from Saengo's neck to her cheeks. How long had the two been talking before I awakened?

Saengo has expressed interest in others before, but it's never amounted to anything. In any other situation, I would happily help her pursue a romantic relationship, but the Ember Princess requires caution. Despite our agreement, she is still technically an adversary, and her motives are unclear at best.

Not that I'm a beacon of experience. There've been people I looked at twice—a boy with dark curls and an infectious laugh, a girl with freckles and a bandolier of knives, a flirtatious apothecary who overfilled the herbs and tinctures I collected for Kendara. But they were passing fancies, brief and insubstantial. Between Company lessons and Kendara's training, I had plenty of obligations to occupy my time and thoughts. Not much has changed.

I don't expect Saengo to feel the same way about her priorities. I simply hope she isn't too interested in Kyshia. Even if the woman could be trusted, she's a Yalaeng. Her engagement to Theyen may be unofficially dissolved, but her marriage is still reserved for political gain. If she breaks Saengo's heart, I can't promise I wouldn't cause an international incident to avenge my best friend.

Sisters, what am I even thinking? All this, just because Saengo *blushed*?

I slowly roll the tension out of my shoulders. Maybe I'm eager to imagine a future for her beyond the Soulless. Beyond all this conflict and danger. Beyond her tether to me.

She deserves a future rich with adventure and love. I just have to ensure it happens.

As Kyshia predicted, we pass through Mirrim's gates without incident. I try not to feel like I'm being carted into a prison, although I spend several excruciating minutes with my hands around my swords, my craft blooming with the awareness of countless souls spread out ahead of us. I still can't separate them into individual points of light, but I can determine when any of them draw close to our carriage.

Once we're inside the city, I ease my grip on my swords.

My nerves are slower to settle. Kyshia is our only ally here. If she decides to betray us, we will have no shelter. Theyen's presence vanished sometime before sunrise. We are well beyond his help now.

The curtains remain closed even though night has fallen, making it more difficult for anyone to see inside the carriage. Kyshia had mentioned finding Saengo room and board at one of the inns owned by the Light Temple. Before agreeing, we made her provide in minute detail the inn's location, floor plan, building structure, surrounding streets, and every possible entryway on each level.

Back in Evewyn, we'd mapped out potential escape points from Mirrim. Theyen had provided a map of the capital, and with his knowledge of the city at street level, we'd noted the weakest points along the walls and calculated the quickest routes to reach them.

While I dislike separating, should anything go wrong, I need Saengo out here rather than trapped in the Bright Palace with me. She might not have been trained as a Shadow, but she is a soldier. My personal insecurities aside, I know that she can handle herself without me.

It's also the better option with the Soulless loose in the city. After my time with him at Spinner's End, I know that he can sense when I'm near. Familiars are different, though, their souls bright and abundant throughout Mirrim. She'll be safe from him so long as she isn't at my side.

The carriage begins to slow, and I risk nudging aside the

curtain. I don't recognize the line of whitewashed buildings, but we're in a back alley to avoid prying eyes. Overhead, the roofs are strung with golden lanterns to ward off the dark. I'd spent most of my time in Mirrim cooped up in the Temple of Light or wandering the nearby streets with Light Temple escorts.

We draw to a stop behind a three-story inn. Even from the back, it's impressive. Shining arches crown the windows, and flowering ivy cascades from a gently sloping roof.

"Does the Temple of Light own many businesses like this?" I ask Kyshia.

"A fair few. I prefer not to rely on donations alone to support the Temple. Suri was a lightwender and has many worshippers who leave generous offerings. But the Soulless is a lightwender as well, and public opinion has already begun to turn. Ensuring we've other means to maintain the Temple is a necessity."

I see her point. Even when donations wane, the priests, priestesses, and all the Light Temple disciples still need to be fed and clothed. The grounds still need to be maintained, and the servants and staff still need to be paid.

The inn's back door swings open, and a lightwender man with a trimmed beard and flowing gray robes strides out. He drops into a bow before the carriage and remains there, bent at the waist, as one of Kyshia's sun warriors opens the carriage door. Overhead, the lanterns go dim, dousing the alley in shadows.

Saengo takes my hand and gives me a meaningful look.

I nod. If anything goes awry, we are to make our way to our designated escape points and rendezvous outside the city walls. We don't wait on the other.

Of course, even though we'd agreed that neither of us would do anything stupid, I know they're empty assurances. If I suspect Saengo is in danger, I won't abandon her. So nothing had better go wrong.

"I'll send a message before midnight and then again at dawn so that you know I'm all right," I tell Saengo.

She nods and then addresses Kyshia. "I'm trusting you to keep her safe."

"That's what I was going to say." I embrace her quickly, and then Saengo rises from the seat, ducking out of the carriage.

The lightwender man, who must be the innkeeper, finally rises from his bow to assist Saengo from the carriage. Then he gestures wordlessly to the open door with another polite bob of his head. Saengo glances over her shoulder as one sun warrior returns her weapons and another shuts the carriage door. I brush aside the curtain, watching until she disappears inside and the lanterns brighten again.

Anxiety roils in my stomach, but there's no helping it. We're here. We've no choice but to see this through. A moment later, the carriage begins to move, this time toward the gleaming structure that is the Bright Palace.

The journey doesn't take long. The driver guides us through the outer gate and then off the courtyard to a wide lane set with smooth stone tiles. Trees bursting with large white blossoms line either side of the lane, along with tall silver lampposts. It's almost idyllic.

At last, the carriage rumbles to a stop. The Ember Princess gets out first, fingers clutching at the leather fauld as if she's wearing fine spidersilk robes instead of aged armor and rough-spun fabrics. I follow her, strapping on my shoulder belt the moment I'm outside.

The sun warriors usher us through a hidden doorway and then up a staircase to a narrow corridor lined in mullioned windows. Beyond, the sky is overcast, the clouds lingering from the evening before, although there has been no rain. The moon is impossible to spot behind the thick cover.

As we approach the end of the corridor, a servant in gold and white robes appears behind us. Her gaze finds the Ember Princess, and her steps are urgent as she hurries forward. My eyes narrow at the way her fingers flutter restlessly about her sash.

Kyshia pauses, silent as the servant murmurs something into her ear. Her back is to me, so I can't see her face, but I can read the stillness in her body, the way she hesitates even after the servant finishes delivering her message. Then she turns to me.

Her expression is neutral, a contrast to the way the servant beside her visibly swallows and glances nervously between me and the floor. She should really find servants who are more discreet.

"There's something I must attend to," she says.

"An emergency?" I ask lightly.

"A small matter. My guards will see you to a waiting room. Once I've finished I'll be back to collect you, and we can speak to the Emperor then."

She doesn't wait for me to agree. She continues down the hallway, the servant close on her heels along with three of her sun warriors. She turns left and disappears from view.

One of the two sun warriors who remain with me jerks her head to indicate I should follow, and we turn right. I'm a bit surprised we're speaking to the Emperor tonight—I'd assumed it would wait until morning. The urgency concerns me a little. Does Kyshia think the Emperor will change his mind if we delay? And does it have anything to do with the "small matter" she's been called away to address?

I would bet my swords that another Yalaeng has been found dead. If that's the case, then it's no wonder they want to see this over with as soon as possible. There's no telling how long the Soulless plans to draw things out. He could work his way through all of the Yalaeng branch families first, or he could come for the Emperor tomorrow.

The sun warriors see me to a windowless room with sparse furnishings and a cold fireplace. When they demand my swords, I weigh the consequences of fighting them compared with the benefits of remaining armed. Eventually, I give in. I'll have to surrender them anyway in order to speak with the Emperor, and the struggle isn't worth it.

The sun warriors lock me inside, two magically burning

sconces my only sources of light. A low table sits in the center of the room, surrounded by four thick cushions. There are no other furnishings. I line up the cushions and sprawl across them, stacking my hands behind my head and closing my eyes.

Although I've barely slept since we left Evewyn, all trace of drowsiness has fled. The only temptation sleep provides at the moment is the possibility of a visit from the Soulless so that I can question him about the matter requiring Kyshia's immediate attention. But the night is early, and he may not yet be asleep. Especially if he's just killed someone.

With my eyes closed, I allow my craft to unfurl beyond the walls of my room, seeking the nearest souls and pushing the physical limits of my awareness. I can't sense anyone directly outside my door, but that's because my guards are wearing sunspear armor. While souls occasionally pass in neighboring corridors, they're indistinct spots of light, distant and formless.

Without a window, it's difficult to tell how much time has passed when someone finally approaches my door. I frown. I don't think it's Kyshia. She would have had to remove her armor, and that's unlikely if another Yalaeng has just been found dead.

I sit up as the lock clicks and the door pushes open. Then I scramble to my feet, my breath catching as my stomach tries to climb into my throat.

Kendara steps inside, carrying a tea tray, of all things. Past her, the sun warriors meant to stand guard are absent. She shuts the door, which only locks from the outside. Even without the sun warriors, Kendara and I both know that she is all that's needed to keep me here.

I stand awkwardly amid the pile of pillow cushions, uncertain of what to say. Kendara isn't dressed in Nuvali colors or the uniform of a guard. Instead, she wears a fitted dark-gray robe, a plain black sash, and loose gray pants tucked into knee-high boots. Worn leather bracers cinch her wrists, and her swords—Suryali and Nyia, named after the sun and moon—are belted at her waist.

As ever, the upper half of her face is concealed beneath a black handkerchief, and her hair, more white than black, is pulled into a tight braid. Her head tilts the slightest bit, and I get the impression she is taking my measure even though she can't see me.

"Who *are* you?" I finally ask, my voice barely a whisper. Who is she that she can send away the Ember Princess's own sun warriors, assigned to watch a soulrender?

I don't expect an answer, and I'm not disappointed. I continue, anyway.

"Why are you—?" My voice stalls.

A large white spider creeps out from beneath her collar and settles on her shoulder. The creature has long, spindly legs and a bulbous lower body with a frost-like pattern in pale silver. Its many, glittering blue eyes watch me, almost as if it's curious.

Kendara sets the tea tray on the table and then gracefully kneels. I watch, bemused, as she arranges the teapot and cups. The spider on her shoulder rubs its front legs together.

"Is that . . . a familiar?" I ask, edging around the table to better see what she's doing. She doesn't look up as she pours two cups of steaming tea. It smells like plums.

"I don't know why you're surprised. You've got one, too."

"Have you always had one?" Was it simply that I'd never seen it?

Kendara gives the spider a gentle pat with one finger. Then she sips her tea and, again, doesn't answer.

More annoyed now than confused, I ask, "Why a frost spider?"

Frost spiders are more comfortable in colder temperatures, like the ice spinners of the far north. Frost spiders can grow quite large as well, although they're nowhere near the size of the spinner Ronin made into his familiar. Ice spinners build webs that span mountainsides.

Where would she have found a frost spider spirit this far south? Knowing Kendara, she had likely chosen it deliberately. She's always spoken of Ronin with distaste. It would amuse her to make a white spider her familiar. She wouldn't regard the creature with any sort of affection. To her, a familiar is a means to an end.

Kendara sets down her teacup, her actions always so measured and exact. Then she stretches out against one of the cushions I'd just been sprawled on. "The palace is buzzing with the news of a soulrender in the Emperor's possession."

I bristle. "I'm not a thing for him to possess."

"Why are you here, fool child?"

"I should be asking you that. You said you'd left Mirrim." I drag a cushion over with my foot and then lower onto it, knees tucked beneath me. Since she can't see me anyway, I give in to what she'd call sentimentality and drink in the sight of her. Even though she's scolding me, I've missed the sound of her voice. I quickly reel in my emotions when my eyes begin to sting.

Still, I can't seem to swallow down the lump in my throat. She sips her tea, reclining on a cushion as if we haven't been apart for months, as if I hadn't believed that I would never see or hear from her again. As if it hadn't wounded me that she let me go so easily, no matter that I understood why.

"I did leave," Kendara says, raising one knee to prop her arm on it. She's being suspiciously casual. "But circumstances demanded I return."

"It's the same for me," I say flatly, hoping my voice doesn't give away my emotions.

Kendara scoffs and places her teacup squarely atop the saucer. Her awareness of her surroundings, unhindered by her blindness, can only be the result of countless years of training. It is a level of skill that I can only hope to reach one day. If I survive the Soulless.

"How desperate are you that you made a deal with the Yalaengs?" she says, sneering. I'm not sure if she expects an answer or if she's just being typically derisive.

"Well, it's a pity you weren't around to advise me against it," I say. "You seem well familiar with them. Are you here to give me more choices?"

I look to the door, and an awareness unspools within me. I sense no other souls nearby. There is no one to hear should anything happen.

My fingers curve against my thighs, hard enough to sting. "Or are you here to end a threat against the Empire?"

TEN

There is no doubt that House Yalaeng considers me a threat. I am a soulrender. That's the only reason they need to have me eliminated.

Maybe every word Kyshia spoke at the teahouse had been a lie—a ruse to get me here. To end me before I could turn my craft against them. The worst part is that I'd known this might be a possibility, and I had come anyway.

My body slowly coils, muscles taut with anticipation. I scan the room for a weapon but there is nothing of use other than the tea. It might be hot enough to scald, which could provide a moment's distraction for me to reach the unlocked door.

Even as my thoughts race, my stomach sinks. Kendara has always placed completing one's mission over all other priorities. She defied the Empire once to save her friend—my mother. Would she do so again to save that friend's daughter?

Kendara smirks. It is neither kind nor reassuring. "If ever I were to kill you, Sirscha, I would give you the chance to defend yourself. A teacher should always allow their student the courtesy of demonstrating what they've learned."

"Is mind reading your craft?" I ask with a resentfulness that's only partially feigned. I hope I've learned to read her well enough that I can trust she's being truthful. Muscle by muscle, my body gradually relaxes.

"Not even truth seekers can divine a person's thoughts," she says, still with that bite of disdain.

"Then why are you here?"

"To offer advice to my idiot pupil." Her voice lowers, and I find myself leaning forward, curious. "Do not trust the Emperor to keep his word, not if breaking it would be a greater benefit. Any agreements with him *must* be put to paper."

"All right," I say warily. Not that I'm ungrateful for the warning, but I can't help being suspicious of her candor. It's not what I'd expect from a loyal subject. "What else?"

"One of his few redeeming traits is that he does not want war. He's had ample opportunity to invade Evewyn, but he's resisted his advisors' heckling to summon the imperial army and march westward. He prides himself on being a scholar and a patron of the arts rather than a warrior."

"I was under the impression it was Kyshia who's been keeping her father from going to war."

Kendara makes a dismissive flick with her fingers. "The Emperor needs someone to blame, and his advisors need a target for their dissatisfaction."

I suppose that's why they were so eager to doubt her loyalty after I revealed my true craft in Tamsimno.

"For the most part, Kyshia's word can be trusted. Although once your deal with her is complete, she won't hesitate to make another one to kill you if she thinks you're a threat."

"I'd expect nothing less," I say, glowering into my teacup. The steam warms my face as I recall the way Kyshia had smiled at Saengo in the dim, enclosed space of the carriage. "So if the Ember Princess goes through with her plan, do you think it could work?"

"I don't know what you've got planned," she says airily, which I don't believe for a second. "But the person you need to be most careful with is His Imperial Highness, Prince Aleng. You can drink that, you know. It's not poisoned. In fact, it's an Evewynian blend. I grew fond of their tea."

My fingers rest against the sides of my teacup. The heat is just shy of burning. "I thought it smelled familiar." Still, I don't drink it. "Prince Aleng doesn't seem particularly involved in the running of the Empire."

Kendara snorts. "Oh, he isn't, but he's been vocal, nonetheless. Like many within the court, he views his father's inaction as weakness. We're all fortunate he's too spoiled and lazy to take a more active role in this conflict. Even so, since he agrees with his father's advisors, they've been pressuring him to assert his authority. If he is present when you speak to the Emperor, be mindful of him."

Abruptly, she rises from her recline with the ease and grace of someone half her age. I shove to my feet as well, my body seized with sudden restlessness.

As she turns toward the door, I hurry around the table and blurt out, "I thought I'd never see you again."

With Kendara, there's simply no way of knowing when, if ever, she'll present herself to me next. If this is goodbye, I don't want to hold on to any regrets.

Kendara faces me again, lips slightly pursed. Then, to my shock, she reaches out and closes her hands around mine. I swallow down the tightness in my throat as her fingers smooth over my knuckles. The skin of her palms is thick and calloused after so many years of training and gripping a weapon.

"Fool child," she murmurs, and there's no mistaking the fondness in her voice. My eyes sting, an ache and a yearning clutching at my ribs. I squeeze my eyes shut, glad she can't see my weakness for her that is so plainly on my face. "You could be the greatest student I ever taught if only you'd let go of this sentimentality."

My voice is barely above a whisper when I ask, "Back in Evewyn, with me and King Meilek and the others, were you always loyal to the Empire even then? Is this where your heart was all those years you were with us?"

Did you ever love me for who I became, or has it always been because I am your friend's child? Regrets or not, even if we never meet again, I'm too cowardly to voice the question out loud.

She squeezes my hand once and then lets go. "Never give your whole heart to a single place or person. Nothing deserves that kind of loyalty."

As she turns away, any other questions I might have fall silent on my tongue. She shuts the door after her, and the lock clicks once more.

For a while, I sit with my back to the door, confused and annoyed.

Part of me wishes Kendara hadn't come at all. My thoughts are muddled, my resolve shaken, my emotions unraveled. I need to be focused when I face the Emperor.

Groaning, I cover my face and work to regain the sense of purpose I came here with, before Kendara's visit. With effort, I narrow my concentration on my breathing—in and out, deep breaths to ground me in the moment.

Sometime later, the lock clicks open. I stand, stepping away before the door can swing inward. I didn't sense the approach of any souls, so I'm not surprised to see Kyshia's two sun warriors awaiting me.

"It's time," one of them says.

Is this what it's like to be led to one's execution?

But this isn't an execution, I remind myself. They need me, at least for now, although I keep in mind Kendara's warnings.

None of them can be fully trusted, but so long as Kyshia and the Emperor agree to commit our deal to writing, then we shouldn't have any problems.

The sun warriors lead me through empty corridors, the walls plain stone, unadorned by the usual tapestries or sun motifs. We must be taking private routes, away from palace inhabitants.

Before long, we reach a thick set of oak doors that open into what must be a secondary throne room. It isn't very large, and it's sparsely decorated compared with the opulence of the imperial gardens where I'd first been presented to the Emperor. On the dais, Emperor Cedral is seated on a wooden throne, the back carved into elegant patterns and the seat a lush red satin. Mounted behind him is a shining sun of wrought gold, a dozen rays spreading outward."

He's outfitted in sunspear armor that's been altered to make it suitable for royalty. Golden accents embellish the polished leather, which he wears over layers of crimson spidersilk. Instead of a crown, his hair is fashioned with a gleaming hair ornament that extends from his topknot like the spines of a fan.

To the Emperor's right is a young man in another set of sunspear armor—Prince Aleng, the Sun's Heir. He glowers at me with the same nose and dimpled chin as his father, but he has Kyshia's eyes. Or rather, their mother's. After Kendara's warning, I hoped he would be absent. Kyshia stands at the Emperor's left. While she still wears sunspear armor, beneath it, she has swapped the simple, rough fabrics for white spidersilk robes and a thick golden sash.

They make an intimidating trio, but I suspect that's the point.

Since this is a private meeting, the only others in attendance are a half dozen sun warriors. In the far-right corner beside the dais, Kendara stands with her back against the wall, looking as comfortable as she had on the cushions in my room. Besides myself, she is the only other person present who isn't wearing sunspear armor.

Although my stomach tenses at the sight of her, I allow my gaze to pass over her, settling on the Emperor. I trail behind the two sun warriors as we approach the dais and drop into a bow.

I don't bother getting onto my knees. The first time I met the Emperor had been in front of the entire imperial court. I'd been pretending to be a soulguide, so I had to be careful of my every word and action.

Now, with the truth out and the awareness that the Emperor would just as soon kill me as use me, I bow only in respect for our bargain.

The sun warriors who escorted me join their comrades at either side of the room, leaving me to stand alone before the three Yalaengs. Priestess Mia had warned me not to look the Emperor in the eye. I disregard that advice now, lifting my chin when his amber eyes narrow at my insolence. He's a lightwender, like Kyshia. Aleng, however, has eyes clear as amethysts—a windwender.

"Soulrender," the Emperor begins, and I swallow back the words that leap to my tongue. *My name is Sirscha. Not "soulrender."* "My daughter informs me that you will be assisting with apprehending the Soulless."

"On the condition that you make peace with Evewyn," I say, just in case he tries to conveniently forget that part.

Aleng's glower darkens further. My eyes narrow first on him and then at the rigid way the Emperor sits, some of that tension bleeding into his expression. At his other side, Kyshia's easy manner in the carriage is gone. She regards me with a cold blankness.

Something isn't right. I try not to look at Kendara, who hasn't moved from her place against the wall.

Emperor Cedral inclines his head, acknowledging his part in our bargain. "With King Meilek, it may yet be possible to repair the friendship between our kingdoms."

Aleng scoffs and addresses the Emperor. "Evewyn's king refused our requests for reparations. How can this be friendship?"

"He accepted all your requests save for two," I remind him. His eyes flash with fury that I would dare speak to him. "Although if amendments have been made since, I wouldn't know about them. I am no longer his Shadow."

The Emperor betrays his confusion for only a heartbeat when his brows furrow. "He didn't send you?"

"He doesn't know I'm here," I confirm. No matter what happens, I cannot allow King Meilek to take any blame for my actions. The consequences must be mine alone. "I'm offering my services as an Evewynian citizen, loyal to King Meilek and his desire for peace. That's all."

Even though he's already standing over me, Aleng raises his chin even higher. He wears the sunspear armor well, but I can tell he isn't used to it. He's been pampered and protected his entire life.

"Father, she betrays her king by coming here. We can't trust that she won't betray us as well."

Ignoring him, I address the Emperor. "I'll accept whatever punishment King Meilek requires of me, but if this ends in peace between our kingdoms, isn't that a benefit for all?"

Aleng still answers, though. "A benefit for a speck of a kingdom like Evewyn, perhaps. We will not simply concede with what you want, not after today."

What does he mean by that? *"Not after today?"* If I'm correct in that another Yalaeng has been killed, was the Soulless more discerning this time in his choice of victim?

"This was not the agreement," I say icily.

"Father," Kyshia begins, but he raises a hand, and her mouth snaps shut.

The Emperor tilts his head toward his son. "I would hear your thoughts."

I clench my jaw, fingers flexing at my sides. I shouldn't have let them take my swords.

Aleng's smile is smug as he continues, this time speaking directly to me. "As I understand it, this new King Meilek has much to contend with, what with your peoples being so divided. Evewyn is too unstable a kingdom to rely on as an ally, and by your own admission, you sought a deal without your king's blessing. Soulrenders cannot be trusted."

I see now why Kendara said he would be the one to watch for. My lip curls in disgust, and my next words are all but snarled. "Princess Kyshia is the one who sought me out, all but begging for my help. House Yalaeng is the reason the Soulless still lives, a lie your family harbored for centuries. And now you mean to revoke the terms of our agreement. You're hardly in a position to speak about trust."

The moment the words are out, I grimace and bite down on my tongue, but I suppose it doesn't matter. Even as disappointing an heir as Aleng is, for whatever reason, the Emperor values his opinion. Aleng will never honor the deal I made with Kyshia.

"You see, Father," Aleng says, gesturing to me with a heavily bejeweled hand, "this is what Evewyn thinks of the Empire."

"Don't mistake my words for those of my king. King Meilek wants only to reconcile."

Aleng continues as if I haven't spoken. "Before we sign any such agreements with Evewyn, this soulrender must swear fealty to the Nuvalyn Empire. We will not risk another soulrender wreaking havoc on the continent, not unless she is under our control."

I suck in a slow, furious breath. Before I can speak, Kyshia finally cuts in.

"I gave her my word and the word of House Yalaeng. Would you have that mean so little?" she demands.

"The Emperor's word was not yours to give," Aleng says. "It hasn't been since you allowed a soulrender into the imperial court, within range of performing unspeakable disaster to His Imperial Majesty."

"Father, you gave me your blessing," she hisses, her composure fracturing. "You know where my loyalties lie. You know what I've done for the Empire. Aleng doesn't care about any of this. He thinks of ruling the Empire as a game, with pieces to discard or use at his leisure—"

"Silence," the Emperor says curtly. He doesn't speak loudly, but Kyshia's mouth snaps shut. Her lips compress, nostrils flaring delicately. "Soulrender, my son believes you should swear fealty to the Empire. What have you to say to this?"

I glare at them, my teeth clenched. In the corner, Kendara shifts against the wall. What must she think of all this? Had she known this would happen? Was that why she'd warned me?

I should have known that Kyshia's word would be worthless, and yet I had hoped beyond all reason that we could make this work. Even if I agree to their demand, they'll likely want me killed once I've served my purpose.

But how could I possibly pledge myself to the Empire? Some years ago, Kendara sent me to a small village north of Vos Talwyn during the Festival of the Twins. People celebrated all throughout the kingdom with days-long feasts, games, and competitions, all to earn the good fortune of the Bright Twin and to appease the Pale Twin.

My task was to enter the archery contest disguised as a villager and win second place. What Kendara hadn't informed me was that the contest was sponsored by the local Sanctuary. Only those already sworn to join the Sanctuary were eligible to enter.

It would have been simple to provide a false name, repeat the vows to get into the contest, and then disappear afterward. Kendara would have expected it.

While I'm always prepared to lie when it suits me, making a vow to the Sisters and then breaking that vow is no minor thing. It didn't matter that I'd never been particularly devout. I couldn't do it. So instead, I bribed one of the judges into letting me enter along with the promise that I would take my vows afterward. Then I won second place and made my escape.

Kendara had been disgruntled. The entire point of the lesson had been to test my fortitude and loyalty, but she couldn't argue that I hadn't completed the task as she'd instructed.

Now, before the most powerful shamans on Thiy, I say, "I will not swear fealty to the Empire."

I can practically feel Kendara's disapproval from across the room. Her voice rings in my head. *Pathetic. Your first real test for Evewyn, and you've failed. Why are you even here if you don't have what it takes to achieve your goal?*

But I'm not like her. I can't pledge loyalty to another kingdom and not mean it. Even with a false name, this isn't the sort of thing one should do lightly, and certainly not with the intent to break it. Who I am—my name, my existence, the weight I ascribe to my own admittedly twisted sense of honor—may mean nothing to others, but these are the few things I've ever been able to call my own. I must treasure them, even if no one else does.

Aleng steps nearly to the edge of the dais. "The Soulless will not take any more of us. Tonight, it was Eren. Tomorrow, it could be me or Kyshia. You will do this in the name of the Empire because it is your duty."

My eyes narrow. Eren is the Emperor's third son. The Soulless had gone after a direct member of the imperial family. This explained the tension in the room, but why would Aleng admit such a thing in front of me when their House has gone to such lengths to keep the murders silent?

"I am Evewynian," I say. "I owe you nothing."

"You are a shaman," he says, raising his voice. The Emperor frowns at his outburst but doesn't disrupt him. "The magic you now wield was a gift from Suryal, as all crafts are. Your roots are here, in the Empire."

"Evewyn is my home, and I decide where to place my loyalty. Not you, not my craft, and not some long dead goddess."

Aleng sucks in a sharp breath at my blasphemy. Even the corners of Emperor Cedral's mouth dip in displeasure. Kyshia is already scowling at her brother, so she merely transfers the expression to me. But I will not meet Aleng's terms, and it's been apparent from the start that he won't honor the deal I made with Kyshia. Given the number of sun warriors present, it's unlikely he'll even allow me to leave this room.

To the Emperor, I say, "It was your House's duty to destroy the Soulless while he was still asleep. Your family had centuries to do it, but instead, you relied on Ronin to take care of it for you, just as you hope to do now with me." I look at Kyshia. "I should have just taken the armor. At least I was prepared to face the Soulless myself rather than cower behind others."

Aleng's fists clench. He looks ready to launch himself off the dais. It's only Emperor Cedral's sharp "Prince Aleng" that makes him step back.

"My son is right. My wish is for peace between our kingdoms, but we cannot trust a soulrender who isn't acting with the Empire's best interests in mind."

"The Soulless was a Nuvali soldier," I remind him. "He was trained by the Temple of Light. He went into battle on the Empire's orders."

"He is a criminal," the Emperor says evenly. "If you will not accept our terms, then we cannot allow you to return to Evewyn."

"Father, if you would reconsider—" Kyshia begins.

"Listen to her," Aleng says, sneering. "She sides with the soulrender over her family. I told you she isn't to be trusted."

"Be silent," the Emperor at last snaps at his son. They glare at one another, but Aleng relents first. Clearly, the Emperor isn't keen on having his family's quarrels aired in front of anyone, much less a potential enemy. To me, he says, "You were given access to the Temple of Light and to this palace on false terms. That you've been allowed to enter again without chains is a testament to our goodwill. Be certain of your decision, soulrender."

His words are clipped, his patience at its end. Well, so is mine.

He's used to servants and subjects falling over themselves to please him. Our first meeting was evidence of that. But I'm not going to ingratiate myself when he plans to either keep me captive or kill me, simply because I won't swear fealty.

"Do what you will," I say, "but between the two soulrenders left on this continent, I'm the one not trying to kill you. Is it wise to give me a reason to change my mind?"

It's a bluff. While I wouldn't mourn the fall of House Yalaeng, another family would simply move in to pick up where they'd left off. But it's only a matter of time before they can no longer contain the news that the Soulless is loose within the capital, especially now that he's killed one of the Emperor's sons. Just as the tide of public opinion is turning against lightwenders, once the Emperor's secrets are exposed, it will also shift against House Yalaeng.

At my threat, Emperor Cedral's eyes narrow, a mild reaction compared with his son, who draws himself up with a furious inhale. At either side of the room, sun warriors reach for their weapons but don't yet draw. Magic teases at my fingertips. It's useless against everyone here except Kendara, but I'm close enough to the dais that I could cross the distance

quickly. If I can get my hands on at least one Yalaeng, prefer-
ably the Sun's Heir, if only to wipe that smug look off his face,
then I might have a chance of getting out of this alive.

Even though the Emperor hasn't yet voiced an order, the
sun warriors move forward, closing in around me. If I don't act
now, I won't be allowed another chance.

I surge forward, bounding onto the dais. The sound of
a half dozen swords being drawn pierces the air. Shouting,
Kyshia grabs her father and hauls him bodily off his throne.
His outraged expression might have been funny in any other
situation, but he isn't my objective.

My gaze is fixed on Aleng and the terror washing over
his face.

Something collides into my shoulder. My legs go out from
under me. I hit the floor beside the throne, neatly rolling on
impact before finding my feet. But as I prepare to lunge again
for the prince, my body stalls in surprise.

Kendara stands in front of Aleng, shielding him with both
swords drawn and pointed at me.

ELEVEN

I recover my wits just as her blade swipes for my head. Flipping backward, I glimpse the sun warriors converging on the dais, but when I shift to block another attack, Kendara isn't there. Instead, she's ushering all three royals through a hidden door behind the dais.

Swearing, I focus my attention on the sun warriors and fail to ignore the stabbing betrayal in my gut. Even though I'm not the one who broke the deal, even though I am her friend's daughter and her pupil of four years, even though I am outnumbered, with neither sword nor craft to defend myself . . . Kendara has made her choice.

As I dodge one attack after another, it becomes quickly apparent that Kyshia was right—I may be confident in the skills Kendara taught me, but I am no match for eight sun warriors. I ram my shoulder into the gut of a windwender, sending her crashing into the two sun warriors behind her, and then I'm running full speed toward the closed doors of the throne room.

Wind blasts me from behind, nearly lifting me off my feet as it hurls me across the throne room. I slam into the heavy oak doors with a pained groan. I've no time to recover as a sun warrior flings a sword. I'm not about to be an insect pinned to a board. Gritting my teeth, I barely avoid the point, which pierces the wood beside my head. My ear stings where the blade met skin.

Reaching up, I jerk the sword free. Then I shove with all my weight against the door. It opens just enough for me to snake through, the edges scraping against my shoulder blades. Shouts ring out from behind me. I round a corner just as flames light up the corridor.

Theyen had said sunspear bones were dense and heavy, impractical for long battles. That means the armor will also slow them down, and my speed has always been one of my advantages. I dart up a flight of stairs, clearing the landing before a gust of wind can snatch at my feet.

We're inside the Bright Palace, which is another advantage. The sun warriors can't use their crafts freely, not without risking damage to the palace.

My pulse pounds, but my breaths remain even. I have to focus. I can't think about Kendara.

I touch the tip of my ear, a cursory evaluation of the injury. It isn't deep, and the bleeding isn't bad. At least now I'm armed.

As the sounds of pursuit grow louder, I spy a statue of Suryal standing within an alcove. It's at least fifteen feet tall, set on a marble pedestal. I launch myself onto it, ducking behind flowing robes carved in stone. Moments later, sun warriors pass in a flurry of flashing swords and angry curses. They bark out orders in Nuval. I only recognize a few words, but it's enough to understand that they're splitting up to cover more ground.

At least Kendara had gone with the Yalaengs. I wouldn't be able to outrun or outmatch her. Pain wrenches beneath my ribs, and I squeeze my eyes shut.

I draw a deep breath through my nose to calm my racing heart. Now really isn't the time to have an emotional crisis. *Think, Sirscha.*

Since the deal with Kyshia is off, I have to fall back on my initial plan—acquire sunspear armor. If Kyshia was telling the truth, then the last suits of armor were relocated to the frost chamber within the winter wing. I don't know where the frost chamber is, but thanks to Theyen, who drew us a map of the Bright Palace from memory alone, I do know where the winter wing is.

Once the corridor goes quiet, my pursuers having moved on, I slide carefully out from behind the statue and drop down from the pedestal. From somewhere far off comes the rumble of dozens of boots over stone. The entire palace has likely been alerted to an intruder loose on the grounds. Wonderful.

Fortunately, it doesn't take long for me to find my way out

a window. Within moments, I'm out of sight, catching my breath against the ridge of the roof. I try not to think of what King Meilek will say when he finds out what I've done. Will he renounce our friendship? Will he banish me? Or will he simply let the Empire do what they will with me? This entire affair has succeeded only in lowering my opinion of House Yalaeng, which I didn't think was possible.

Scanning the rise of towers and sloping roofs around me, I quickly calculate my location. I'm not far from the winter wing. Pushing off the ridge, I slide carefully down the tiles and leap a gap onto the neighboring roof, the soft soles of my boots muffling the impact. Sentinels patrol the walls enclosing the palace grounds, and avoiding every guard tower is impossible, so reaching the winter wing will take a bit of finesse and luck.

I sit in the shadow of one such tower, waiting for the right moment before dropping onto the narrow ridge of a roof above what I know to be a long, narrow corridor leading into the winter wing.

After a quick sweep of the grounds beneath, I swing off the side, twisting my body to maneuver through a narrow window. The stone scrapes my cheek and then my ear, the injury there stinging as fresh blood tickles my neck.

Only a handful of guards are posted in this part of the palace, and they're easy enough to dispatch. I've a feeling the lax security in the midst of a palace lockdown has more to do with Kyshia's assistance rather than my good fortune. Maybe in case discussions didn't go as planned? Whatever the reason, I locate the frost room without difficulty.

Inside, the room is empty save for four suits of armor displayed on wooden posts. A single window, too narrow for anyone to slip through, cuts down the length of the wall. I peer through it. I can make out the hulking structure of what Theyen had said was a banquet hall with an attached ballroom. To the east of that are the stables, which are just out of view. But something must have happened, because soldiers stream in that direction, urgent voices carrying upward.

I catch a few Nuvali words I recognize, like "drakes" and "soulrender." I frown. Why would they think I'm in the stables? The roar of several drakes pierces the night air.

Had someone set the drakes loose? My stomach drops. I'd suggested a diversion to Saengo if anything went wrong.

When she hadn't heard from me as I promised, she must have assumed the worst and taken it upon herself to act. The stables are the easiest section of the palace grounds to access from the outside, but even so, coming here was foolish and risky. I'm going to hug and scold her the moment we're together again.

With soldiers funneling toward the stables, I offer a quick prayer to the Bright Twin that Saengo has gotten clear of the area and is making for our escape point like we agreed. Not wasting another moment, I select a set of armor that looks like it might fit and begin pulling on the pieces.

I only get as far as the breastplate, tassets, and bracers before my nose twitches. I smell smoke. It's sharp and bitter and growing stronger by the second. Peering out the window again, I quickly spy the source—curls of black smoke have begun unfurling from the windows at either side of the frost chamber. Confused, I remain still for several heartbeats, listening. I don't hear anyone. More pressingly, my craft doesn't sense anyone nearby.

Who could have set the rooms around me on fire? It can't be Saengo—she would have warned me first. Swearing, I abandon the rest of the armor, retrieve my sword, and hurry to the door. Shielding my nose and mouth, I rush into the corridor, which has filled with smoke. While the fire won't destroy the talisman bones, it will delay the Emperor from using them until they can be once again fitted into armor.

Voices sound from beyond the haze. Eyes stinging, I shove into a doorway, grateful to see a large window that's open to the night air. In the inner courtyard below, soldiers swarm for the winter wing, splitting off from the stables.

My craft flickers at my fingertips, searching for the nearest souls. To my surprise, I find nothing.

Magic surges beneath my skin, insistent, steady. Still, I sense nothing. The realization seizes me—the sunspear bones don't just protect against soulrenders. They also contain my craft, trapping it within me. The possibility had occurred to me, so I try not to worry overlong about it. As I told Saengo, so long as the Soulless can't reach my soul, I don't need my craft to defeat him.

With the soldiers likely having discovered the stables were

a diversion, I make my way there. As expected, although some have remained to search the area, it's been mostly left to the stable hands and servants to regain control of the drakes set loose from their pens.

Although I'd been warned the armor is heavy, I'm still surprised by the weight. It feels like I'm carrying an entire other person against my back. I roll my shoulders, trying to get accustomed. It's not good to feel off-center when standing so high off the ground.

I'm about to swing down from the roof when a scream startles me. My fingers tighten on the ledge, my feet dangling in midair. A woman has just emerged from a hidden servant's door. She stares directly at me, eyes wide and face ashen. Then she shrieks again and spins on her heel, vanishing back inside.

"Damn it," I mutter as I hit the ground running.

Voices and shouts surge from the walls and shadows at my back. I race down a broad lane that will lead me to the exit. High on the walls above, sentinels call to one another. Within moments, arrows spear the ground at my feet. I hiss as one slices through the cloth at my shoulder, grazing skin, and another nearly pins my foot to the earth.

Magically raised winds howl down the lane, whipping my braid around my face and trying to snatch my feet from beneath me. But while I can barely see where I'm going with the dust that stings my eyes, it also scatters the arrows raining down on me. The gate looms ahead, a ridiculously ornate structure. With a groan, I launch myself up the side of it, the elegantly wrought likenesses of drakonys and suns providing easy purchase as I clear the gate and drop down onto the street, finally free of the grounds.

A heartbeat later, I duck as wind blasts into the gate with a violent rattle of shrieking metal. I don't stick around. I head down the street, slipping between buildings.

Despite the time, people litter the streets, likely having overheard the commotion within the palace grounds. Some gawk, others scream as I race past them.

A resounding *bang* shudders through the air as the gates are flung open, and the ground trembles with the pounding of drakes. The guards are in pursuit.

I need to get to higher ground so I can be certain I'm heading in the right direction. But as I begin pulling myself up a trellis overgrown with ivy, a voice rises from the tumult, high and scared.

"Sirscha!" It's Saengo.

I go still, ice spilling down my spine. My breaths sound suddenly loud.

"Sirscha! Help!"

At once, I release the trellis. Retracing my steps, I grip my sword and turn my craft inward, seeking the bond between me and Saengo. I'm dismayed to find that muffled as well. Our connection is still there, but it's indistinct, like her candle flame is shrouded in fog.

"Please," I whisper. The weight of the armor feels even

heavier, fear heightening my awareness of every obstacle between me and my friend.

Please. Please let her be okay. Why didn't she escape after setting the drakes loose? Even if Kyshia respects the sanctity of a familiar, that doesn't mean everyone else does, and after the spectacle we'd been forced to perform in front of the entire Nuvali court, they'll all know that Saengo is my familiar. They'll know that the best way to hurt me is to hurt her.

The moment I reach the open street, the ground beneath me shifts, cracks streaking across the earth and splitting open. I stumble in the heavy armor but swiftly regain my balance, crouching low to keep from falling. At least two dozen soldiers stand at either end of the street, and more have taken up positions on the rooftops, their figures little more than shadows in the dark. I'm surrounded.

Most of them wear standard Nuvali armor, not the sunspear leathers. But it doesn't matter anyway unless I mean to shed the pieces I'm wearing.

None of them speak, but their weapons are drawn, waiting. My gaze scans their faces, searching for Saengo's. A strange noise disrupts my panic, a sound like grinding stones. Something emerges from behind the soldiers, who shift aside to let it pass.

My eyes widen. The creature that steps into the golden glow of nearby lampposts has the shape of a man, but in monstrous proportions, with planes of earth and stone. The creature bears down on me, dirt cascading from the creases and crevices of its body. It's the height of two grown men. My throat closes, the fear jolting my limbs into movement. I leap into a roll just as massive arms crash down with a sound like rocks shattering.

"Wait," a voice calls out that I recognize as Aleng's. A sneer twists my mouth. If he hurt Saengo, he won't have to wait for the Soulless to find him.

A hush falls over the gathered soldiers. I remain in a crouch, my senses alert. The stone creature slowly backs away, the ground trembling with each step.

My eyes narrow, and I draw a steadying breath—only to find I can't. Confused, I try again. It's no use. I can't breathe. Panic blossoms anew in my gut.

One of the shamans surrounding me is a breathsiper, a windwender who can steal the air from another's lungs. When I stand, the earth seems to collapse beneath my feet, transforming into loose sand. I jerk backward, but it's too late. The sand swirls around my boots, sucking them in. I try to slip my feet free, but the sand surges around my legs, dragging me down to my knees.

I drop the sword, useless now as my chest grows tight and my heartbeat roars in my ears. I'm trapped.

As my mind races for an escape, I search their ranks again for Saengo and Aleng. The soldiers all keep their distance, relying only on their craft to subdue me.

I have to remove the armor. My craft is my only means of surviving this. Gritting my teeth, I tug first at the ties of my left bracer. My lungs burn, the pain creeping through my chest. While Kendara had given me exercises for lengthening the amount of time I could hold my breath—and then tested my progress by tying me up and dropping me into a lake—I haven't practiced in quite some time.

"Your Imperial Highness," someone says in the quiet, stilling my fingers.

Aleng at last steps into view from behind the line of his soldiers, his clear amethyst eyes bright with triumph. I glare and wrench off the first bracer, tossing the leather into the dirt. With determined fingers, I tear off the second one as well. Already, my craft stirs, the awareness of souls slowly sharpening. I can only barely sense the soldiers around me. They're still too indistinct to grasp.

I reach for the tassets next. Two pillars of earth shoot from the ground at either side of me. With my feet trapped in the quicksand, I can't dodge. The earth slams into my upper arms and then closes around me like a vise, securing my arms against my side. Trying to resist only makes my vision blur, desperate for air.

"Sirscha," Aleng says, and I freeze, head spinning, because he's speaking in Saengo's voice. "Help me, please. Sirscha, won't you come?"

If I could speak, I would snarl in fury. He's the breathsipher. Breathsiphers don't just steal air, they can also steal a person's voice so long as they've heard it once. Saengo had barely spoken when we'd presented ourselves before the Emperor those many weeks ago, but apparently, it'd been enough.

Even knowing it's useless, even with my vision going dangerously dark, I strain against the earth encircling my arms. The sword is still lying within reach. If I could just free one arm, I would fling the blade into his smug face.

Behind him, Kendara steps into view. With that hand-kerchief concealing half her face, it's impossible to tell what she's thinking. But I suppose it doesn't matter. Betrayal and rage claw at my closed throat. Kendara owes me no loyalty, and yet . . .

I trusted you, my mind screams. *How could you do this? Is this all I'm worth to you?*

Past the soldiers, curious shamans linger beneath store eaves or in dark corners, surveying the spectacle. Aleng's smile is sharp with malice, and at his side, Kendara stands silent, her familiar a white spot perched on her shoulder. Nothing in her body language indicates she's bothered by the fact I'm dying before her.

Is this really how I go? In the middle of a street, sur-rounded by enemies and so far from home? *Pitiful, Sirscha.* All that desperate yearning—for more than what was given me, to become someone worthwhile, someone worth remem-bering—and for what? To die, alone, in the dirt and the dark, without even the breath to fight back.

TWELVE

An arrow pierces the night. It slams into Aleng's leather breastplate, between two sunspear bones, just above his heart.

My throat opens, and sweet, blessed air rushes into my lungs. The earth enclosing me falls away, crumbling to the ground. I nearly collapse, too relieved to be embarrassed by the sounds I'm making as I desperately inhale. I glance first at from where the arrow had come—a rooftop, where a soldier lies slumped against the tiles with Saengo standing over her, bow in hand.

The relief is so powerful that my whole body sings with it. Then I look again to Aleng, his body braced against Kendara's, his face contorted with pain. With shaking fingers, I retrieve the sword, but it's too late. His soldiers close ranks around him, and he's dragged out of sight.

My heart squeezes, Kendara's name trying to force its way past my teeth. But I squash the weakness and focus instead on getting free.

As I tug my booted feet from the suction of sand, a thick fog spills across the street. It happens impossibly fast, the fog so dense that I can barely make out the dim glow of the nearest lamppost—a brumys's power to shield their prince's escape.

"Get to the roof!" someone shouts, and the remaining soldiers splinter further, pursuing Saengo, who has already vanished in the fog.

Those who stay behind form a circle around me, numbering just over a dozen. Most of the sun warriors in sunspear armor fled with their prince to protect him. Only a handful remain alongside regular soldiers. Praying that Saengo is headed for one of our escape points, I loosen the tassets so that the only piece of sunspear armor left on me is the breastplate. Their souls grow clearer, the fog barely a hindrance.

With the soldiers spread out around me, I easily spot the terranys. Her eyes glitter like chips of emerald as her creature of rock stirs. Stone grinds against stone as it charges forward.

Because of the breastplate, using my craft feels like when I first awakened it. It takes all my focus, but the light of her soul shines clear and I grasp it tight.

She stiffens, mouth falling open on a stifled gasp. The creature collapses midstride, scattering into rubble that tumbles against my boots. The other soldiers shy away, alarmed.

But the sun warriors don't flinch. One of them charges forward and then abruptly disperses into a coil of flame. The heat burns away the fog as it surges toward me.

I release the earthwender's soul and barely dodge the fire that scorches the ends of my braid. With a deep breath of scalding air, I turn and run. There's no fighting someone who can transform into flame, not without being able to use my craft on him.

Since Saengo headed east, I go south toward another possible escape point along Mirrim's wall. Heat rages at my back, licking at my boots. The sun warriors don't hold back now that we're no longer inside the Bright Palace. As I pass a cart of cabbages, the entire lot goes up in flames.

Cursing, I dart into an alley between two brick homes. I glance back in time to see the coil of fire converge once again into the sun warrior. Thank the Sisters flame eaters can only hold the form for a short period of time.

The sun warrior follows me into the alley, the other soldiers close behind him. Hurrying down the dim space, I round a corner and rush past a garden of fragrant lemongrass and lime trees. I turn into another alley, this one narrow enough that I have to shift sideways and shuffle through.

From the other end comes the din of voices and the lure of dozens of souls. I emerge onto a bustling market, late-night shoppers filling a broad, brightly lit street. Stalls are shoved up against one another on either side, many with colorful awnings and large signs. Displays of magic and the pungent smell of deep-fried sweets draw small crowds. Nearby, children up far past typical bedtimes play around a water bucket with two toy battleships.

I dive into the bustle as a jet of flames soars over my head and those of nearby marketgoers. At first, they think it's a demonstration, and they stop, smiling as they seek the source. But then the soldiers stream out of the alley, shoving people out of the way and scattering familiars that hiss or screech at the disruption. The sun warrior transforms once again into a serpent of flame, and the screams begin, those nearest stumbling over their companions as they flee.

The presence of innocent bystanders doesn't deter the flame eater, and my options are limited. I either outrun him, which might be possible, or I wait until he's solid again and take him out quickly.

Gritting my teeth, I turn to face my pursuers. Scorching heat blasts toward me. I duck and roll before grasping the bucket with the now abandoned toy ships and flinging the water.

Steam scalds the air as the water strikes the flames with a crackling hiss. It's not enough to do much harm but it's enough to startle him. The sun warrior coalesces as he hits the ground, blinking water droplets from his eyes and steaming faintly.

Before he can transform again, my fist slams into his cheek. He grunts, searing palms shoving at my shoulders. His fingers burn where they touch my clothes, but I don't relent, punching him again. As his hands melt away into flames, I smash the butt of my sword into his temple.

His arms solidify and his body goes limp. I only have a moment to breathe in relief before two other sun warriors bear down on me. Flipping backward, I avoid the swipe of a blade and then shove aside a man standing far too close and gawking. These sun warriors don't seem to mind if they take an innocent limb or two so long as they can kill me.

All at once, silence descends.

The road, still filled with people in the midst of fleeing or hiding, is deathly quiet. The only sound is the sudden hiss of burning food in an abandoned stall. Every living person now stands frozen, their souls gripped tight.

I swallow, fingers clenching around the hilt of my sword. I hadn't sensed him coming. The breastplate dulls my craft, but now that I know he's here, now that I know to search the sea of souls for his, it seems impossible I hadn't noticed his approach. His soul crowds out all others, an immense and ancient power with a weight that's physical, heavier even than the armor strapped to my chest.

Slowly, I back away from the sun warriors. The sunspear bones protect them, but there is no shield against the horror of what he's capable of. Fear shines in their eyes as they raise their swords and turn in a circle, frantically searching the night.

I see him first, because I know where his soul is. He appears from behind a group of girls who are hunched in mid-run, still as statues. The silk of their robes flutters in a slight wind. The Soulless is dressed simply in dark-gray robes and a straw hat, bizarrely nondescript compared with the clothes he'd stolen from Ronin's wardrobe back at Spinner's End.

He strolls through the remains of the market, past two woman holding wicker baskets, a man who'd been trying to steal a shawl in the chaos, and a child clutching a toy to his chest, all of them incapable of doing anything more than watching with wide, terrified eyes. The Soulless removes the straw hat, discarding it in the dirt. Half of his hair has been swept up into a modest topknot, with the rest falling freely around his face and shoulders, nearly as long as mine.

His steps are steady. Controlled. Even in motion, there is an unnatural stillness about him. His face, limned in lamplight, is pale and angular, those amber eyes glinting like candle flames. Nothing in his placid expression gives away the fact that he holds in his grasp dozens of souls at once.

The sun warriors finally spot him. They shift from foot to foot, knees bent, weapons raised. Going by the slight tremor in their swords, they must be rallying every bit of their courage and training to face him.

But this is what Kyshia had wanted to happen. She'd wanted the Soulless out in the open, with her sun warriors impervious to his craft. A pity the majority of them fled to protect their prince.

The sun warrior on the left rolls her shoulders as her skin begins to ripple and change. Within seconds, every part of visible skin has hardened to rough, gray rock. She's a stoneskin. The other sun warrior summons water from every available source—the bottom of gutters, pitchers from food stalls, what's left of the bucket water, now spilled across the dark street. All of it merges into a shining stream that circles him like a shield.

The Soulless doesn't look concerned. He continues forward, his steps measured.

The sun warriors attack, and a half dozen shamans who'd been frozen jerk forward to intercept. Taken by surprise, the stoneskin slams into one of them, an elderly man with a cane. He goes flying, hitting the ground in a crumpled heap. With a gasp, she shuffles back as more shamans shift to stand between the sun warriors and the Soulless.

They move as if in pain, their eyes clenched tight, their limbs jerking. There are too many, swarming the two sun warriors. They shove the shamans aside, disabling who they can, but every attempt to attack the Soulless results in another shaman taking the blow. They simply can't get close to him.

I don't understand how he's making them obey him. Is his power truly so immense that his magic is his will?

Regardless, I'm not going to get a better opportunity than this. I grip my sword and dart through the teeming bodies. None of the controlled shamans interfere, focused only on subduing the two sun warriors.

The Soulless stands motionless in the midst of the tumult, calm as the eye of a storm. His head is haloed in red from a string of lanterns strung overhead, and his hands are clasped at his back. A plain sword is tucked into his sash. Time to find out if he knows how to use it.

His gaze shifts to mine as I attack. He draws so quickly that I'm momentarily surprised. His blade meets mine, the clang of metal striking metal ringing above the clamor. I try to step in closer, my elbow striking for his jaw. He dodges, and my elbow meets his arm instead. I retreat a step, but he doesn't let me get far, his sword sweeping outward.

I knock the blade aside with my own and smash my boot into his gut. Grunting, he stumbles and then nearly stumbles again as I try to sweep his legs out from under him. I wish I had my dual swords. The sword style Kendara taught me works best with the shorter, lighter blades. One sword never feels quite right, although it serves me well enough when I need it to.

The Soulless's footwork is quick and precise. This is not the man from a few months ago, who looked fragile enough that he might crumple from a firm blow. But even then, even recovering physically from his time within Ronin's cocoon, that fragility had been a façade. His true power lies in his craft, which is still impossibly vast.

Leaving Spinner's End and traveling across the length of the Empire has strengthened his muscles and stretched his endurance. These things I anticipated, but I'm not sure why I'm surprised he's a skilled swordsman. I should have expected this. He'd been a soldier after all, even if that had been life-times ago.

But whereas I have spent years strengthening my body and honing my skill, he has spent centuries in a cocoon, and for all his skill, he is also out of practice. It isn't long before my blade twists his sword from his grip, sending it clattering to the ground before my foot connects with his side. He staggers with a quiet groan. I aim my knee for his ribs just as a searing pain spears through me.

I gasp, nearly dropping my sword as my other hand flies to my chest, fingers digging into the leather breastplate. My craft surges within me, fighting back. Pain wedges beneath my ribs, and yet, it's not the agony I felt back at Spinner's End when he first grasped my soul. Even with just the single piece of sunspear armor, it affords me a measure of resistance.

With a cry, I break free of his grasp. I draw a ragged, furious breath and raise my sword, not sure if I mean to kill him or just knock him out. But before I can act, once again, pain shears through me. My legs fold and I bite my tongue as my knees hit the ground. Magic pulses within me, swelling beneath my skin and tearing at the Soulless's grip.

The Soulless straightens, pushing loose strands of hair from his face with a small, amused smile. A smudge of dirt stains his cheek.

"You will submit," he says, sheathing his sword.

He'd been humoring me, allowing me to believe I might be able to defeat him with only a sword. Or perhaps he'd wanted to test the limits of his newly regained strength. Whatever the reason, while he may not be a match for me physically, his craft is still all he needs.

I'd discarded the other pieces of sunspear armor that

would have perhaps allowed me to win this fight. For what little good it did me, I'd been trapped and dying. I'd had no choice.

"I won't," I say through gritted teeth just as my craft breaks his grip once again. I stagger backward, raising my sword as the echo of pain aches in my chest.

"You will, or every life in this street will be on your head."

I glance around, renewed fury cresting within me. The stoneskin is missing, having fled or worse, and the water-wender is lying flat on his back in the road, held down by a dozen unwilling hands. He struggles, shouting for them to fight the Soulless's power, but how can they?

It's possible I could kill the Soulless right now. If I fight hard enough against his craft, if I move quickly enough to drive my sword through his chest before that wicked power can curl its poison talons around my soul again . . .

I'm probably fooling myself. I don't know if a fatal blow to anyone else will kill the Soulless, and I'm not sure that's a gamble I can make with so many souls in his grip. He won't ever truly be gone until the Dead Wood is destroyed.

But it might be enough to disable him and bring him under control. Could I act fast enough, before he can kill all these people? There are even children among them, eyes wide with terror, wholly aware of what they're doing but unable to resist his terrible will.

I swallow with difficulty, my throat too dry. Then, grudgingly, I lower my sword at my side.

All around, the shamans collapse like puppets with their strings cut. Panicked, I turn in a circle, my craft seeking their souls. But they're not dead, simply unconscious. Except the sun warrior, who struggles beneath the weight of so many bodies suddenly piled atop him. I press shaking hands to my stomach, unwillingly cowed by the Soulless's power.

"Follow," he says, turning away.

Bitterness coats the back of my throat. I loathe that he can present his back to me without fear, that he can order me about like I'm one of his puppets, caught in the snare of his craft.

When I don't immediately obey him, he adds, "Don't forget, Sirscha. Every soul in this city is mine to take any time I wish it."

"So you're content to be the monster they've made of you?" I ask.

"Yes," he says easily. "I am their monster, and they are right to fear me."

The last thing I expect is for the Soulless to take me to an inn. I suppose if he's been hiding in the city, he'll have needed a place to stay. To eat and rest and pass the time when he isn't skulking about in the shadows, stalking Yalaengs. It's disturbingly human of him.

The inn is located close to the city gates, although it's instantly clear that the neighborhood isn't occupied by the affluent. It certainly isn't somewhere Kyshia would have stayed, although the building looks like it needs her resources far more than the one where we left Saengo.

Being so close to the gates, it wouldn't be far to run if I tried to escape. But the memory of those people, all of them trapped within the Soulless's grip, stays the thought.

We approach the inn, passing shamans strolling in pairs through the night. To strangers, we could be just another couple seeking quiet and privacy. The thought is revolting.

But even with the whole kingdom looking for him, no one actually knows what he looks like, and before tonight, other than myself, all who've seen him are dead. In a kingdom of shamans, he's just another lightwender. Even with the increased security and scrutiny of lightwenders, he can still hide in plain sight.

"Those people . . . " I begin as we enter the inn. I fall silent, following him through a cramped barroom with creaking floorboards. My boots stick uncomfortably against splotches of spilled drink that have long dried.

Even at this late hour, and despite the holes in the walls and a roof beam that looks liable to collapse, nearly half the tables in the cramped room are occupied. Although I have to focus my craft past the sunspear armor, I can also sense a mass of sleeping souls in the rooms above our heads.

"They're fine," he says. It takes me a moment to realize he's answering my unfinished question about the people in the night market.

He guides me to a tiny table in the corner with two stools as chairs. Reluctantly, I sit, but my thoughts are back with all those people he'd left unconscious in the street. Part of me wants to ask how he did it. Forcing someone to obey is as simple as applying pressure to their soul, making them aware how close they are to death. But controlling them through will alone, without words—is that something I could do as well?

I push the thought away. It hardly matters right now.

"How long have you known I was in the city?" I ask, running one finger along the grimy tabletop. I flick a crumb with my nail.

"Since the moment you entered Mirrim," he says. His voice is quiet and steady, although his lip curls when the crumb lands on his sleeve.

I'd wondered if he might be able to sense my arrival. Even in a city brimming with souls, the Soulless seems capable of separating them in a way I can't. Just as in Spinner's End, he always seems to know where I am so long as I am within his range of awareness—and his range is considerably larger than mine.

We fall silent as an aged man in an apron approaches. A dirty kerchief ties his hair back, but his hands look clean as he places a steaming bowl of white rice and two bowls of clear pork soup before us.

At my questioning look, the Soulless responds, "I took the liberty of ordering us a meal before I left to fetch you."

He says it like he was simply stepping out to pick me up. I scowl that he'd expected to return here with me and that, because everyone continues to underestimate him, even knowing what he's capable of, he was right. And now here I am.

THIRTEEN

The innkeeper returns with a bottle of cheap wine and two tin cups. Then he bows politely before drifting off to another table.

"The bed is lumpy and the rooms are cold, but the food is good," the Soulless says, as if to explain why we're here.

I swallow back the words, *I didn't ask.* This is wholly surreal. Less than an hour ago, I thought I was going to die at the hands of the Nuvali prince, and now I am sitting in a run-down inn, watching the Soulless eat as if we are old acquaintances.

Although still unnaturally meticulous in his movements, our fight has left him looking a little more human. His hair is mussed and his clothes marked with dust. The idea of the Soulless doing something as mundane as eating is so weird, but it's a necessary reminder that he is still just a man. He is powerful. He is monstrous. But he is also human.

Maybe I could kill him with a blade after all. I'll have to find an opportunity to test it.

The dim lighting deepens the weary shadows beneath his eyes. Looking at him now, I decide he can't possibly be fully recovered from the centuries trapped within Ronin's cocoon. And yet, he has traveled across the continent in order to reach his quarry.

He must be exhausted. His stillness and his carefully controlled movements are as much a guise to conceal his fatigue as they are him reacquainting himself with his body.

Although I've no appetite, I don't know when I'll have a meal next, so I pick up the soup spoon and sip the broth. To my surprise, it's quite good.

As I eat, I consider the fact that he'd known I was in Mirrim from the moment I entered the city. Which would mean he also knew I was in the palace.

"The fire at the Bright Palace," I say, eyes narrowing.

"It would have been inconvenient if you got ahold of that armor." His gaze flicks down to the breastplate, distaste tugging at his lips. "You may as well get rid of it for what little good it did you."

What it did was help me to resist his grasp on my soul. Not only that, but unless I concentrate, it also muffles other souls so that I no longer have to worry about killing someone by accident. It helps to not feel so overwhelmed by my own craft.

I ignore his suggestion, wary of whether he will force my hand. He doesn't. So I eat, keeping my eyes on the Soulless and my ears tuned to the murmur of conversations nearby. It isn't difficult to eavesdrop.

". . . her golden carriage earlier this evening," someone a couple tables away is saying. "They think she might be hiding in one of those fancy inns she owns."

His companion snorts. "Don't be stupid. The Ember Princess has been holed up in the Temple of Light. My aunt was just there this morning. She's pretty sure she saw her walking through the gardens."

"No one's seen more than the back of her robes for weeks," the first man says. I glance over. He has a scraggly gray beard and frayed robes washed too many times. "Weird, isn't it? I'm telling you, there's some truth to all this Soulless stuff—"

"Stop working yourself up," his companion says before slurping loudly at his noodles. He burps before continuing. "They're lying. The Emperor wants us afraid and obedient."

"Watch your mouth," the first man hisses, glancing warily around the room. His companion only snorts again and continues eating his noodles.

I watch the Soulless to see if their conversation interests him, but his attention is only on his food. He washes down his last mouthful with the wine and then offers me the bottle. I ignore it, fishing through my broth for the last bit of pork. There wasn't much meat to begin with.

He waits until I set down my soup spoon, and then he stands.

With a warning in his voice, he says, "Come."

I glare at him before grinding my teeth and obeying. I briefly contemplate taking my time slurping down the last of the soup broth, but it would be childish, and there are things I want to ask him that would be better suited for privacy.

After two flights of stairs, he leads us down a hallway with a suspiciously dark stain along one wall and pauses before a door. From the depths of his gray robes, he produces a plain brass key and fits it into the lock. There's a click, and the door swings open on hinges that screech loudly. Quietly slipping out the door when he's asleep won't be an option then.

He gestures for me to enter first. Warily, I do.

The room is tiny, with a low ceiling and an even tinier bed shoved into a corner. It's neatly made, and a low-burning fire warms the hearth. For how small the room is, the window takes up most of the wall opposite the door. It's wide enough to provide a fantastic view of the city, with even the Bright Palace visible in the distance. I wonder if he still enjoys watching the stars. They're perfectly visible from the bed.

A stool is set beside the fireplace, and I move it beneath the window before sitting down.

"How are you paying for all this?" I ask. He shuts and locks the door before pocketing the key again.

I don't need a key to escape this room. With the size of the window, it'd be easy enough to open, but I am uncomfortably aware of the number of souls in this inn. Every soul here is in danger if I try to leave.

"Ronin's finances are considerable," he says, crouching by the fire. He adds several pieces of wood from the small pile neatly stacked behind the door.

"How did you get into the city?"

He doesn't reply this time, only continuing to prod at the flames. I don't know how House Yalaeng is keeping his presence here a secret, but after what just happened at the night market, there's no way they'll be able to suppress the news from spreading now.

There will still be skeptics like the man downstairs, scoffing at the idea of the Soulless's return. But for those who witnessed his power and were subjected to it, there are simply too many of them for House Yalaeng to silence.

Besides that, he'd killed the Emperor's son. It won't be long before that's discovered as well.

"I must thank you," the Soulless says quietly. He watches the flames grow, licking up the sides of the fresh logs.

"For what?" I ask, wary.

"For the room you discovered in Ronin's library."

I stiffen. Ronin kept a secret archive attached to the library, which I'd managed to unearth. Unfortunately, I could read very little of what he kept there because almost everything had been written in a dead language, presumably Ronin's native tongue.

"There were many things of interest to read," he says. "Family trees, records of holdings, deeds and accountings that I must assume aren't common knowledge."

"Is that how you've been tracking down Yalaengs?" I ask, even though the answer is plain. The Soulless is as old as Ronin was, and I know very little about the Soulless's past or how educated he might be. It's entirely possible he can read the language Ronin wrote his records in.

I frown when the Soulless stands, but he only reaches for the pitcher of water on the mantle. He pours himself a cup, content to study the flames. There's something different about him since I last saw him at Spinner's End. Even highlighted by the soft glow of firelight, his eyes remain hard, a coldness there the warmth can't reach.

What bit of his humanity he'd retained through his love for his brother is gone, along with his brother's soul. Now, there is only anger and resolve.

"You've waited centuries for your revenge," I say. "Why take your time killing random Yalaengs with no influence over the Empire's decisions?"

"Because I can," he says without inflection. "Because the Emperor should know what it's like to wait, uncertain of anything except his own death, and some days . . ." His eyes grow even harder. "Some days, not even that."

"You're killing innocent—"

"You would mourn two obscure Yalaengs and a handful of their guards, but not the soul you so carelessly extinguished?" he says, his voice a low growl. He doesn't look at me, but still, I swallow tightly, my spine rigid, constantly aware of what he's capable of.

I'd thought the soul I pried from his talisman was his familiar. I'd thought freeing it would destroy him and free the souls in the Dead Wood, but I'd been horribly mistaken. The soul he'd kept trapped within a talisman for centuries had been his brother's, which he intended to return to life, once he figured out a way. If such a way even existed.

I'm sorry for your brother, I think. *But he needed to be freed as well.* I'm not stupid enough to say that out loud, so instead I say, "I don't mourn them, and you're forgetting three others. You've killed more than just two Yalaengs and some guards."

Kendara's message to me had stated four Yalaengs dead. Since then, he's also killed Prince Eren.

His lips curls, just briefly. "I didn't kill them."

I roll my eyes and open my mouth to argue, but then I pause. What reason would the Soulless have to lie? He would readily accept responsibility for killing Yalaengs and has stated more than once his intent to do so.

He glances at me. "Does it really surprise you that they're using me as a cover to get rid of each other?"

"But how?" I ask. I'm not going to simply take his word for it. "How could they replicate what you can do?"

"You're the assassin. How would you do it?"

I cross my arms, head tilting in consideration as I indulge the question. To replicate the Soulless's power, the victim and anyone around them would have to be killed silently, without struggle and without blood. It would have to look as if their souls had been simply torn from them.

"Poison," I decide. It's the only way to kill without a physical weapon. "It'd have to be a poison that's untraceable, or at least, untraceable enough to pass a cursory inspection of the body. But it would have to be administered equally to everyone within a given space . . . Or perhaps even dispersed into the air without anyone noticing."

The Soulless's mouth twists into a humorless smile. "They squander their power. They are undeserving of the station they were born to, a privilege seized by their forebears and the blood they spilled to acquire it."

I rest my back against the wall, discomfited. I already believe that House Yalaeng should be removed from power. If they choose to kill one another, that's their own business so long as they don't get me involved.

Except they did just that when Kyshia asked for my help, and I foolishly agreed. And after tonight, House Yalaeng will know that I am in the Soulless's company. He probably thinks he was rescuing me. My nose wrinkles at that. But after Saengo divided Aleng's forces and I had the use of my craft, that flame eater had been the most difficult to deal with, and I'd taken him down just fine.

Regardless, it will not help my assertion that I'm not on the Soulless's side.

The thought of poison suddenly reminds me of Kendara's white spider. Just thinking her name makes my breath catch, an ache rising swiftly in my throat. She was going to let me die, right there in front of her. My face grows hot with renewed anger. The betrayal hurts more than any of the injuries I'd sustained completing her ridiculous tasks—and there had been many.

When this is all over, if I survive, I'm going to find her and make her face the choice she'd made. *"If ever I were to kill you, Sirscha, I would give you the chance to defend yourself. A teacher should always allow their student the courtesy of demonstrating what they've learned."*

I will gladly demonstrate exactly what I've learned from her.

Closing my eyes, I allow myself a moment to regain control of my emotions. I'm not going to break down in front of the Soulless, and the last thing Kendara deserves are my tears. When I open my eyes again, I shift my thoughts back to her familiar. She'd chosen a frost spider, and Kendara never does anything without reason.

"What do you know of frost spiders?" I ask abruptly.

If the question confuses him, he doesn't give any indication of it. "Frost spiders?" he repeats. "They prefer colder climates. They're nocturnal, and their venom turns the underside of their victim's tongues blue."

"So they're deadly," I say, that fact thrumming through me.

"Very, although it's notoriously difficult to extract and, even then, it's a slow-acting venom. It takes time to work its way through the system." He glances at me again. "Come across a frost spider recently?"

I look out the window, ignoring his shrewd gaze. The

night sky is overcast, only a few stars peeking through the clouds and the moon a haze of silver high above the Bright Palace. The Emperor is probably scouring the streets searching for us. I pray that Saengo has already made it out of the city.

I can't even believe I'm considering it, but if Kendara's familiar provided the venom to frame the Soulless, then . . . What could that possibly mean? Is she murdering people at Aleng's command? Or are her motivations her own?

"You think they're doing it with frost venom?" the Soulless muses. "It could be effective if the venom was distributed at supper and the victims died later in the evening. Difficult to trace unless you know what to look for."

Their deaths would've been attributed to the Soulless. I doubt anyone would take the time to inspect the underside of the victims' tongues. Or if they did, such revelations wouldn't be shared beyond the Emperor and his medical examiner.

The Soulless falls silent as I watch the darkened street below our window. It's quiet and still, with only the soft glow of a distant lamp illuminating a small familiar curled up at its base, asleep. If I concentrate, I can sense Saengo's candle flame, and the fact that I can use my craft at all is proof she's alive. But "alive" and "safe" are two different things. Worry for her knots my stomach.

She feels far away. It's hard to gauge with the sunspear breastplate, though, which I won't remove in his presence.

Besides, Saengo and I went through too much to acquire it.

"You will rest," the Soulless says, dragging the blanket off the bed and dumping it at my feet. "We've a long day tomorrow."

After spending centuries within that cocoon, trapped in a deathlike sleep, I wonder how much rest his body actually needs. He does look exhausted. And if he needs to sleep, once he's unconscious, he'll be like any other human—vulnerable.

"A long day doing what? Planning another murder?" I ask.

He doesn't smile, but his eyes take on an amused glint. He unties his sash and begins to remove his gray outer robe. I swivel on my stool, facing away from him.

His low laugh makes the back of my neck prickle unpleasantly. "You're modest. How surprising. You're imagining how to kill me in my sleep, but you can't look at me in my underrobes?"

It has little to do with modesty and everything to do with how very much I'd rather be anywhere else than with him. Nudging the wall, I turn around again, eyeing him askance. The Soulless doesn't remove any more layers of clothing. His underrobes are thin blue linen and look suspiciously like the robes the servants wore at Spinner's End.

When he gives me an expectant look, I sneer and rise from the stool. Grabbing the blanket on the floor, I stretch out in front of the small fireplace. I roll onto my side, facing the flames, and use my arm as a pillow. Seemingly satisfied, the Soulless settles into the narrow bed. The bed doesn't look much more comfortable than the floor, honestly, but I don't mind sleeping on hard surfaces.

I wait, listening for his breaths to grow even. Although I'm not the least bit tired, my eyes drift shut and my mind grows fuzzy, dragged into dreams.

FOURTEEN

We stand within the Dead Wood.

In this dreamscape, the earth is dry and silty, like sand. The trees are bone white, and the branches end in grasping human hands that claw at empty air and one another. Overhead, the sky is a cauldron of angry black clouds.

There is no wind, but a chill breathes down my arms and the back of my neck. I shiver and tug at the sleeves of my tunic.

Some paces away, the Soulless steps over roots that writhe like snakes, his hands clasped at his back, looking perfectly at ease. Sprouting from his shoulders are hundreds of thousands of gossamer spider's threads, each a link between him and the souls bound to him and the Dead Wood. He's dressed in dark-gray robes of a much finer cut, with an embroidered sash wrapped tight around his waist.

His hair falls loose around his shoulders, and he pays

no mind to the way the trees recoil from him, clearing his path. The branches wrench away, the faces within the bark screaming wordlessly as they strain against their prisons. Still, the Soulless continues, his steps leisurely, as if he's strolling through a blooming grove rather than a graveyard.

Slowly, I follow him, wary of the branches that tear at one another with grisly broken fingers. As far as my dreams with him go, this is as close a representation of the Dead Wood in the waking world as it has ever been.

"Did you just pull me into a dreamscape against my will?" I ask, uncertain.

My mind races with questions at how he could do such a thing. Was it like forcing unconsciousness on those people in the night market? Some bizarre spiritual asphyxiation?

No, that doesn't seem right. He's here as well, accompanying me through this strange dream—this is to do with the sharing of our craft and the way our souls resonate with one another. Disgust roils in my gut.

"You must learn how to hone your craft into a blade rather than swinging it—"

"—like a club," I say, recalling the insult he'd given me back at Spinner's End. I realize too late that I probably sound petulant, and I glare at his back.

He doesn't mock me further, though. He only says, "Once you can do that, you need only point the blade, and your magic will respond."

Stepping past a network of roots that slither away from

the Soulless's feet, I lift my hands and flex my fingers. Even within a dream, my craft surges at my command and sparks at my fingertips, hungry for attention. The desire to use it wrings through me.

"You're eager to learn, but you're afraid of what you can do." The Soulless pauses between two trees, his mere presence bending the trees outward. If the Dead Wood is the monster that hides in the shadows with ready claws and bloody teeth, then the Soulless is the master it cowers away from.

I drop my hands. "Any decent person would be afraid of what we can do."

"A decent person uses fear as caution, not cause for hatred."

I scoff. "Are *you* going to teach me about hatred?"

"Am I not qualified? How many lifetimes has it been my companion? It is my sustenance and my guide." His voice is a low rumble that sends the roots skittering. "They fear us, and they believe this justifies the extermination of our craft. You have not lived in this world long enough to understand what it is to lose everything and everyone that has ever mattered to you."

His words force my thoughts to turn to Saengo. The distance that I've felt yawning between us these past months is only in my head, I know that, and yet that doesn't make it any less real. I don't wish to lose her in any measure, but if living a life away from me would make her happy—a life away from the constant reminder of the shackles of our bond—then I am prepared to be gracious about it.

"Here." The Soulless gestures to a sudden space that's appeared between the trees—a circle of tightly packed earth, much like the sparring circles at the Company.

I raise one eyebrow in question.

"Sit," he says. "Practice feeling the shape and breadth of your craft. Learn how far you can push it. There is no one here but us."

The last thing I want to do is indulge him. But despite myself, I am intrigued. If he wishes to teach me, would I be an idiot for refusing?

Warily, I step into the open space. I sit, legs crossed. To my surprise, the Soulless doesn't stay to watch. He turns his back and continues his aimless stroll, the roots and branches scuttling out of his path.

When he vanishes from view, I tilt my head back, eyes narrowed on the trees. Without the Soulless, they are suspiciously still. They're not even really here—they're only a manifestation of the Soulless's making, a projection of the souls trapped and bound to his power. I wait a moment longer, and when they remain unmoving, I finally risk closing my eyes.

I rest my palms on my knees as I draw a slow, deep breath and turn my focus inward. My craft rushes forward, a ready flood cresting within me. I don't try to control it. It fills my limbs and surges outward, overflowing into a pool of light and power.

This isn't like when I'd let loose my craft at Spinner's End and was nearly crushed beneath the weight of the souls' collective rage. Here, it really is just me and him. Instead, this is more like when Saengo broke Aleng's hold over my lungs and all that painful tension was released, allowing air to rush back in.

It's . . . freeing.

Time passes strangely in this dreamscape, so I don't know how long I sit there. Every second stretches interminably as I listen to the harmony of my magic singing in my ears, I feel the warmth of it beneath my skin. I learn its unique ebb and flow, the way it rushes to my command and stalls at my hesitation. I wrap it around me, tracing its shape and breadth.

Slowly, the fear of being overwhelmed recedes, replaced by repetition and familiarity. My craft is no longer a feral beast to be kept chained and caged. It is a creature that, though wild, will come when called and curl its tail around my ankle.

When I wake in the morning, I am thoroughly unsettled.

As the only other known soulrender, one who has mastered the craft, the Soulless makes an obvious mentor. Even so, it leaves me conflicted.

We take breakfast at the same corner table we'd eaten at the night before, and then the Soulless packs his few things and returns the key to the innkeeper. Since I'm not getting rid of the sunspear breastplate, I wear it beneath my outer robes. Even as a single piece of armor, it wouldn't be difficult for

Nuvali soldiers to identify. As a result, my clothes fit strangely, lumpy and bulging in odd places. Aside from a judgmental sweep of his gaze, the Soulless doesn't remark on it.

Once we leave the inn, it doesn't take long for me to realize he's taking me toward the gates. Is one of the Yalaengs there? His business in Mirrim is far from finished, so why would he be leaving the city?

We approach the gate, and my question the night before as to how he entered the city is answered. Every soldier at the gate goes still. Those meant to be checking for permits or pulling aside lightwenders for questioning begin waving people and wagons through, their eyes wide, their movements jerky and frantic. If the people trying to get in and out of the city notice, they don't care enough to stop and ask, too eager to get on with their day and their business.

The Soulless has acquired another hat from somewhere, and with my cloak pulled over my head, we walk out of Mirrim, just like that. I swallow down my disgust, both with him for controlling the soldiers and myself for my curiosity at how it's done.

No matter how tempting the power may be, it is a violation that shouldn't be permitted. It isn't right, exerting one's will onto others. Just because we are capable of doing something doesn't mean we should.

For much of the morning, we continue down the main road. It's busy at this time of day, and we pass a constant stream of wagons, carriages, and riders going about their business.

The Soulless ignores all of my questions and speaks only to remind me that even though we're no longer within Mirrim, the busy road is still rife with souls.

We stop around midday at a roadside teahouse, smaller and more welcoming than the one where I'd met with Kyshia. The Soulless disappears into the stables and returns with two drakes in hand.

"Whose are they?" I ask as he mounts a plain brown drake with yellow speckles down its spine. I run my fingers over the smooth scales of the other drake, dark green with two black horns.

"Ours," he says placidly.

I look toward the road. The traffic is light but steady. After what he did at the gates, I suppose he isn't much concerned with being discovered, seeing as no one has the power to stop him. Still, his boldness is surprising and a little unnerving.

"What did you do to their owners?" I ask, trying to get around him to check the stables.

His hand falls on my shoulder, fingers like steel as they dig into my skin, even through my robes. "They're fine, and we must be going."

"Did you hurt them?" I demand, jerking free of his grip.

I roll my shoulder at the slight ache that remains. Like the sunspear armor, the sword I'd taken from the Bright Palace was too conspicuous. It would be easily recognized as one belonging to a palace guard, so I had to abandon it this morning. My only weapon against him is my craft, and after last night, for the first time, I almost feel in control of it—but that probably has to do with the sunspear breastplate as well.

"No," he says, golden eyes narrowed in irritation.

We glare at one another as I search the stables with my craft, finding the souls of other drakes as well as two people. Satisfied that he hasn't left any dead bodies for some poor stablehand to discover, I relent and mount the drake.

As we return to the road, he says, "Your concern for those who would see you dead grows tiresome."

"Your constant threats are tiresome as well."

At first I think I must be mistaken when he makes a noise like a snort and peers at me from beneath the brim of his hat. I don't know where he found the thing, but it casts a lattice of shadows over his face.

"If I stop threatening you, will you stop being so soft?" he asks.

"Fight me without your craft, and I'll show you soft," I say evenly, as if we're discussing the weather.

"You think using our craft is cheating when it is more a part of us than any sword will ever be. It is your greatest weapon, the one you should be honing with dedication and practice, and yet you treat it as a weakness."

It annoys me that I don't disagree with him. When I'd fought the trees those months ago—when I'd mistakenly believed the talisman was the key to the Soulless's defeat— that was the closest I've ever felt to truly embracing my craft and what I can do. After last night, I'm beginning to hope that

I might be able to feel that way again, but without fear.

"This would be easier if you stopped fighting me," the Soulless says. "If you give me your word that you won't try to escape, then perhaps we can come to a more favorable understanding."

I bark a single laugh. "Why would I give you my word when I don't trust yours?"

His gaze darts to mine, golden eyes glimmering beneath his hat. "I never say something I don't mean."

I snort. Everyone lies. The Soulless is no exception. The only vow he's made that I can trust is his promise for revenge against House Yalaeng. Although it has been centuries since he and his brother were experimented on by the Light Temple, ultimately resulting in his brother's death and the creation of the Dead Wood, he is intent on seeing the Empire pay.

But he did make another vow. *Your betrayal will be paid. Every soul I take, every fool waiting for you to save them will be the cost.*

A sudden sick feeling churns in my gut, and I ask what I'd been wondering for weeks now, a question I'm not certain I want answered. "What did you do to the people left at Spinner's End?"

I search what I can see of his face for . . . I don't know what—remorse, sadness, anger? There is nothing, only that same unsettling stillness.

"They are dead."

His words pierce like arrows. I swallow several times,

the roiling in my stomach rising into my burning cheeks. My heart pounds.

I recall the faces of those who'd been left behind—the soldier who'd escorted me to my room, the maid who'd violently startled when I walked in on her setting out my dinner, the falconer who'd been all too eager to let me receive the Soulless's messages. They'd been terrified. They'd needed help. They'd wanted *me* to help them. I'd told them I would try.

My eyes close, the leather reins biting into my palms as I sway with the rocking motion of the drake beneath me. If not for the knowledge that it wouldn't work, I would wrap my magic around his soul and tear it from his body.

"Why?" I finally ask, the single word a raw whisper. I hate how weak it makes me sound.

His jaw tenses. "Recompense."

"They were innocent."

When he looks at me again, his eyes are alight with anger. "So was my brother."

My mouth opens, but I snap it shut again as we pass a series of wagons. I lower my face, wishing for a hat of my own as I school my expression into something more neutral. A small family sits in the back of one wagon, atop bales of straw. A little girl with gray eyes waves timidly.

I force myself to smile back, but it transforms into a scowl the moment the wagon passes. I'd thought the soul in his talisman was his familiar, but I don't regret setting his brother free. That doesn't mean I don't understand his grief, though.

Saengo's death at Talon's Teahouse might not have been by my hand, but it had been my fault all the same. A shaman had thrown a knife at me, and I had ducked, not realizing that Saengo was standing behind me. I should have protected her, and instead—

In any case, my mistake and his grief don't justify what he did to those at Spinner's End. Nothing would justify that.

"Take it as a lesson," the Soulless says, bitterness in his words. "That is what happens when you make promises you can't keep. When you are determined to face an opponent you cannot defeat, people die. Do you think any of them would have done the same for you?"

They wouldn't have. He knows it, and so do I. All my life, people have proven time and again that they wouldn't care if I simply disappeared. Those like Jonyah would have welcomed it. Even when I stood beside King Meilek as his Shadow, I wasn't some hero on a quest to save the kingdom. I was the monster they tried and failed to kill. Me . . . and the Soulless.

But I've long since decided to stop allowing others to define who and what I am. I'm not a hero, but that doesn't mean I will stand aside and let people die in front of me. Choosing to be decent isn't an act of bravery.

"How long will we be gone?" I ask. The last thing I want is to turn his attention to Saengo, but he must realize that I can't be away from her for any considerable length of time. How I'm going to keep her safe while getting away from him is a different issue, though.

"Your familiar will be fine."

Either the Soulless is a mind reader—and as far as I know, that's not a craft that exists—or he's exceptionally observant. Biting back the urge to ask how he knew what I was thinking, I say, "Does that mean you can cure the rot?"

"It means don't test my patience and you may find out."

Glaring, I don't speak to him for the rest of the afternoon, although I do wonder if we're headed to Luam. Before the trade city can become more than a glimmer of sunlight on water in the distance, we turn southwest. We take a well-worn path through patches of forest until we reach the eastern bank of the Xya River. From there, we follow the river south.

Boats are a constant presence on the river, merchants and fishermen ferrying their goods back and forth from Luam. This means we are never alone, giving me little chance to escape from the Soulless without risking others, which is, of course, his intention. I don't bother asking where we're going.

When we bed down for the night beside the trees, just shy of the riverbank, the Soulless once again steals me into his dreamscape. I suspect he can only do this due to our proximity, although he doesn't explain when I ask. Instead, he orders me to practice.

I want to spit at his feet, but learning to control my craft will lead me closer to defeating him. So I do as he says, quietly promising that he will regret teaching me.

The following night, when I've grown comfortable with the swirling current of my craft, I manage to forcibly awaken myself from the shared dream. Unfortunately, it also awakens him, but it is a victory, nonetheless. I am no longer a prisoner in his dreamscapes.

We travel steadily south. On the third day, I steal a sword from a boat someone left moored on the riverbank, but the Soulless takes a family captive until I discard it. When I ask why he's so worried I'll stab him in the back if he's supposed to be invincible, he predictably ignores me. Later that evening, during a lull in river traffic, I consider escaping on my drake but worry he'll kill the drake in retaliation.

Even as I entertain every possibility in which I could escape or disable him, I also want to know what he's up to, if only so that I can disrupt his plans.

By the third day, it becomes apparent that we're headed for the border between the Empire and Kazahyn. I briefly wonder if he means to help the Kazan, but then I dismiss the idea. While his target is House Yalaeng, both kingdoms fought against him in the battle that took his brother's life. I doubt he cares much for who comes out on top in this conflict, so long as he accomplishes his own objectives.

The last time I made this journey had been on a boat with a combined Nuvali and Kazan force. With the aid of shaman crafts to hasten our travel, the journey from Luam to the border had taken less than a full day and then another couple days to reach the southern coast.

On drakes, at a more sedate pace, it takes us four days to reach the border. The mountains come into view well before that, though. Much of Kazahyn's geography is dominated by a mountain range. The Kazan build their cities underground, the surface generally left untouched save for the occasional farms and various port cities along the coast like Tamsimno.

Around noon on the fourth day, the Soulless stops without explanation. We leave our drakes to graze in the underbrush as he motions me forward on foot.

Curious, I trail after him to the tree line, where the ground shifts from soft earth to rocky shore, sloping down toward the river. Since the Soulless is looking southward, I follow his gaze. It isn't difficult to spot what he must want me to see.

Farther down the river, a blockade has been set up with sleek boats manned by shamans in Nuvali uniforms. Merchants and fisherman are being forced to reroute through smaller waterways. The only boats allowed through are those ferrying supplies to the encampment downstream. The flash of white and gold banners peek over the treetops.

Once we return to our drakes, I ask, "Why are we here? Is there a Yalaeng in the encampment you've come to kill?"

"Yes," the Soulless says, which takes me aback.

I was only being snide. Although I'd considered the possibility during our journey here, I thought it unlikely given that every Yalaeng of consequence would be holed up in Mirrim. As the Soulless rummages through his pack for the last of the fish I'd caught and cooked earlier, I settle against a large jutting root, my thoughts tangled.

Whoever is inside the encampment must be important

for the Soulless to travel so far from Mirrim, away from the imperial family and his true objectives. A general perhaps?

The question now is what to do about it. I can't allow the Soulless to continue murdering people, much as I agree they probably deserve it. Once we're inside the encampment, weapons will be readily available.

All I need is a sword, a diversion, and an opportunity.

FIFTEEN

As the Soulless eats, I close my eyes and seek Saengo's candle flame.

It takes a fair bit of concentration with the sunspear armor, but she feels far away—although not nearly as distant as she should. This troubles me, as does the fact that Theyen will know by now that something went wrong. I hope he isn't planning anything. He has a record of being too brave for his own good.

Maybe Theyen found Saengo and returned her to Evewyn. It's a comforting thought, and I cling to it. My fingers drum mindlessly against the breastplate, which I've only removed a few times to wash myself in the river. The surge of my craft when I remove it no longer feels overwhelming.

I'm not sure how long Saengo and I can be apart before my craft begins to fail and her physical form fades. It's been almost a week since I saw Saengo last, and with every passing hour, my anxiety over the state of her rot grows. No matter what happens today in the Nuvali encampment and no matter what lies the Soulless might tell about her well-being, my priority afterward will be to escape and find Saengo.

I study the Soulless, something I've had ample time to do these past few days. He looks out of place, even dressed in that straw hat and plain robes. Something about him simply doesn't seem natural.

"Your bond with the Dead Wood," I begin. "How close do you have to be to the trees in order to retain your craft?" His bond with the trapped souls is very different from mine with Saengo's. Even so, if they connect him to his magic, then there might be some similarities as well. But with how immense his power is, how long can he remain apart from the Dead Wood before he needs to return?

"Don't worry," he says, chewing a small bite of fish. "I've enough magic for some time yet."

He gingerly reclines against a tree, and while it would look casual to anyone else, I know differently. The travel wears on him. Despite that we get the same amount of sleep each night, he tires more easily. His movements grow slower in the evenings when we bed down for the night. His pale skin only accents the shadows beneath his eyes.

A few times, I've caught him massaging his legs or slowly flexing his hands. Even though we're traveling slowly, his body isn't accustomed to being in a saddle for so many hours in a day.

Despite his physical limitations, he hasn't been as useless

as I initially expected. He doesn't eat much, but aside from the fish I caught this morning, everything else we've eaten has been caught with his powers. He always skins and cleans the animals himself and then builds a fire to cook the meat with a crude spit, since we've no equipment. He also knows which plants are safe to eat and which to avoid. He's obviously spent time in the wilderness, and although his skills must be rusty, he doesn't seem to suffer for it.

I haven't even had to step in to help. In fact, he hasn't asked me to do anything other than follow, eat, and sleep. I'd caught the fish out of boredom, not to be useful.

He rests for only a short while before rising again. We weave through the trees, easily avoiding scouts whose souls we can sense from far enough away. Our steps are careful and unhurried. I'm a little impressed by his ability to move so soundlessly, although I'm not sure if it's because he's been trained or because he's so deliberate in his movements.

The section of forest nearest the river isn't heavily guarded, first, because the river would leave any enemies exposed and scouts patrol the shore and, second, because this is the northern end of the camp, well within Empire lands.

Once we're close enough to the encampment, we drop to our stomachs, edging forward on knees and elbows to avoid notice by the perimeter guards. Fortunately, they're currently engrossed in conversation and not paying any mind to who might be lurking in the trees.

The Soulless still hasn't explained anything to me, but I'm

not an idiot. We're taking stock of what we're up against. In silence, we watch as soldiers come and go, some by river, others shuffling about their daily duties. Far in the distance, mere specks soaring and diving through the clouds are what I think might be wyverns. The Kazan encampments must be right across the border.

We remain hidden for about an hour, but it isn't long before an important detail becomes evident—we haven't seen a single lightwender.

There must be some here, of course. Nuvali medics are nearly exclusively light givers. Perhaps they're being restricted to a single location. I can't imagine the lightwenders would be pleased with being treated like enemies. Just as the Empire had hunted all soulrenders, just as Queen Meilyr had persecuted all shamanborn, all lightwenders are being punished for the actions of a few. Would the cycle never end?

After a time, the Soulless nods wordlessly over our shoulders. We carefully retreat in silence.

When we've found our way back to our drakes, I ask, "Are you going to tell me who we're here for?"

The Soulless returns to his spot before a tree with bits of moss climbing up the bark. He crosses his legs and meets my gaze. My shoulders tense at the look I see there. "Princess Kyshia."

The answer catches me off guard. That's not at all what I was expecting. "But she's in Mirrim."

"She is not," he says simply.

I open my mouth, close it again, and then cross my arms, frowning. The men at the inn had said something about seeing Kyshia at the Temple of Light on the same morning she'd been with me and Saengo on our way to Mirrim. She's obviously using decoys to protect herself and confuse her enemies. So it's not impossible that she has since left Mirrim again, leaving another decoy in her place.

But how had the Soulless known she would be here? I'm not sure how I feel about Kyshia being his next target. Despite her promises of safety and trust, the moment her father and brother broke our deal, she'd fled, leaving me to my own devices. Never mind that she'd likely thinned the guards around the frost chamber to ease my way there. I would have died if not for Saengo.

But what else should I have expected? Even Kendara had done nothing.

"All right," I say, "assuming she is here, why Kyshia? Why now? I thought you meant to take your time."

"I'd intended to leave her for among the last, but given that she walked you into a trap, I've reevaluated my list."

"It wasn't her doing," I say, even though I've no reason to defend her. "Her brother broke the deal. The Emperor seemed willing until Aleng spoke."

"Now you know the extent of the Emperor's character and that of his children," he says flatly. "She should not have offered you a deal in the first place without full confidence in her power."

Hard to argue with that. I kick a stone into the underbrush before sitting. One of the drakes is curled up close by, fast asleep. It snores softly, snuffling a bit in its sleep. The drakes are exhausted after so many days of travel, all to reach the Ember Princess.

Why would Kyshia even risk coming down here? Maybe, after Eren's death and then having her authority so soundly overruled by Aleng and the Emperor, she no longer felt it wise to remain in Mirrim, even with her family. Or *especially* with her family, given the Soulless's assertion that he had nothing to do with three of the murders.

But coming here instead was just as questionable. She would rather risk the enemies here than those in Mirrim. I would pity her if not for the fact she all but left me to die. The Soulless isn't wrong that she walked me into a trap, even if she hadn't known what it was. I was an idiot to trust any promise from a Yalaeng.

If the Soulless is right—and I can't imagine he'd have bothered coming all this way if he wasn't absolutely certain—then Kyshia must have fled Mirrim the same night she brought me before her father, perhaps after learning I'd disappeared with the Soulless.

He had done exactly what they wanted, revealing himself for me. But they hadn't been ready, had instead been too busy dealing with one soulrender to be wary of the other, and now Kyshia probably believes the Empire has two soulrenders to contend with. They are ever the inventors of their own troubles.

"There are a lot of innocent lives in that camp," I say. "You can't kill them."

"This again," he says, although his sneer is half-hearted at best.

"Your vendetta is against House Yalaeng, not those just following orders. Were you and your brother any different when you went to war for the Empire? You can't punish them for simply making do with what the Empire has given them."

His expression settles again into blankness, although the edges of his mouth tighten briefly, something I would have missed were I not watching his face for a reaction.

After a long silence, he finally says, "Come up with a plan by nightfall for how to get to the princess without my craft to clear our path, and I will hear it."

Despite myself, I'm surprised by his concession. It's several hours to nightfall, and since the Soulless doesn't seem inclined to move, I acquire more fish and build a fire to cook them. All the while, I consider my options and grow increasingly concerned that Saengo's candle flame still feels closer than it should.

Once Saengo managed to escape Mirrim, she would have hidden and waited for me to appear as well. If she'd spotted me with the Soulless, perhaps she followed us south? She's certainly not anywhere within my own range of awareness, but how she's managed to escape the Soulless's notice is a mystery. If she is truly nearby, I pray to the Sisters she has the good sense not to do anything foolish.

Even with the blockade farther south, the river maintains a steady stream of traffic. Every so often, a scout sails by, near enough to the shore that I grow tense with apprehension—not for us, but for whichever poor soul should happen upon us.

Fortunately we pass the remaining hours without incident. The Soulless moves only once all afternoon, when I began probing at his soul with my craft. His eyes opened to give me a cutting look—a warning not to test him.

When daylight fades, I rise. "I'll be right back."

"I'll know if you attempt to run," he says, not even looking at me.

I don't dignify the threat with a response. I'm not sure how far he can stretch his powers. It had been remarkable in the night market, but after four days of travel, four days on top of how much time he's already spent away from the Dead Wood and his visible weariness, I do wonder if that's affected the range of his craft.

If I simply delay him long enough, would he lose all access to his powers? Or would they weaken enough that I might stand a chance?

Those are questions for another day. Right now, I'm not trying to escape. Instead, I head toward the Nuvali encampment and two souls I sensed earlier who I suspect aren't just scouts. The Bright Sister seems to have smiled on me, because when I draw close enough, my craft senses they're still there. I approach quietly, crouched low in the wildflowers that grow thick and high.

When I find them, the two soldiers are half dressed and dozing, shielded from view of the encampment by a tight cluster of trees and the overgrown wildflowers. I mentally snort.

I almost feel bad knocking them out, but at least if they're discovered, it won't immediately raise any alarms. It's clear what the two had been up to.

Once I'm far enough away, I change into one of their uniforms and then gather my clothes into a bundle and return to the Soulless. He hasn't moved from his spot beneath the tree. When I drop the second uniform on the ground beside his knee, his eyes open. He glances at the clothes and then up at me.

"This is your plan?"

"It's better than strolling into camp and killing or controlling everyone. You'd raise the alarm at once, and she'd be gone before you ever reached her. We'll have to keep our eyes down, though. I didn't see any lightwenders earlier, so if they catch sight of our eyes, it'll be a dead giveaway."

He frowns, but he doesn't object.

Once he's changed, we make our way back to the edge of the encampment. By now, night has fully descended, and we're well shielded by the dark. A different pair of perimeter guards stand around a single torch, speaking to one another in low tones and looking bored.

"Come on," I murmur, standing.

The Soulless is unnervingly obedient as he follows me from the trees. The guards aren't surprised to see us, but we lower our eyes and avoid the circle of torch light, letting the shadows do the work of shrouding our faces.

"You're late," one of the guards says, sounding more sullen than angry. Since I've no idea what he's talking about, I only bow apologetically and quicken my steps to make it seem like I'm in a hurry.

"Leave them be," the other guard says. "Goddess knows we need some distraction lately."

They both snicker, but at least they don't try to stop us. When we pass the first few tents without anyone raising any alarms, I release a slow breath and pick up my pace. While the Soulless keeps his head down, nothing in his demeanor suggests he's concerned if we're caught. In truth, I'm surprised he's indulging me.

When we were at Spinner's End, the Soulless had divulged details about his past in order to earn my cooperation, not through threats and force but through a shared understanding. Maybe that's what he's doing now by letting me have my way, especially after what he did to those at Spinner's End— proving that he isn't completely unreasonable so long as he accomplishes his purpose for being here.

Since it's past dinnertime, the encampment is generally quiet. Most have bedded down for the night after a long day, but clusters of soldiers are still gathered around the remains of cooking fires, drinking and chattering in low tones about who-knows-what. Maybe wondering when they can return home and if this conflict with Kazahyn will end before more blood is shed.

We weave around tents, taking a meandering path through the camp to avoid torches and campfires. But our destination is the large, white tent that rises well above the others with the banner of a blazing sun crowning its peak. I doubt Kyshia would be inside the general's tent—that would defeat the purpose of hiding—but she would be close by. Part of me is skeptical she's even here, and an even greater part hopes she isn't.

We pause once we're close enough to get a clear view of the white tent. Soldiers stand guard at either side of the entrance, beside low-burning braziers. In the broad space before the tent, a fire has been set up, around which two more soldiers sit on halved logs, passing a wineskin between them.

Their uniforms are slightly different than the rest, and I would bet they're actually sun warriors. Yet another pair dressed like servants fuss with some drakes, leading them in a curiously patrol-like circuit around a few neighboring tents. A final soldier loiters beside a torch.

"Now what?" the Soulless murmurs. I've a feeling all this subtlety amuses him when he could subdue everyone with barely an effort.

I gesture with my chin at the tent all these soldiers appear to be guarding rather than the general's. I don't sense anyone inside, but I also can't sense four of the seven people present. There's no reason for this many people donned in sunspear armor to be gathered around an empty tent, which means the Soulless must be right. My stomach drops. If Kyshia is in there, she'll be wearing sunspear armor as well, which will at least give her a fighting chance.

The Soulless's eyes narrow on the tent I indicate. Somehow, I'll have to catch him unawares before he reaches Kyshia.

"Don't kill anyone," I remind him.

His gaze flicks to mine, but it's hard to read his expression in the dark. He doesn't answer, so I repeat myself.

"I'm only here for one person," he says, and I nod.

Squaring my shoulders, I stride out into the open. The Soulless shadows my steps. At once, every soldier present comes alert. Likely, this area is meant to be off-limits.

The shaman by the torch moves forward just as the ones by the campfire begin to stand.

"You lost, soldier?" one of them demands as I hurriedly bow, mostly to hide my eyes. The Soulless mimics me. "What's your name?"

A sun warrior in sunspear bones disguised beneath the standard uniform approaches us. His boots are loud in the relative quiet, and he drags his heels a little when he walks. The moment he's within range, I rise from my bow and slam my palm beneath his chin. His head snaps back with a painful clatter of teeth. Before he can recover, I plant my fist into his jaw, and then snatch his sword from its scabbard as he crumples.

The two dressed as servants and the soldier by the torch instantly drop, bodies thumping heavily against the dirt. They're likely regular soldiers, since they're not wearing sunspear bones. I spare a heartbeat to ensure they're not dead and then ram my knuckles into the nearest sun warrior's throat to cut off her shout for help. I tackle her to the earth as magic stirs around me in a swirl of wind and stinging dirt. We hit the ground, me on top with wind whipping at my cheeks and eyes.

Something flashes in her hand. I seize her wrist and twist. With a choked cry, she drops the knife. I grasp the hilt just as a powerful gale nearly lifts me off her. She scrambles back, but as I hit the ground beside her, I swing my leg and my boot catches her beneath the jaw. She collapses, unconscious, the wind dying around us.

Behind me, the Soulless has dispatched one sun warrior and is battling the second. His sash is wrapped around the sun warrior's neck, but the way the Soulless's jaw is clenched tight and the veins strain in his neck means this sun warrior is a breathsipher. Just as the Soulless is attempting to strangle him, the sun warrior is suffocating him in turn.

It's only been a handful of seconds, but it won't be long before we're noticed. With one last glance at the Soulless, I shove aside the flap of what I hope is Kyshia's tent and duck inside.

The moment the canvas falls into place behind me, I stumble. A sudden tingling sensation overcomes me. Weakness steals into my limbs, fatigue cramping my muscles. Wisps of golden light lift from my chest, my arms, my legs, siphoning through the air toward Kyshia, who stands at the other end of the small tent, fully dressed in her sunspear armor.

I suck in a tremulous breath, take one staggering step forward, and fling the knife. Kyshia ducks—I hadn't been aiming to hit her—and it's enough to break her concentration. The golden light fades, strength surges back into my body, and I lunge the few paces between us, lifting my sword to her neck before she can use her craft again.

She's a light giver. Light givers are capable of stealing the life from within one person and passing it to themselves. Or vice versa, typically to keep an injured soldier alive until a light stitcher can properly heal them.

"You betrayed me to your father and brother, and now you try to kill me?" I demand, sucking in a deep breath to chase away the last of that uncomfortable tingling in my muscles.

Kyshia edges slowly away from the tip of my blade but there isn't much room. It isn't a very large tent. "I didn't betray you, but I'm not in a position to deny the Emperor."

Outside, the sounds of struggle have ceased. Footsteps approach the tent. When Kyshia opens her mouth again, I hiss for her to be quiet. With sudden understanding, she nods, eyes narrowing on the entrance.

Behind me, the tent flap stirs. In a flash, I pivot on my foot and thrust the sword.

SIXTEEN

Two hands clamp down on either side of the blade before the tip can pierce the Soulless's chest.

My teeth clench, and I brace my feet for leverage as I shove harder. The Soulless only sneers, his arms trembling faintly but unyielding. He's far stronger than I gave him credit for. Blood seeps down his wrists.

Then pain rips through me. I stagger, one leg almost folding. The Soulless releases the blade as the pain retreats. Backing away from him, I lift the sword again, even though it's pointless. I'd had one shot to surprise him, and I'd failed.

"You're predictable," he says, almost bored. He lifts his hands, surveys the damage, and then drops them to his sides, seemingly unconcerned. He steps into the tent.

Kyshia, who has backed herself into the corner, stands straight and tall, chin lifted. She means to die with her dignity.

At least she won't go easily—her soul is protected from his craft. The only piece of sunspear armor she isn't wearing is the leather helm, which sits on a low table beside her cot and a bulky shield with the Nuvali sun in gold. It's no wonder—the helm is a ridiculous thing with the bones protruding from the sides like horns.

"We got in here your way," the Soulless says. "Now we will finish this my way. You will kill the Ember Princess. If you refuse, I will kill her, followed by every soldier in this camp."

"She's wearing talisman armor," I say, glaring.

"And you have a sword," he says flatly. "I've heard you're good with it."

I glance at Kyshia, who looks between the two of us with guarded, angry eyes. She must be afraid, but she gives no indication of it. If she has any fighting skill, I've yet to see it, but if we were to fight, I'm confident I would win.

But I don't want to kill Kyshia, even if she did leave me to die. "Her family should be removed from power, not murdered."

"They would not have hesitated to murder you and your family had you been Nuvali," the Soulless says.

I swallow tightly. They'd done just that to my mother's family—murdered them all and then finished the job when they sent assassins into Evewyn to find the soulrender who'd escaped. Even so. "We can choose not to be like them."

He scoffs. "Not fighting back is not the act of bravery you think it is. They kill each other already, using our names and craft to shield their crimes."

"Defense and murder are two different things," I say.

"It's no use trying to reason with a monster," Kyshia says quietly. To her credit, her voice does not shake. I wonder if attempts on her life are something she's familiar with.

I transfer my glare to her. "So you would rather I do as he says and kill you? You shouldn't have left Mirrim. At least there, you'd have the protection of your father and brother." *And Kendara,* I think bitterly.

"Not likely," she says coolly, "seeing as Aleng is dead. I ensured it before leaving."

As my eyes widen in surprise, the Soulless lets out a low laugh. "You don't deny it."

"Why should I? You're here to kill me either way. What does it matter?"

"Wait," I say, putting up the hand that isn't holding the sword. "You killed . . ." After Saengo's arrow pierced Aleng's chest, he'd been quickly taken away by a host of soldiers. And Kendara. "You used Kendara? She was obeying *your* orders? Are you responsible for the other murders as well?"

Indignation and anger at all the manipulation rises within me. I point the blade at her, part of me wildly tempted to do as the Soulless wants.

"Neither I nor Kendara had anything to do with Eren's death. Nor did he," she says, jerking her chin toward the Soulless. "Our father didn't believe Aleng was ready to be Emperor. Even the court agreed, no matter how much they dislike Father's decisions. Aleng would rather drink and gamble and tumble a warm body than strategize a military campaign or run a kingdom. Everyone knew it."

"Then why was he present in our meeting?" I ask. And why would Kendara warn me about him specifically?

"Because he didn't want to lose his position as the Sun's Heir. He thought opposing our father in this conflict and throwing the kingdom into war would establish him as a leader." She says the word with disgust, some of her composure fracturing. "He had some support within the court as well, and the fool would have happily made himself a puppet if it meant keeping the comforts of his position."

"So when it became evident that the Soulless was in Mirrim, he used it to his advantage?" I ask. The Soulless's expression of faint disdain hasn't changed throughout her explanation.

"Yes. He worried that Father would replace him, so he began by eliminating some of his competition—cousins first, obscure Yalaengs but still within the line of succession. And then he grew bold enough to go after our brother. He had to be stopped."

"By using his own method and framing the Soulless for it?" I ask.

"You were the bait. Aleng has hardly been out of sunspear armor since the murders began."

My teeth ache with how tightly I'm clenching them. So the plan wasn't just for me to draw the Soulless out of hiding. It was a cover to get rid of Aleng as well. I suppose she'd arranged for something to go "wrong" during the fight with the Soulless, but Aleng had ruined everything by refusing Kyshia's deal.

Maybe he'd suspected the plot and intentionally undermined her. But Kyshia and Kendara were likely prepared for this, and when Saengo shot Aleng, Kendara had improvised.

I'd nearly died in the process, though, and I hate the part of me that wonders if Kendara had known either Saengo or the Soulless would come for me. It would explain her inaction, an excuse my heart is eager to grasp at, a hope that Kendara hadn't *really* planned to let me die by Aleng's hand. Not if her task had been to kill Aleng herself.

In any case, Saengo had come. Medics would have had to remove at least half of Aleng's armor to treat his wound. And if, in fact, they framed the Soulless for it, Kendara would have had to arrange the deaths of those around him as well once the poison took hold.

"So much could have gone wrong," I say, uncertain of whether to believe her. It's a lot, and she's already proven a willingness for dishonesty when it suits her.

"It was a gamble worth taking. This is what leaders do, Sirscha. The death of a few for the peace of many. Would you have done any differently in my shoes?"

The Soulless looks at me now, evidently curious about my answer. I glare at them both, fingers tightening around the sword.

"Maybe," I decide.

When it came to life and death, mercy could cost you everything. Except for the soldier on the ship whose soul I accidentally ripped, every person I have killed has been in self-defense—the shaman at the inn, Jonyah and his sell-swords, Ronin. Ronin had been a threat to all the kingdoms, but I acknowledged that I should have subdued him instead. It's easy to have regrets once we've been met by the consequences of our actions.

Kyshia makes a soft sound, a humorless half-laugh. "I told Kendara to meet me here." She cocks her head at me. "I thought perhaps this could happen, but she should have arrived by now. She said removing my brother as the Sun's Heir would be her last task for House Yalaeng. I didn't think she was serious."

Even though I haven't sorted out my feelings for Kendara, I hope she's telling the truth. I hope Kendara severs her ties with House Yalaeng.

"Maybe she wants to see you dead as well," I say.

"It's possible," she says, her chin jerking higher. "But you're not going to kill me."

She speaks it with such confidence, and part of me is just contrary enough to want to prove her wrong. But whether or not Kyshia deserves to die, I'm not going to be the one bloodying my hands to do it.

"No," I say. "I'm not."

Pain shears through me. I gasp, fingers convulsing around the sword hilt. Magic swells beneath my skin, rushing to break the grip of his craft, but I hold back. If he's focused on me, then he might not notice Kyshia edging toward the knife I'd thrown, still speared through the canvas.

"Your naïveté is embarrassing," the Soulless says. "You think if you save her, she'll owe you something or feel any sense of gratitude? This ridiculous idea of honor and morality only works when everyone agrees it does, but you're playing by two different sets of rules."

Pain is a current flooding through my veins and throbbing at my temples. Still, I don't break his hold on my soul.

"They are *drenched* in the blood of soulrenders they have killed. You say defense and murder are different. Were those soulrenders given the chance to defend themselves? What is this if not in defense of every person they have not yet killed?"

"This isn't about them," I say through my teeth before at last throwing off his magic. I gasp, sweat sliding down my spine and every bone in my body aching. The Soulless glares but doesn't attack again. "I wouldn't mourn her or her father or any of them. And I don't expect a debt for not killing her. It's not about . . . earning approval or gratitude."

Once, perhaps, it might have been, when I'd been so desperate for acknowledgement. When I would have given nearly anything—my life, my morality, my honor—just to prove that I was worth something.

But not anymore. That's no way to live a life, making decisions based on whether it will earn me respect or acceptance. Everything I've done and everything I will do—these choices may speak to my character, but they do not speak to my worth.

No one gets to decide what I'm worth.

"It's not about them," I repeat. "It's about me and the choices I make—who I choose to be." Even if seeing House Yalaeng wiped from existence *would* be viciously satisfying.

I may not be a monster, but that doesn't mean I'm a saint.

"How foolish," the Soulless says, unmoved. "But it's too late to—"

The blare of a horn cuts him off, followed immediately by an inhuman roar that sends a tremor down my spine. The three of us go quiet, listening. Shouts have erupted through the encampment, growing louder, along with the rumble of boots and drakes.

There's another roar, almost a screech that makes me wince, along with a deep, rhythmic sound, like the beating of heavy wings. I've heard these sounds before.

"Wyverns," I whisper. Kyshia shoots me an alarmed look, but I brush past the Soulless to peek outside, if only to provide a visual for what my craft already tells me.

The mayhem is at the southern end of the camp, nearer the border, but it's growing closer. Already, soldiers emerge from their tents, hastily buckling their swords to their waists as they race past. No one seems to care anymore that this area is restricted, which means the bodies in the dirt are quickly spotted.

Two soldiers stop to check their comrades who are lying unconscious where the Soulless and I had left them. One of those on the ground stirs, already rousing.

I whip around, letting the tent flap fall shut. "We have

to leave."

The Soulless turns for Kyshia, but I dart around him, placing myself between them.

His voice is whisper soft. "You are becoming more trouble than—"

An arrow slices through the canvas, piercing his back. His body jerks, and his face goes white. I startle back, eyes wide. The Soulless's lips compress before he suddenly coughs, blood speckling his chin.

With a snarl, he reaches back, spine twisting, and grasps the arrow shaft. Blood soaks through his cloak, thick and dark, as he rips out the offending bit of wood. More blood stains his gritted teeth.

I swallow. I'd known that the Soulless's life was unnatural and his soul fractured beyond repair. I'd wondered if running him through would be effective, given how difficult it's proven to kill him. But seeing the evidence before me is still completely disarming.

The arrow had likely punctured a lung or some other vital organ. And yet, he still stands, casting the arrow a look of disgust before tossing it to the ground. A sick feeling twists my stomach—not because he isn't dead from a fatal wound but because I recognize the fletching on the shaft. It's the same as the one that struck Aleng.

The sound of voices has grown louder and closer, and while the souls of soldiers continue to rush past toward the wyverns, others swarm around our tent. It's clear they've worked out what's happened. They know the Soulless is here.

"Did they plan this?" someone outside asks in a panicked voice. "Are the shadowblessed working with him?"

My gaze lifts from the Soulless's wound to his face, but I doubt his lack of action has been anything other than the Pale Sister laughing at me once again. The Soulless wipes slowly at the blood on his lips, and all at once, the voices outside the tent are cut off. I suck in my breath as every glittering soul gathered outside the tent winks out.

My craft reels from the shock of it. The silence that follows is quickly broken by terrified voices, a flurry of orders, and rushing feet.

"Arrows ready!" someone shouts.

I share a glance with Kyshia before we drop to our stomachs. I roll, seizing the shield beside her cot and squeezing both of us beneath it as a flurry of arrows pierce the tent. The sound of tearing canvas fills my ears. Kyshia cries out when an arrow catches her leg through the leather.

"They're going to kill you," I shout at Kyshia, but although she's finally lost enough composure that her fear is evident in the whites of her eyes, she only shakes her head.

"I ordered them to kill him if he appeared, regardless of my life," she says, breathless, and then squeezes her eyes shut as another volley of arrows rip through the tent.

I grunt in grudging respect. Nearby, the Soulless is on his knees, hands pressed flat to the earth. His pale face is a mask of impending rage, his amber eyes all lightning and fury. One arrow is lodged in his calf, one in his arm, and two more in his shoulder and back.

I peer over the protection of the shield. Nearly one whole side of the tent has torn away under the assault, revealing the camp in a riot of shadows and torchlight. A fire blazes in the distance, illuminating the line of archers. They stand a fair distance away, with tents having been knocked down to provide a clear line of sight.

My hands clench into fists as my craft strains outward, but I can't sense the souls of those archers. The breastplate doesn't help, but I'm certain they should still be within the Soulless's radius of power. That he hasn't killed them yet confirms my suspicion that the longer he is away from the Dead Wood, the more his power diminishes.

Or perhaps "diminish" isn't accurate. All those soldiers he'd just killed are still outside the tent, their bodies piled gracelessly in the dirt. But the reach of his craft is certainly shrinking.

As the archers ready another volley, I frantically scan what I'm able to see through the ragged canvas. Where is Saengo? There's no mistaking that single arrow with green fletching lying where the Soulless tossed it, the tip dark with his blood. Nuvali archers use arrows with light brown fletching.

I nudge Kyshia toward her cot. If we tip it on its side, it can provide a broader surface of protection. She begins shuffling sideways.

"The sky, the sky!"

With a horrible snap of beams, the entire rest of the tent is suddenly ripped away. An enormous black wyvern circles overhead, powerful talons flinging aside the remains of Kyshia's tent. Then the creature dives again, ripping through another nearby tent and its unfortunate occupant within.

The Soulless groans as he removes each arrow, glaring up at the sky with eyes that nearly glow golden. My gaze falls on the discarded helm that has fallen off the table and onto the ground beside the cot. Without thinking it through, I surge for it. Kyshia gasps, scrambling to support the shield on her own just as I jam the helm over my head.

At once, my magic retreats to a whisper. I sense nothing but the faint trace of souls beyond the ruins of Kyshia's tent. The Soulless snarls, his carefully controlled exterior crumbling beneath each unexpected obstacle. He obviously didn't coordinate this attack with the Kazan, but more importantly, he can no longer grasp my soul.

His magic probes at the armor's edges, trying to wrench past its defenses. Pain prickles in my chest, but it isn't enough for him to take hold.

With the tent gone and her way clear, Kyshia drops the shield and makes a run for it, limping from her wound. When the Soulless tries to follow her, I swipe my sword into his path. He pauses, his expression one of wild fury. The cloudy night sky and the distant fire paint riotous shadows across his face. Perhaps for the first time, he isn't hiding behind a veneer of calm and perfectly restrained power.

The archers have scattered beneath the diving wyverns, and the other soldiers keep their distance. Satisfied that he can't repeat what he did in the night market, I attack.

He ducks, barely avoiding the blade as it whispers past his neck. He staggers out of range, his bleeding calf making him clumsy. He might be able to withstand both blades and arrows, but he can still be hurt. The wounds clearly pain him enough to slow him down. Enough, perhaps, that I might get to see just how much his body can take without killing him.

As I lunge at him again, jumping over the remnants of a tent beam, arrows stream skyward. More wyverns swoop over the camp, their riders lighting the ends of their arrows with oil and flame. They're aiming for the encampment's supply wagons and storage tents. Drakes scream as they run wild, loosed from their burning stables. When one of the wyvern riders passes low overhead, I glimpse part of their clan sigil on the saddle. To my relief, it isn't the Fireborn Queens.

"This is what you would protect?" the Soulless asks with a gesture at the camp—the fire, the flashes of steel, the screeches of wyverns, and the screams of the dying. "They will never stop fighting one another. Ronin learned this lesson and sought to end it his way, but they are not worth protecting. Stand by me, and we will never again be subjected to their tyranny and warmongering."

I don't answer him, perhaps because I don't know how to. Perhaps because I don't actually disagree. I simply can't abide his methods.

He dodges my sword but can't avoid my knee, which meets his gut. His bad leg stumbles as I attack again. He hisses at the wet slide of my blade against his ribs. I press in, twisting the sword before dancing back to duck his fist. For a man who should be dead half a dozen times over, he's still fast, his knuckles grazing my cheekbone. His leg smoothly follows in a kick.

I throw up my arm, but the impact knocks me off my feet. I roll nimbly, recovering my footing in time to block another punch.

"Get down!" a voice calls from behind me. I've only a moment to comply before an arrow hits the Soulless's chest with a wet thud, just beneath his collarbone. The fletching is green.

My heart lurches into my throat as I turn, scanning the mayhem for Saengo. She stands a short distance away, her silhouette illuminated in the light of an overturned torch. She's already nocked another arrow. The Soulless rips out the one in his chest, a grunt and the way his face briefly tightens the only indications that he feels the pain. With Saengo giving me cover, I raise my sword again.

The Soulless's gaze slides past me to Saengo. Pain wrenches through me, resonating across the bridge of our bond. With a gasp, I whirl around to see Saengo drop her bow. Her hands fly to her chest.

"No," I whisper, icy terror spilling through my ribs. My chest wrenches again with the echo of her pain, and I bite back a cry. Saengo should be far enough away, farther even than the archers who'd nearly collapsed Kyshia's tent. She shouldn't be within his range. She isn't . . . She isn't human.

She's a familiar, infected by the rot. His corrupted magic is already inside her. Saengo falls to her knees.

The sword slides from my fingers and I run, sprinting across the distance. My feet trample strewn supplies and smashed tents, and my shoulder collides with a soldier fleeing the battle, but all that matters is that I reach her. Everything else is insignificant. I can't hear my own breathing, my own pulse—it's as if the world has stopped and all that exists is Saengo on her knees, doubled over and shuddering with pain.

At last, I drop to her side and reach for the collar of her tunic with trembling hands. She is panting, her skin cold and clammy as I wrench the fabric open.

In the flickering torchlight, blue lines of infection writhe beneath her skin like the roots of the Dead Wood. The rot slithers up her neck in thick venomous ropes.

Saengo collapses against me, gasping like she can't draw breath. My chest feels like it's being cracked open, yet it's nothing compared with what she must be feeling. My magic latches onto the connection between us but struggles to hold on. With a frustrated cry, I tear off the helm and then fumble with the breastplate until that, too, lies discarded in the dirt.

Point it like a blade, I think desperately as my magic takes hold of the ragged edges of her soul. But no matter how much I pour into her, it's like trying to fill a bottomless cup.

My magic should be sealing the cracks in her soul, driving back the rot as it's done every time I've healed her since the night I killed Ronin.

But while her skin glows as if holding the sun inside her, the infection persists. Those vivid blue lines writhe and grow, weeds refusing to stay pruned and surging forward the moment I ease back even a little. As it is, I'm barely keeping the rot at bay.

I shake my head. He can't have her. This isn't how it ends. Saengo won't die *again* because of me.

The sound of wings penetrates my frenzied panic, and gusts of wind whip dust into the air. My head snaps up to see a wyvern dive low, its outstretched talons reaching for a soldier fleeing on a drake. I clutch Saengo to me, continuing to pour my magic into her, but the way she's glowing makes us easy to spot from the sky. If the next wyvern rider decides to make us their target—

The wyvern falters. Its huge body jerks, and suddenly, its wings fold. It crashes into the camp with a screech and a sound like a mighty thunderclap. I gasp and crouch over Saengo, shielding her from flying debris and raining earth.

The wyvern has crushed the last remaining tents in this part of the encampment, overturning braziers and spilling ash and embers. Splintered cots lie in shambles, and dented copper bowls glint in dancing firelight. I tuck one arm beneath Saengo's back and the other behind her knees, ready to flee, but the creature doesn't thrash about or even stand.

Instead, it rolls onto its belly, quivering from its frilled head to its feathered tail as if leashed in place.

Its rider groans from where she'd been thrown against the tattered remnant of tent canvas. She tries and fails to stand, her mussed white hair falling over her face.

A moment later, the Soulless steps calmly past the shadowblessed rider. He climbs onto the wyvern's wing joint and settles into the saddle.

I watch, despair and fury warring within me. Tears spill down my cheeks, but I glare at him with as much hatred as I can. Saengo's fingers curl into claws, digging into my arms and drawing blood. Still, my magic isn't healing her as it should.

"Accepting your power is the only way to protect your friend," he says, his voice cutting through the dark and the mayhem. "If you wish to save her, then bring me the Ember Princess."

SEVENTEEN

S aengo is dying.

If I'm being honest, she's been dying for months now. From the moment I took her with me through the Dead Wood, and before that . . . Before that, well, she'd already died once.

This time, there will be no coming back. No miracles. No hidden crafts to awaken. There is no cure for a broken soul.

The fear threatens to crush me, but I fight to remain focused. Saengo needs me, and I'm not ready to give up. I will never be ready.

Soldiers have begun gathering around us, wary and uncertain. I don't know where the other shadowblessed riders have gone. Perhaps they fled after the Soulless took control of that wyvern. It doesn't matter to me, and I pay them all little heed.

Saengo twists violently, scratching at my arms when I

clutch her tighter so that she doesn't hurt herself. Her lips move, but I don't know what she's trying to say. Blinking the tears from my eyes, I channel every bit of magic I possess into her, grateful at last for its immensity, for the surety gained from the nights this past week spent learning its shape and breadth.

"What is it, Saengo?" I whisper, unable to speak any louder for how my voice breaks. Saengo wrenches me closer. Her cheeks are flushed, her skin feverish. Still, she opens her mouth to try again.

I lower my ear to her lips, eyes squeezed shut, and catch a single word breathed against my skin: "Mountain."

At first, I don't understand. And then—

"The Spirit of the Mountain?" I draw back in confusion and anguish. How can I possibly get her there in time? It would take us days just by boat. Whatever the Soulless did to her—is doing to her—she would never make it in time. And despite my power, I wouldn't last, either.

Helplessness grips me, but I quickly shake it off when my focus wavers and the threads of infection gain ground beneath her skin. This is not a battle I can outlast.

"What does she need?" To my surprise, Kyshia kneels at my side.

At the sight of her, fury seizes me. My hand shoots out, closing around her throat. Her eyes go wide as she tries to back away, fingers digging into my skin to wrench free. I only squeeze tighter. I don't need my craft to kill her, and if her death saves Saengo, then isn't that a worthwhile exchange?

I'm peripherally aware of the alarmed shouts, soldiers drawing swords and readying crafts. But Kyshia abruptly stops struggling, instead throwing out her hands at either side to still the soldiers from attacking.

She meets my gaze, that beautiful face twisted in a painful grimace, and mouths, "Please."

Saengo jerks in my lap, moaning as she closes her fingers around my shirt with rigid, painful movements. Closing my eyes, I release Kyshia.

She gasps, a wheezing, desperate sound, but she doesn't back away. She takes only a moment to regain her breath and then repeats, voice hoarse, "What does she need?"

Grief thickens my voice as I say, "The Spirit of the Mountain."

Kyshia swallows gingerly, fingers brushing over the bruise no doubt forming around her neck. She doesn't reply because she knows as well as I do that it's an impossibility. We're simply too far away.

Then she abruptly stands. "My dragokin!" she shouts.

I shake my head. No dragokin would be fast enough—a wyvern, perhaps, but not a dragokin.

It isn't long before a soldier weaves a glimmering white-scaled dragokin through the wreckage of the camp. Fragments of tents and supplies lie strewn everywhere. More than a dozen fires, some from the shadowblessed and others from overturned torches and braziers, have yet to be extinguished.

Kyshia and her generals should be pulling together this mess and scrambling to patch up their defenses in case of another attack.

Instead, the Ember Princess accepts the reins of her dragokin and then holds them out to me. I ignore it, pressing my forehead to Saengo's burning skin.

"The camp of the Fireborn Queens," she says, and my head snaps up, something like hope not yet daring to break through the haze. She points southeast. "It's just across the border. Take Dalee. She's fast."

"Is Theyen there?" I ask, already hoisting Saengo's weight against my shoulder as I lift her to her feet. Saengo moans, the glimmer of my magic and our bond continuing to simmer beneath her skin.

Kyshia shakes her head. "I don't know, but it's your best shot."

I nod and murmur to Saengo. I don't know if she can hear me, but I still tell her, "I'm taking you to Theyen. Hold on, okay?"

Kyshia helps me get her in the saddle. Then I pull myself up behind her, holding her still as Kyshia strips the sash from Saengo's waist. She ties it around me and Saengo and then secures it with a tight knot. I keep one arm around Saengo to steady her and take the reins with the other.

"Go," Kyshia says before I can decide whether or not to thank her. So I simply nod again and jam my heels into the dragokin's flanks.

Behind us, Kyshia shouts for the soldiers to let us pass, but her voice soon fades with the distance as the creature—Dalee—speeds through the camp. She's larger and leaner than the drakes I'm used to riding, capable of handling more weight while moving at quicker speeds. She moves easily and smoothly over the debris, her powerful legs leaping over shattered wagons and around burning crates.

Saengo slumps against me, twitching and twisting. I grip her firmly and pray she doesn't accidentally unseat us. The dragokin doesn't seem to mind the movement, and with all the ceremonial armor dragokin wear, she's probably used to carrying much heavier weight. I let her take the lead, going as fast as we dare, faster even than is safe as we dive headlong into the sparse trees and high grass.

"Hang on," I whisper to Saengo. She is a beacon in the dark, lit up by the continuous flow of my magic. Even if the shadowblessed didn't have perfect night vision, they'll see us coming from a fair distance away, a golden light racing through the dark, slowly but surely fading.

It feels like we've ridden for hours, although it can't have been that long. The wind roars in my ears to the steady beating of Dalee's feet against earth. To my horror, I begin to tire. I fight it, pushing onward. If not for the nightly practice within the Soulless's dreamscapes, I'm not sure I would have lasted even this long.

"S-Sirscha," Saengo struggles to speak, her breathing thin and her voice ragged. "Listen—"

"No," I snarl, my arm tightening around her waist. "Don't you dare. Don't even think about trying to say goodbye." I draw a tremulous breath to control the way my throat closes and my eyes burn. "You'll be fine. Just listen to my voice, okay? Once—" My voice breaks, and I swallow back the sob that wants to rip free of my chest. "Once this is all over, we'll . . . we'll convince Theyen to take you on a flight on his wyvern. You'll love it so much that you'll never miss the ground again."

"Sirs—"

"King Meilek will make you his royal falconer and Millie his personal messenger, and she'll become so self-important that we'll never get her to behave again. Then we'll pick plums from your father's orchards and help the cooks bake pastries until we're kicked out of the kitchen for eating too much of the filling. And then—"

Saengo's body begins to convulse. My magic stutters, falters, and the bridge that connects me and Saengo collapses for a heartbeat.

Terror chokes me before my magic flares again. I force every bit of it I can through our bond, so faint now that it's barely holding. I'm afraid that if I continue to force it, it will break again, but I can't stop, either. The rot is winning now, blue veins wriggling over her jaw.

Weariness settles into my bones, burrowing deeper as my magic weakens.

At last, the scatter of distant lights begins to solidify into the vivid orange glow of braziers. Campfires speckle an encampment spread out along a gently rising slope. The Kazan don't need light to see in the dark, and their fires are more for warmth and cooking than visibility. I've no doubt their perimeter guards know we're coming, what with the way Saengo glows as we race onward like a star streaking through the night sky.

I'm not even sure if that's the Fireborn Queens. I pray it is, or one of their allies and not the ones who just attacked the camp because I can't keep this up. I'm not strong enough. The moment we're within distance to make out the shapes of tents against the mountains, all trace of composure abandons me and the tears I've been keeping at bay finally break free.

Then, darkness swarms around us. Dalee makes a sound of alarm, her legs stalling and slowing as we're enveloped in pure blackness. The dragokin spins in a circle, hopping and whining in distress, with her senses cut off. Gathering my wits, I tear off the sash Kyshia had wrapped around us, grip Saengo, and drop from the saddle before Dalee can throw us off in her panic. So that she doesn't trample us, I slap my palm hard on the dragokin's flank.

She roars and takes off through the blackness. I can't see her, but the sound of her beating feet fades into the night until all I can hear is my pulse thudding in my ears and Saengo's thin, reedy breaths.

I lower Saengo to the ground and shout, "My name is Sirscha Ashwyn! I'm looking for Hlau Theyen!"

The murmur of voices breaks through the quiet, but it's impossible to tell where they're coming from.

"Please, we need help," I say again, clutching Saengo, who has gone limp in my arms. I can't even see her. I can only feel her against me, feverish and too still, a candle flame on the last threads of its wick.

The darkness dissipates. I flinch as the night comes into clear relief. Three shadowblessed guards surround us. One of them is a woman I recognize from Theyen's retinue in Vos Talwyn.

"It's true," she says to the other guards. "This shaman—Sirscha—often kept Hlau Theyen company in Vos Talwyn." She takes in Saengo first, limp in my arms with lines of infection crawling up her cheeks, and then me.

I'm not sure what she sees in my face, but it must be bad because she doesn't say anything else. A shadow gate opens behind her, and she vanishes through it.

I'm not yet ready to feel relieved, but I rest my forehead against Saengo's hair and whisper, "It's going to be okay. Hang on. Please."

My strength has reached its end. I feel it draining from me, water through a sieve. The bridge between us is now little more than a spider's thread.

"Should we move her to a bed?" one of the other shadowblessed asks, sounding tentative.

I shake my head just as Saengo begins to tremble again. It's not convulsive this time, just a single tremor that rocks through her whole body. The vibrant blue veins of the rot darken to black.

"Saengo," I whisper harshly, shaking her. She is otherwise deathly still. "Saengo!"

A gate opens. Theyen steps out, accompanied by the woman who'd left to retrieve him. His gaze finds mine at once.

Somehow, I choke out the words, "The Spirit of the Mountain."

Theyen doesn't need any other directions. He stalks forward, scoops Saengo's body into his arms, and vanishes into the gate.

EIGHTEEN

I remain kneeling in the grass, bent over and head bowed. My arms shake, the exhaustion so complete that even the tears have stopped. I can only breathe and pray and try not to collapse. I can't feel Saengo's candle flame, but that doesn't mean anything. I pushed my craft too hard. I've barely any magic to sense the souls of the shadowblessed, even though they stand mere paces from me.

With Saengo half a continent away, it only makes sense that I can't feel her. It doesn't mean anything else. It *can't*.

All around me, the silence is thick with confusion and unvoiced questions. The shadowblessed guards seem at a loss for what to do now.

"I'll inform the general of what's happened," one of them says in low tones. The sound of her footsteps recedes through the grass.

Drawing a slow breath, I dig my fingers into the earth. Dirt slides beneath my blunt nails, but I dig them deeper, seeking control over my body and my emotions. Then, when I think I might be able to stand without falling over, I rise to my feet.

I swipe my sleeve over my cheeks, still damp, and count the seconds in my head. The two remaining shadowblessed guards don't speak. They must think I've lost my wits.

The guard who went to fetch Theyen shuffles closer and offers a comforting touch against my shoulder. "We'll bring you some water," she says before nodding at the other guard. He turns and hurries toward the encampment.

"Thank you," I say, and I'm not just referring to the water.

She seems to understand because she smiles gently. "Hlau Theyen speaks well of you, and he doesn't make a habit of such things."

If this were any other time, I would laugh. Now, I say, "He's been a good friend." Not just good—he's been a far better friend than perhaps I deserve.

I seem to be cursed, anyone foolish enough to befriend me rewarded only with misfortune. First Saengo and then Phaut. I don't want that for Theyen or King Meilek, but I am too selfish to let go. I don't want to be alone again.

"Whatever's happened, I'm sure your friend will be okay. Do you need to sit?" the guard asks.

I shake my head. In truth, I should probably lie down, but my entire being rebels at the idea of resting before Theyen returns. Even if it takes all night, I will stay here and wait.

Fortunately, it doesn't take that long. Shortly after the other guard returns with a waterskin, a gate opens.

The two snap to attention as Theyen emerges. My feet shuffle forward, anticipation and fear lending my limbs some much-needed energy.

He says nothing, merely extending his hand. I take it at once, and the gate closes around us. For the first time, I welcome the sightless, soundless dark. I can't even hear my own breathing. While the idea of being lost here is always terrifying, at the moment, even that is overshadowed by my fear for Saengo.

It doesn't take long before Theyen pulls me from the gate. I drag in deep breaths of fresh mountain air, the scent of trees and earth filling my senses. Releasing his hand, I press both my palms against my stomach to quiet the slight nausea trying to take hold.

"In here," he says, his voice a low rumble in the dark.

Once my head has stopped spinning, I look around properly. We've emerged outside a small temple of white stone with windows of elegant wooden screens depicting cranes in midflight or pristine mountain oases. There's none of the extravagant décor or gilded architecture more common in Mirrim's temples, nothing but a simple wooden marker beside the front door.

The building sits nestled against the base of a cliff. A thin waterfall cascades down the stone directly behind the temple.

A narrow dirt path leads into the forest. As I squint into the dark, a pressure begins in my chest—a gradual but deliberate tug right behind my ribs.

I ignore it as we approach the temple. The trees grow tall and wild, crowded so closely against the walls that the building would be difficult to spot if not for the moonbeams dancing off the roof tiles.

Inside, we discover a small square room where a wooden altar sits beneath a painting of the Mountain in swooping black ink. On the altar rests an empty silver tray and a canister of unlit incense.

Now that the Mountain has been closed off to worshippers, both the offering tray and the donation box are empty, and a thin layer of dust has settled over the dark wood. Theyen crosses the room, heading for an open doorway left of the altar. From beyond it comes the sound of running water.

We cross the threshold and find ourselves in a walled garden behind the temple. Mist hovers around the waterfall, which spills down the cliff and into a pool, where Saengo is submerged up to her shoulders.

Having spotted her, I hurry along a cobbled path through overgrown ferns and young trees thick with summer growth. The walls at either side of the garden are thick with ivy, and the trees from the surrounding forest thrust their branches over the top as if to peer inside.

The air around the pool glitters silver where the moonlight scatters against the spray of water. I swallow tightly and approach the pool's edge. The pressure in my chest becomes more pronounced, more insistent. I might be able to brush it off as my body's reaction to seeing Saengo alive and well if not for the fact that the tug behind my ribs wants to lead me *away* from the temple.

It's distracting and annoying, given that all I want right now is to see Saengo. I have to be certain that she's healing before I give any attention to whatever's calling me on this Mountain.

Saengo's head turns at our approach. She offers me a weak smile but doesn't rise from the water. The infection is still black and stark against her pale skin.

Tentatively, I reach out through our bond and am nearly crushed by the relief when I feel her there, still connected, if only barely. Gently, I trace the fragile edges of her soul where the rot has wreaked its terrible magic. While Saengo is finally healing, it is much, much too slow. With time, the rot will still win. We've only delayed the inevitable.

I school my expression so that the realization doesn't show on my face, even as my stomach tightens and my heart aches. Saengo raises a hand to brush a damp strand of hair off her cheek, water streaming from her soaked sleeves. She's still fully dressed. As I step into the spray around the pool, warmth envelopes me. Faint tendrils of steam rise from the surface. The water is hot.

"Why doesn't she heal?" Theyen asks softly. He stands behind me, away from the heat and the mist.

I have to swallow a few times before I think my voice will be strong enough to answer. "Because the Soulless has driven the rot too deeply into her soul. I . . . I don't think I can heal it this time."

Every time I pushed back the rot, I sealed the cracks in her soul with my own magic. But the rot was an axe constantly chipping away at her, and with each new crack, her soul grew more brittle, more fractured. This had only ever been a temporary fix, certainly not maintainable forever.

I thought we would have more time. Whatever the Soulless did to her tonight has driven the rot far beyond what my meager patch jobs can handle. Now, I worry that if I push too hard, even with the magic that she channels for me, her soul might shatter.

I bite down on the inside of my cheek, the physical pain a reminder that I can't break down in front of Saengo. She needs me to be strong. To have faith, even if faith is something I never quite learned how to hold on to.

Saengo leans over, the water splashing at her chin and mouth as she reaches for something beneath the surface. A moment later, her hand emerges holding a dagger.

My feet jolt forward, my instincts screaming at me to snatch the weapon from her hand before—

Saengo tosses the dagger, and it lands near my feet. The wet blade glimmers silver in the moonlight. Uncertain, I pick it up and dry the blade against my sash.

"If we know how this ends," Saengo begins, which makes my breath catch, "then you only have one choice. Use the knife, take my blood, and defeat the Soulless."

Behind me, Theyen goes rigid. My face flushes with heat, anger burning away the edges of my exhaustion.

"I will not," I spit out, flinging the blade aside. It stabs into the dirt, the hilt lost to the dark.

"This is how we defeat him, Sirscha," she says evenly. Every word breaks my heart. She sounds firm, as if she's already decided. "Together. This is how I help you become powerful enough to stop him."

"No," I say, raising my voice without any of Saengo's composure. She may have made her choice, but I haven't. There is no force alive that could make me agree to this.

How do I tell her that she is the greatest reason I'm even still here, fighting against an enemy as impossible to defeat as the Soulless? I don't want to exist in a world where I survived at the cost of Saengo's life.

Taking the life of the person who meant the world to him had broken the Soulless, and it might break me, too.

"People are depending on us, Sirscha," she says, her voice horribly soft. "We can't be selfish. Think of King Meilek and Evewyn. All the shamanborn who have only just been freed. More return to Thiy every day, and they deserve a chance at happiness." Her gaze flicks over my shoulder. "Think of Theyen and the Fireborn Queens."

Theyen puts up a hand. "Actually, I agree with Sirscha. This is a bad plan. She might not even survive, and then where will we be?"

Saengo closes her eyes, and at last, some of her frustration breaks through the calm. With the bond between us so weak, I can't sense what she's feeling, but I imagine the helplessness. The hopelessness. We can't continue this way.

"For now, just focus on healing," I say. "Please."

She doesn't respond other than with a slight nod. I turn away, feeling a bit like I'm running away from the conversation, but there's no point having it in the first place. I won't agree. Once Theyen and I are back inside the altar room, I rummage around in the drawers beneath the altar until I find several half-burned candlesticks.

"I don't suppose you have anything to light these with?" I ask Theyen.

He pulls a silk pouch from his sash and produces two matches from within. Once the candles are lit and secured to the altar, I also light three of the incense sticks.

"How far up the mountain are we?" I ask as I place the incense across the silver tray. The tips release white smoke that curls around the painting of the mountain. That pressure in my chest tugs again, urgent.

"A fair distance, although we should still be wary of being discovered by patrols." He looks pointedly at the lit candles and incense. Normally, I would agree, but if we're to stay on the Mountain and if she is, in fact, helping Saengo heal, then we should pay our respects.

"How did you know this temple was here?" I step back, press my palms together in prayer, and offer the altar a deep bow of gratitude.

"Ask Saengo. She told me to follow the path, so I did."

I study the painting, my brows pinched. I'm wary of unseen forces wanting me to follow their lure, especially after the Soulless called to me from the greenhouse at Spinner's End.

But Saengo felt at peace here, and I can't sense anything malevolent. There's only a vibrating sort of power that presses in from all around, from the trees to the air to deep within the earth.

With a sigh, I turn to Theyen. "Will you stay with Saengo? There's something I need to check out."

I peek out the door and into the garden. Saengo hasn't moved from her position in the pool.

"What is it?" Theyen asks as I step past him, crossing the altar room and out into the night.

The path is barely visible, but with that insistent tug behind my ribs, I'm not worried about losing my way. "I'm not sure, but I won't be long."

I start up the path to where it disappears into the trees. Before I can take two steps, though, Theyen grasps my wrist.

"Are you certain it's safe? Don't lie to me."

Despite the gravity of the entire night, despite that my eyes are probably still red and puffy from crying and I could sorely do with a nap, I smile. "When have I ever lied to you?"

"Lying by omission counts," he says harshly. His eyes glimmer a little in the darkness, hinting at the pale blue irises.

I'm not sure what's he's referring to at first. Then I lift one eyebrow. "You can't be talking about me being a soulrender."

His lips compress, like he wants to say something, which is frankly baffling. Theyen has never before held back from speaking his mind to me.

"King Meilek only knew because he was there when I figured it out myself," I say, and I wonder if Theyen actually wants to be consoled. "Otherwise, I haven't told a soul other than Saengo."

He doesn't look appeased, only annoyed. "For Saengo's sake if not your own, have a little care for your life."

My smile grows crooked. Part of me wants to tease him for caring, but a better part of me knows Theyen must be serious to sound so uncharacteristically earnest. So I nod and wait until he removes his hand.

"It's safe," I assure him. "We're standing on the back of an ancient elemental. What could go wrong?"

As he glowers, I give him a final reassuring smile and head off into the night.

With how hard I pushed my craft earlier, my body tires far more quickly than I'm used to, but I force myself to keep moving. It occurs to me that I didn't even ask Theyen what I had so abruptly pulled him away from. I should apologize once I go back. He could have been in an important meeting or with his family or something.

And yet, he hadn't even hesitated when he saw the state Saengo was in. I'm grateful for him and for the security of knowing she'll be safe if Nuvali patrols happen upon them or if the Mountain drops me into a hole. I don't think she will, but seeing as I've no experience with elementals, I'm prepared for anything.

The path soon becomes overgrown and difficult to navigate, especially in the dark, but weary as I am, I trust in my senses and the meager moonlight above. After a time, although I can no longer see the path or whether I'm even still on it, my gut tells me I'm moving in the right direction. That presence remains, soothing my concerns, gently nudging me onward.

The trees grow thickly here, their branches twined overhead so only the barest of light can break through. It is a strange echo of the path Saengo and I took into the Dead Wood all those months ago.

My craft still feels overstretched, my magic slow to recover, but it's enough that I can sense some of the souls nearby, birds and the like. After a time, the trees give way and I pause before the shadowy maw of a cave. The mouth is set into the cliffside, just large enough for one person to walk through.

Steeling myself, I slowly enter the cave. My fingers brush the rocky wall to keep my bearings. Since it's too dark for anyone other than a shadowblessed, I raise my other hand to ensure I don't walk into anything or bash my forehead against a low ceiling. Every step is slow and careful, mindful of sudden drops.

I haven't gone far when the wall begins to curve. Before long, something pale and blue glimmers faintly ahead. Several somethings. As I draw nearer, the lights grow in number, speckling the walls and ceiling. They aren't very bright, but they're enough for me to be certain of my surroundings.

I'm in a tunnel that gradually curves to the right so that I can't see where it leads. When I peer closer at the lights in the wall, I'm amazed to discover they're alive. Tiny worms glow a faint blue as they tunnel in and out of the stone.

Saengo would be charmed. I'll need to bring her here as soon as she feels up to moving. After another few minutes of steady walking, a sound finally rises through the silence—the burble of running water.

I increase my pace, eager to reach the end of this interminable tunnel, but when I finally find the exit, I come up short at what lies beyond.

It's an enormous cavern. Far overhead, a hole in the ceiling allows a silvery beam of moonlight to illuminate the strange and lush oasis spread out below. A narrow brook runs from one end of the cavern to the other, a merry sound in the hushed space. Trees and vines climb up the cavern walls, and saplings grow in clusters along the water's edge. Large flat rocks are piled at the cavern's center, almost like a staircase leading up to a stony outcropping that overlooks the brook. Nearly every stretch of ground is coated in a rug of green moss, vibrant even in the dim silvery light.

It's beautiful and bizarre. I take a cautious step forward, careful not to crush the knots of red-capped mushrooms and purple blossoms that thrust out from among mossy rocks. The water seems to glow from within, although there's no discernible source. As I slowly approach the pile of rocks, a heavy calm presses into my shoulders, like the comforting weight of a familiar blanket.

A warm breath slides through the cavern. All the leaves begin to rustle, filling the air with a quiet susurration. The water churns over pale blue stones. From somewhere within the chorus of sound, someone speaks my name.

It isn't quite a voice, more like the shape of one. If I hadn't been listening for some indication of the Mountain's presence, it would sound like no more than the whispering leaves, the kiss of branches, or stones carried along with the current.

The Spirit of the Mountain is an elemental, not the soul of a once-living creature but an earthen power awakened by shamanic magic when Thiy was still young. She is, technically, as alive as any spirit can be.

I climb the stair-like rocks onto the outcropping, which allows me a higher vantage point to survey the cavern. Dust motes glimmer in the shaft of moonlight, adding to the illusory quality of the place. Like I could wave my hands in front of me and dispel the trees with bark as white as winter frost.

All of my worries feel distant. I could lie down on one of these moss-covered stones and rest a while, let the water carry away all the problems of the world outside this haven.

But the ache of my muscles and the dim light of Saengo's candle remind me it's a dangerous notion. Outside this cavern, my best friend is deathly ill and awaiting my return.

Softly, as if speaking any louder might disturb the peace, I ask, "Can you save Saengo's life?"

Another breath moves through the cavern, the leaves trembling in its wake. That almost-a-voice responds, "Saengo is not alive."

NINETEEN

The words are ice against the warm calm trying to settle around me. I close my eyes, and my fingers dig into my palms as the Mountain continues.

"She lives a half-life." The wind shifts, almost playful as it tugs at my braid. "Nothing and no one can restore a familiar to true life. Saengo knows this. We have spoken."

At this, my eyes fly open. Saengo hadn't said anything about that. In fact, she'd said the opposite—that she wasn't able to speak to the Mountain yet. When had that changed?

Warmth caresses my cheek like a loving hand. "There is another question in your heart," the voice says.

Moonlight streams through the opening in the cavern ceiling, and I wish with all my being that this sense of peace was real and not the fabrication of a power beyond my understanding.

I swallow. "Can you help me destroy the Dead Wood?"

The Mountain takes her time answering. The wind teases at my sleeves as the leaves whisper and water splashes along the bank.

"You are a powerful soulrender," she says at last. "Powerful enough that I felt your craft awaken."

That isn't an answer, but still, it emboldens me. To be acknowledged by an elemental must mean something, surely?

"You once made a deal with a shaman. Is it possible to do that again, with me? Or does it only work for soulguides?" I'd rejected this option mere weeks ago. If the cost of her help is Saengo's life, then nothing will have changed. That's not a bargain I will ever make.

But there can be no doubt that she called me here, as surely as she must have called Saengo. There must be something she can do that won't require Saengo's sacrifice.

"All lightwenders can touch souls in one way or another, although only one of your kind has ever been bold enough, or powerful enough, to bond with an elemental—a soulrender like you."

The words jar me. I frown, looking around as if I might expect to find the Spirit of the Mountain perched on a rock, watching me.

There's no one, of course, despite the certainty of her presence all around me.

"Suri was a soulguide," I say, uncertain. "She could guide souls back to the living. Soulrenders only destroy."

The dust motes dart through the air in a flurry, the brook splashes, and I get the sudden impression the Mountain is laughing. "Suri was the most powerful soulrender in existence. The boundaries of your craft were not so rigid then, but even so, her magic bent to her will in ways never seen before and never seen again."

I sit with this revelation, but so many emotions battle within me that I simply feel numb. Suri is lauded as one of the most powerful shamans Thiy has known. It's not so difficult to imagine that she was so powerful, her gifts so unique, that people assumed she was a whole new kind of lightwender.

I turn my hands in my lap, palms up, frowning down at the small scars and calluses that map out my years of training. These are the hands of a soulrender, and soulrenders only bring destruction. Everything that's happened since I awakened my craft is proof of that. The Soulless is proof of that.

My fingers curl gently against my palms. But if Suri was always a soulrender, then she'd exemplified the best of what our craft could achieve. Maybe even what *I* could achieve . . . if only my abilities didn't better echo the Soulless, who exemplifies the very worst of our craft.

What would the Nuvali do with this information? Would they alter their ideas of what a soulrender can be? Would they deny it as false? Or would they tear down Suri's monuments and strike her name from history?

Thinking back on the compendium of shamanic callings I'd found in Ronin's library, I recall the part about how

Suri could sever the bond between familiar and shaman, completely disabling her opponents. If that was, in fact, a soulrender ability, then . . . Is that what I've been doing all this time when I release the souls from the Dead Wood? Severing their bond with the Soulless? There's still so much I don't know.

"Would it work then? For us?" I ask. The Mountain isn't just any spirit. She doesn't need a shaman. She's a powerful force all on her own. "Would it be similar to the bond between shaman and familiar?"

"Yes," she breathes, a hum of sound in the warm cavern air. "But it's not any lightwender who can survive a bond with an elemental."

The warning shakes my resolve, and I have to take a moment to process this possibility. Then I give a tight shake of my head. I can do it. The Mountain just said I'm powerful enough that she felt the awakening of my craft. That has to mean something.

"What about Saengo? I won't risk her life for this."

"Not even for the sake of Thiy?"

My jaw tightens, and a sick feeling churns in my gut. I can't. I can't. *I won't.*

Before I can force out the words, the Mountain continues.

"She will not be harmed," she says in a voice like gently shaking branches. "She will be a bridge between us, and when it is over, she will no longer be your familiar. She will remain as she is now, but her soul's tether will be bound to me."

The idea of no longer being connected to Saengo is both terrifying and comforting. But isn't this what I'd wanted for her? Isn't this what I'd been anticipating for months now? The reason I'd put distance between me and Saengo, useless as that had been?

From the moment we returned to Vos Talwyn, probably even before that, I've been preparing myself to let her go. After all that I've taken from her, here is my chance to give a semblance of it back.

At least she'll survive, even if I don't.

"How would it work?" I ask.

The wind caresses the hair at my temples. "I will channel your magic in her place—all of it concentrated into a single blow. It would be enough to put the souls of that cursed wood to rest."

My craft still feels a bit raw after pouring nearly every bit of my magic into Saengo, but I can already feel it recovering, far faster than Saengo is healing. But if the Mountain channeled all of my magic *all at once* . . .

"It was like a fire burning too fast and too hot," the Soulless had once said. Pushing your craft beyond its natural limitations will always have consequences.

"And my craft?"

A breath like falling leaves whispers against my ear, "Extinguished."

My heart pounds. I have to be sure I understand. "Forever?"

"If you survive . . . yes."

"Their souls burned out."

I draw a deep breath. There is no other way. So long as Saengo is safe, it won't matter if this costs me my craft. Severing the Soulless from his source of magic will leave him just as powerless. So long as I'm alive once it's done, I can defeat him with swords alone.

But would Saengo agree? Would she want her soul forever bound to the Mountain?

"I have to speak with Saengo," I say.

"Choose carefully," the Mountain says, gently urging me back the way I'd come. "It is not a decision you can undo."

My thoughts are curiously quiet as I make my way down the mountain. I suppose I've always known that to be rid of the Dead Wood, the cost would be great. But while I would want to stop the Soulless for the sake of everyone who calls Thiy home, even if the only person this saved was my best friend, I would still do it.

When my ambition had been to become Shadow, I'd been prepared to risk my life to obtain it. I believed that in order to prove my worth, I needed something quantifiable, something concrete—acknowledgement from the queen, becoming Shadow, even saving the shamanborn in Vos Gillis. Something I could point to and say, "Here. Here is your proof," even if the only person I was speaking to was myself.

Now, I am a soulrender. I was, however briefly, the King's Shadow. But even if I was none of these things, even if I was still nothing more than Sirscha Ashwyn, an orphan with no true name and not a single possession save the clothes on my back, I would still be someone of worth.

Once, I'd been prepared to die in protection of my kingdom and my people. Now, after everything that's happened since that night at Talon's Teahouse, I no longer want to die for such reasons. Instead, I want to live for them.

For King Meilek and the Evewyn he will nurture under his rule. For Theyen and a future where he isn't chained to his enemy for the sake of peace. For Saengo and the promise of an entire lifetime spread out before her.

But if I have to die, then to die for her would at least make it worth it.

When I return to the temple, I find Theyen reclining on a stool that he found who-knows-where. He sits against the wall, facing the altar, his eyes closed.

He awakens when I enter. On the altar, three new sticks of lit incense have joined the others.

"Just in case," he explains with a shrug. He straightens on the stool, arching his back in a slow stretch. I take a moment to actually notice what he's wearing—teal robes with stalks of bamboo embroidered across the wide sleeves and a translucent black sash. He's always conscious of his clothes, though, so it's impossible to tell if the robes were for the benefit of a meeting or simply his daily wardrobe.

"How is Saengo?" I ask, moving to the back door. Saengo is sitting at the edge of the pond, her legs still submerged in the water but a blanket wrapped around her shoulders. I can't imagine where Theyen found that, either.

"Still healing," he says.

"Thank you for staying," I say with a grateful smile.

Saengo looks up when I approach. She's not quite as pale as she'd been, the hot water putting some much-needed color back into her cheeks. The infection has receded to just beneath her jaw and, to my relief, returned to blue, although the color is still stark and darker than usual.

"How do you feel?" I ask as I settle onto the grass beside her.

She shrugs one shoulder. "Alive."

I scoot closer, and she rests her head on my shoulder. She's discarded most of her clothes, draping them over nearby branches to dry. Beneath the blanket, she wears only her inner robes for modesty. The fabric is still damp.

"Thank the Sisters," I murmur, resting my cheek against her hair.

"And the Mountain?" she says. When I nod, she adds, "Did you talk to her?"

I'm not sure how she knows, but she did say she could sense the Mountain's intent. And since the Mountain had mentioned speaking to her, she must somehow be able to communicate with the spirit without needing to enter that cavern at the Mountain's heart.

"I asked for help, and she made me an offer," I say. Saengo tilts her head to look at me, brows furrowed in interest.

Quietly, I tell her about the conditions of our potential deal—with the Mountain channeling my magic, I could destroy the entire Dead Wood in a single strike, but the sacrifice would be my craft. I don't mention the part where I might not survive.

"But you'll be bound to the Mountain," I say. "I confess I'm not entirely sure what that means, though."

"We spoke about it the last time I was here," Saengo admits. Her cheeks go pink as she wrinkles her nose. "I'm sorry for telling you otherwise. I wasn't sure yet what to say to you or . . ."

"It's okay," I say. "You don't have to tell me anything."

"I want to," she insists. "We spoke, but only briefly. I would be protected from the rot, but more importantly, I would no longer be a weakness for you."

I nudge her gently with my shoulder, but she continues before I can make any protests about which of us is a weakness to the other.

"Once I'm bound to her, it would be my choice to stay or go—and when that happens."

I go still. Even my breath stalls in my lungs. The idea of Saengo choosing to go, to follow death after I had unwittingly pulled her back from it, terrifies me in a way I can't voice.

Don't, I want to say but can't because that isn't my decision to make.

"Don't worry," she says, perhaps sensing my fear. "I've no plans to go any time soon, but I would have to spend most of my time here on the Mountain. I wouldn't be able to stay away for any extended amount of time, and I certainly wouldn't be able to leave Thiy." She sighs. "So I guess piracy is off the table."

I try to smile but can't quite manage it. "Are you certain this is what you want?"

She lifts her head from my shoulder and shifts to face me, her legs splashing in the water. "I already decided a while ago. I just hadn't known how to tell you. This is what I want. This is how I make my life my own, in whatever way I can."

I reach up to tuck her hair behind her ear. When I try to smile again, it comes easier this time. "Then I want this for you as well. You should have told me sooner."

"I didn't want you to feel like I was abandoning you."

I wince. That, too, was likely my fault as she'd no doubt picked up on my feelings these last couple months.

"Saengo Phang," I say, poking her shoulder. She laughs softly and smacks my hand away. The sound makes my heart ache but in a good way. I wasn't sure I'd ever hear it again. "If you're happy, then it doesn't matter what I feel. But in case it matters, I would have understood. I *do* understand."

She tilts her head, studying my face. "The question now, dearest Sirscha, is whether this is something *you're* sure about. You'd have to go back to being human. No more powers. Is that what you want?"

"This is the right decision," I say firmly.

Saengo smiles and lies back in the patchy grass. Her legs remain in the water, but she uses the blanket as a pillow. When she yawns, I rise to my feet.

"Try to sleep," I say, to which she nods, her eyes already closing. I should sleep as well, but strangely, I don't feel quite so exhausted anymore.

I find Theyen in front of the temple, sitting cross-legged beside a small cooking fire, where he's warming a pot of rice porridge. When he sees me, he holds out a bowl he's already filled.

"Thank you," I say, taking the food. Once I'm settled on the ground, I take a careful sip of porridge. It's warm and thick, savory with slivers of ginger and scallions. He must have returned to his clan's camp for these supplies. I suppose it would be no trouble for a gate to go back and forth, but even so. "You didn't need to."

"Just eat."

I do, suddenly ravenous, and the rice porridge is delicious. When Theyen reaches into a pouch to sprinkle some spices into the pot and then gives it a stir, my brows rise. I assumed he brought the food already prepared by the camp cook.

"You know how to cook?" I ask.

He gives me a slightly exasperated look. "Don't sound so surprised. Even a prince should know basic survival skills."

Even after how much Theyen has done for me, I don't actually know all that much about his clan or his family. His other friends. If he even has other friends. I really am truly terrible at this friendship thing.

I twirl my spoon through the rice porridge before affecting a casual voice and asking, "Who taught you? One of your sisters? Your mother?"

The Fireborn Queens are matriarchal, so his mother would be the clan leader. I'm not sure that she would deign to personally teach him something as mundane as cooking rice porridge, but what do I know of the Kazan clans? Maybe Kazan royalty is different.

Then again, knowing Theyen, maybe not.

"Are you trying to make small talk?" he asks, sounding a bit incredulous. "Because you should stick with your limited set of skills, which don't include making conversation."

"As opposed to you?" I ask, laughing.

"I can be diplomatic when I choose to be. I am a prince, after all."

I look pointedly at the silver circlet against his white hair, which he is never without. "I hadn't noticed. Anyway, I was just asking. Don't answer if you don't want to. I'm fine with brooding in silence as well."

"That *is* one of your finer skills," he says, and I mime flinging my spoon at him.

After a few seconds, though, he surprises me by saying, "My sister taught me."

"You mentioned two older sisters. Do you have many more?"

He sighs, like he's resigned himself to the topic. "Only the two. They do the bulk of the work with helping our mother manage the clan."

"And you get stuck dealing with clan allies and the border conflict with the Empire?"

"Assisting," he corrects me. "Which I prefer. Being out here is better than having to endure endless meetings in Penumbria."

"I thought you didn't like the sun."

One side of his mouth curls into a reluctant smile. "It isn't so terrible."

I sip loudly on my rice porridge, which earns me a quick, annoyed glance.

"I prefer the stars, though," he says, tilting his head back to gaze skyward. "They're . . . peaceful."

I finish off my bowl and then set it aside. Leaning back on my hands, I join him in watching the stars. The sky isn't quite as clear as that evening in Evewyn, but it's enough that the stars are a glittering swathe in the dark.

After a while, I say, "I'm sorry for . . . for calling on you so abruptly. I imagine I must have taken you away from something important. There's no need to stay if you're required elsewhere."

His reply is soft. "It was no trouble, and they can manage without me a little longer."

Smiling, I ease onto my back so that I can better see the stars without having to crane my neck. After a moment, Theyen does the same, stretching his long body beside the fire and the small pot that he's already removed from the flames. I almost laugh when he takes the time to smooth out his robes to keep them from wrinkling too badly.

I'm terribly grateful for him. He must have a dozen or more things to attend to, especially after a Kazan clan attacked the Nuvali camp, even if it wasn't connected to the Fireborn Queens. Speaking of which—

"I never quite apologized for . . . well, for ruining your engagement with the Ember Princess. Or should you be thanking me? I can't quite tell what it is you want at this point."

He sighs and says dryly, "It's just as well. I needed an excuse to break the engagement, anyway. I simply hoped it wouldn't involve war or retaliation."

I grimace. "Well, I'm sorry."

He doesn't answer, and I can only take that as acceptance. It's a warm night, and after a while, my right side grows uncomfortable from the heat of the flames. I shift away from the fire and then flick a stone that was jabbing the back of my head.

"If King Meilek became engaged to a shadowblessed, would you object?" Theyen asks.

At the unexpected question, I turn my head to look at him. We're lying a bit awkwardly around the fire, our heads closer than our feet. He doesn't look my way, though, and all I can see is his profile limned in warm firelight.

"*Is* he engaged to a shadowblessed?" I ask, uncertain.

"Not that I know of."

"Are you volunteering?"

"Would you be able to stand me as your king?"

"Prince Consort," I amend. "And I'm pretty sure that's something you should discuss with King Meilek."

"I'm asking you right now."

I roll my eyes and go back to watching the stars. "I suppose if he were to marry a shadowblessed, I would hope for his happiness. I know a love match is impossible, but I don't think it's too much to ask that they not loathe each other, either. It would also be a step forward for Evewyn's alliance with Kazahyn and prove to the shamanborn that he is willing to embrace the magical races."

After a beat of silence, he asks, "So it wouldn't bother you?"

"Why would it bother me? He is my king. I'm hardly in a position to object."

"You're his friend. He would listen to your counsel."

I consider this. Theyen might be right, but it still feels presumptuous to even think I could offer him guidance on who he should marry. "I . . . would want him to do what he feels is best for Evewyn." Then I frown and glance at his profile again. "Would it bother *you* if he married a shadowblessed?"

"It makes no difference to me."

I roll my eyes again and determinedly search the stars for familiar constellations. "Then why are you asking?"

"Just asking," he says, parroting my previous words. "Never mind. Let's not talk of this."

"You brought it up."

"Well, now I'm ending it. Just look at your stars or your . . . sack of seeds or whatever."

I laugh, and after a moment, Theyen gives a small laugh as well. The silence that follows is a comfortable one.

While I can't find the Demon Crone's Pouch, still, I offer the goddess a prayer for safety in the days to come.

TWENTY

As I lie on the hard dirt beside a dying fire, I think about the Soulless as sleep finally creeps over me.

My senses open to the current of my magic, and then go deeper still—diving into the flow and the depth as it gradually returns to what it had been before I pushed it so hard. Then I think about the Soulless, seeking the kernel of his magic still buried within me. That fragment of him is a predator in the high grass, quiet and still. Waiting and watching, ever present.

In my dream, we're in Evewyn. The forest is quiet and green, bright sunlight streaming down in flashes of gold.

The Soulless stands beneath the full summer boughs, his fingers sliding in and out of a sunbeam as if examining the texture of the light and heat.

"Congratulations," he says, closing his fingers into a fist. "Did you mean to pull me into this dreamscape, or was it an accident?"

"I hoped it would work," I say, rising onto my toes. The grass is plush and yielding beneath my boots. Now that I've actually succeeded in pulling him into a dream of my own making, having him here feels . . . intrusive. I hadn't specifically chosen the forests of Evewyn, but I guess my subconscious had supplied the setting while I acquired the participants.

"And to what do I owe the honor of being summoned?" he asks. There's a bite to his voice, a threat like steel against my neck. "I was expecting you to find me at Spinner's End, but seeing as your craft is intact . . ."

I have to swallow back the instinct to snarl my own threats at him. "I simply wanted to ask you something."

"Which is?"

"I want to know if you are set on this path."

He pauses with his hand still caught in the sunbeam. He reminds me of a child delighted by the glitter of light over water. It's a dangerous illusion.

"And why would you want to know that?" he asks in return.

There is no wind here. No bird calls or rustling leaves. Next to the brilliant sunlight and vivid green leaves, the quiet is eerie. I suppose I'll need to work on my dreamscapes. Or maybe not, since I won't be in possession of these powers for much longer.

I decide not to think about that.

"What happened to you and your brother deserves vengeance, but those responsible are long dead. You're killing people who have only ever known you as a name in a story."

"So I should do nothing?" he asks. "Let their crimes go unpunished and unremembered?"

"House Yalaeng will be held accountable, but not like this. Work with me first to destroy the Dead Wood, and then we can carve out a space that is safe not just for us but also for the soulrenders yet to come—where they won't be feared and hunted and made into monsters."

He tilts his head, a shrewd gleam in his eye. "I applaud your passionate words, but they're wasted on me. What do you have planned, Sirscha?"

He turns in a slow circle, examining our surroundings as if trying to glean clues from my half-formed dreamscape. Thank the Sisters we're not standing on the Mountain or in her temple.

"I didn't think I could change your mind," I admit, "but I wanted to give you that chance, anyway." It was more than I'd given Ronin. I should have shown him mercy, even if part of me wonders whether it would have done any good.

"How courteous," he says mildly.

Now that I'm certain Saengo wants to bind herself to the Mountain, I have to ensure that sacrificing my craft is my only option. The Soulless could be so much more than his vengeance. Instead, he is a shade of a man, a ghost of House Yalaeng's making come to call.

Besides, even if I'm willing to do what it takes to destroy the Dead Wood, I'm not exactly eager to potentially kill myself.

The Soulless's eyes narrow, and he takes a step toward me.

I back up, my craft swelling within me as I thrust myself out of the dream.

I jolt awake, my hand slapping the ground at my side in search of a weapon. Then I remember where I am, and I slump onto my back again with a quiet breath. A thin blanket is draped over my legs, and although I spot the remains of Theyen's cooking fire, Theyen himself is gone. He must have left after I fell asleep.

The sky has only just begun to lighten, streaks of pink and gold painted in the eastern sky. Kicking off the blanket, I rise to my feet and take a moment to stretch the kinks out of my back.

I fold the blanket and then tuck it beneath my arm before heading inside. The cold pot of leftover rice porridge sits on the corner of the altar, along with two clean bowls. When I lift the lid of the pot, I find plenty left for a suitable breakfast.

Saengo is exactly where I left her, asleep on the banks of the pond. Her blanket is still wadded up beneath her head, but she's no longer submerged in the heated water, partially or otherwise. Without disturbing her, I examine what's visible of her neck.

The rot has only barely receded, still more than halfway up her neck, livid and menacing. I tamp down the anxiety stirring in my gut and quietly drape my blanket over her. Then I stretch out on the grass beside her and close my eyes.

I must have fallen asleep again, because when I open my eyes sometime later, the sun has fully risen. Saengo yawns, groaning a little as she stretches her arms over her head.

With a sleepy smile, I return out front to rebuild the fire and warm up the rice porridge. I force Saengo to finish two full bowls before I'm satisfied.

Then we spend the day as we haven't in ages—talking, foraging, lounging in the weeds and the wildflowers without a single responsibility. We talk about a future after the Dead Wood and the Soulless, one that won't include traveling the world as we intended but that will be ours all the same.

It's not an escape—there's too much at risk to forget about what's happening beyond the Mountain. But it is . . . an interlude. A pause. To breathe. To let Saengo heal. To come to terms with a potential ending that I'm still too cowardly to tell her about.

I take Saengo to the cavern where I spoke with the Spirit of the Mountain. Just as the Mountain hadn't revealed to me what she and Saengo had spoken of, I trust that whatever was said between us will remain that way. Then I leave Saengo there to explore while I hunt our dinner. When the sun begins to set, we return to the temple.

Once darkness descends in earnest, I build a fire in the garden for light, away from the spray of the waterfall. I'm just finishing when my craft senses the abrupt appearance of a soul outside the temple.

When Saengo's head jerks toward the sound of footsteps inside the altar room, I say, "It's Theyen." I call out a greeting, which dies in my throat when he enters the garden.

He's usually immaculate, but his snowy hair is dirty and matted beneath his circlet. His teal robes are edged in dust, and there's a long line of blood splattered across his shoulder. It's red, so at least I know it isn't his—shadowblessed blood is gray. More blood spots his sleeves, and the leather of his boots is mottled, as if slightly melted.

I'm on my feet in an instant, Saengo beside me. "What happened?" I ask, dread a yawning pit in my stomach.

"The Nuvali retaliated for last night's attack," he says. He hands Saengo a rolled bundle of blankets. "More bedding. They're clean."

"Thank you," she says faintly, clutching the blankets to her chest.

"But the Fireborn Queens had nothing to do with that attack," I say. "Are you wounded?"

"I'm fine. The Empire doesn't care which clan attacked them or that the Soulless was responsible for what happened in Princess Kyshia's tent. Their Ember Princess nearly died."

I swear, loudly enough that a bird startles from a nearby tree. The fighting is all so senseless when they should be united against the Soulless. This is what he wants—the kingdoms at each other's throats, destroying one another while he takes out House Yalaeng, unimpeded.

"There's to be a meeting," he continues. "King Meilek requests your presence."

"Why? I'm not his Shadow anymore."

"He said something about not accepting your resignation."

I pass a hand over my face, not sure if I should be grateful or angry. "Of course," I finally say before turning to Saengo. She's already fluttering her hands at me, urging us to hurry.

"Go," she says. "Being alone for a few hours is hardly a grievance."

"I'll be back soon," I say as she pulls me into a quick hug.

Once we're outside the temple, Theyen opens a gate. The darkness closes around us, and I clench my teeth until my temple throbs. My fingers dig into Theyen's arm, which can't be pleasant after he's clearly been through a battle, but he doesn't object. Fortunately, it isn't long before the gate spits us out again. I suck in a lungful of air as Theyen awkwardly pats my back.

We've emerged alongside the Xya River, just outside the sprawl of a military encampment, torchlights blazing into the distance. We're in Kazahyn for sure, on the lower slope of a mountain. Neighboring peaks tower against the horizon like forested giants.

The banners rising over the encampment fly the image of a falcon clutching a plum blossom. It's a little jarring to see the Evewynian flag restored to what it had been before Queen Meilyr's reign. But it's comforting as well, because it's a visible reminder that her reign is ended. It's hope for more changes to come.

Boats are moored all along the riverbank. Evewyn's larger ships are probably docked in Tamsimno, this time as allies. How strange that must be to the shadowblessed living there.

I imagine there must be some resentment, which King Meilek and Theyen will have hopefully smoothed over.

Theyen stalks away toward the encampment, and I follow closely. We're close enough that the perimeter guards must have seen the gate open because they only bow politely at our approach, letting us pass without comment.

"Do you know which clan attacked the Nuvali camp?" I ask as we weave between green and gray tents. Weary soldiers congregate around campfires, eating a quick meal and cleaning their weapons in anticipation of the next battle.

Some soldiers bow or nod at the sight of us. Others turn their backs and pretend not to see.

"The Windcallers," Theyen says. "Not one of our allies."

With more light from the dozens of torches scattered throughout the camp, I take closer stock of his appearance. Dark flecks that are either dirt or dried blood dot his neck and jaw. The red streak across his shoulder has dried stiffly, and the delicate bamboo embroidery along his sleeves is stained and torn.

I grit my teeth in frustration that I wasn't here to help. Surveying the conditions of the camp, I ask, "Where did they attack?"

While the soldiers look weary, the camp itself seems to be in order. It's certainly not the wreckage of the Nuvali camp after the wyverns attack.

"North of here," he says. "This morning."

Meaning once night had broken. Shadowblessed can't use

their crafts during the day, so the ideal time to attack would be just after dawn. I mutter another curse.

Theyen catches my eye. "It wasn't anything we couldn't handle. Even without our crafts, we have our wyverns and our weapons. We're not helpless."

"I didn't say you were," I say, recalling what it had felt like to watch from the deck of Queen Meilyr's ship as dozens of wyverns bore down on us. The shadowblessed make a fearsome enemy, and attacking them during the day was the smart and obvious choice.

"We were fortunate that King Meilek arrived in time to offer assistance," he adds, and his mouth twists into a dark smile. "The Nuvali were surprised to see shamanborn among us."

At this, I look around again with renewed interest. But most of the soldiers sit with their heads bowed over their swords or bowls of cold rice, and it's difficult to pick out the glimmer of jewel-toned eyes in the firelight. I hadn't expected shamanborn to volunteer to fight for Evewyn so soon after being released from the Valley—and they *would* be volunteers. King Meilek would never force conscription on them.

Although I hate that I even think it, part of me worries the shamanborn might be plotting to undermine Evewyn by siding with the Nuvali. While I can hardly fault them for wanting some form of revenge, I hope this isn't the case. I want to trust that they're fighting for their own futures as much as Evewyn's, but as I learned in Mirrim, as King Meilek's

Shadow and a soulrender, I don't always get the luxury of trusting in hope.

"So someone found out the Ember Princess was hiding at the border?" I ask.

Theyen nods. "We've been in communication with the border clans, those we aren't allied with, so that we can at least offer one another support. But one of their spies must have spotted her arrival, because they took the chance to eliminate her without warning the rest of us. The more we fight one another, the more lives lost in this ridiculous conflict, the less chance our kingdoms have of coming to terms."

"I wish I'd been here to help."

"You have your own problems."

"Still—" I cut off when a woman glances up to watch us pass. Her eyes shine blue like cut sapphires. Her mouth falls open and my feet stall, and then I wheel back around to face her. "Kudera?"

"Sirscha!" She rises from where she'd been crouched around a dying fire. She's dressed in Evewynian green, but it isn't a soldier's uniform. "I'd hoped to find you."

"What are you doing here?" I ask, bewildered. "You weren't in the battle, were you?" Kudera isn't a soldier. She couldn't even use a sword when I met her in Vos Gillis.

"Sisters, no," she says, putting up her hands. "We could only enlist if we were King's Company graduates from before our imprisonment. But King Meilek took volunteers for more mundane tasks around camp, so here I am."

Relieved, I feel a bit foolish for not realizing that King Meilek would never allow untrained citizens to go to war. They would be a liability to the trained soldiers of the Royal Army, whether they could use their crafts or not.

"How are the shamanborn getting along here?" I ask. Behind me, Theyen looks impatient, glowering at my detour.

Kudera's eyes flick in his direction, wary, before she answers. "If you mean how are they getting on with the rest of the army, King Meilek has Blades stationed throughout the camp to keep an eye on things, and we're generally kept apart so it hasn't been so bad. But I heard talk among the soldiers that it was nice having craft users on our side in the fight today."

"Let's hope that holds up," I say. "You stay safe, all right?"

"Don't worry about me. I've been practicing with how to use water as an attack ever since, you know, you helped us escape, and I'm getting pretty good."

"You'll have to show me once we're back in Evewyn."

She readily agrees before squeezing my hands in parting. Guilt pricks me for my earlier thought that they might be here to undermine Evewyn. Still, it was tremendously good of them to come so far and fight for a kingdom that had imprisoned or killed their friends and family. I can't say I would have done the same. I only hope that Kudera and the other shamanborn are here because they genuinely want to be and not because they feel they have to prove anything to King Meilek.

No one should have to risk their lives just to prove their right to exist.

Theyen is eager to keep moving once Kudera returns to the fire. "This isn't a social visit," he says.

"That was one of the shamanborn Phaut and I helped to escape from jail in Vos Gillis," I explain.

At this, Theyen's annoyance abates. "And she still chooses to defend Evewyn? That kind of loyalty is hard to come by."

Perhaps, but sometimes, loyalty can be born out of a desperation to belong. Some people will go to great lengths to fill that lack inside them. I should know.

It isn't much farther to King Meilek's tent, which is large and green, with a Blade posted outside at each corner. They acknowledge us with a nod, and a fifth Blade guarding the entrance pulls back the flap for us to enter.

Inside, strung silver lanterns provide ample light for the host of people already standing around a table, although King Meilek isn't among them. I recognize two Kazan leaders—allies of the Fireborn Queens—as well as King Meilek's advisors, all of whom snap to attention at our arrival. They greet Theyen with deep bows, as befits a prince and ally, and then me with cursory nods. For King Meilek's sake, I return the gesture with perfunctory politeness.

Then my gaze falls on a figure seated in the corner, slouched over a stool with her elbows resting on her knees. Heat rises up my neck as I stalk across the tent. Kendara doesn't look up when my shadow falls across her covered eyes.

"Shouldn't you be in the Nuvali camp protecting your princess?" I demand, uncaring of our audience. Let them know that Kendara is a double agent. If she could kill her own crowned prince, then I can't trust that she wouldn't do the same to King Meilek.

Kendara's head tilts, and an infuriating smile twists her mouth. "So becoming Shadow hasn't taught you to be more respectful to your elders."

TWENTY-ONE

"I owe you nothing, least of all respect," I say, lowering my voice only because I've succeeded in drawing the attention of everyone in the tent. While I don't care if they know Kendara can't be trusted, they certainly don't need to overhear any details of what I've been up to. "You stood before me as I nearly died, and you did nothing."

I take in the fading streaks of black through her white hair, the age lines that bracket her mouth, and the strong slope of her shoulders. She's dressed similarly to the last time I'd seen her, in a gray tunic with no distinguishing colors. She looks healthy and hale, and I hate that I'm relieved. I hate that I want her to be okay even after what happened in Mirrim.

"I see it hasn't made you any less dramatic, either," she says.

My nostrils flare as I inhale deeply to control my rising temper.

She leans forward, and her voice is barely audible as she adds, "I warned you about him, idiot girl, but you fell into his trap because you're soft."

"And for that, you would have left me to die?" I hiss furiously.

"I trained you," she says evenly.

I want to scream. It's as much of a compliment as she's capable of giving—she trained me, hence, she trusted that I would be fine. But really, she's only complimenting herself, and it doesn't alleviate my anger as it had been Saengo who saved me.

Since I can't very well keep arguing with her in front of everyone, I say, "Kyshia says you were expected in the Nuvali camp."

She waves a dismissive hand. "I did my part for them. Now, I'm here. And don't get all touchy about me not going to save her. I knew you wouldn't let the Soulless do anything to her. Like I said, you're soft."

"Have you been in touch with King Meilek all this time?" I ask, thinking about her initial message revealing the deaths in Mirrim. Had she continued passing information along to King Meilek in order to even be here? That is, unless King Meilek trusts her so implicitly that he would allow her to be present during this meeting without a full accounting of where she's been all these months.

As usual, Kendara doesn't bother answering me. She only says, "Afraid I'll take back the position of Shadow?"

You're welcome to it. I keep the words in check. Kendara is too good at her job. There's no way to be certain that her muddled loyalties won't put King Meilek in danger.

It surprises me he didn't tell her about my attempt to resign. Does that mean we won't be discussing the fact that I disobeyed him and got myself all but kidnapped by the Soulless? I hope so.

"Don't worry," she continues with a smirk. "King Meilek tells me my former rooms have already been occupied. I'll have to find another vacancy."

Someone pulls back the tent flap, and I turn, dropping into a bow along with everyone else as King Meilek enters. He's accompanied by Kou and Captain Liu. He offers everyone a polite greeting, but at the sight of me, a smile splits his face.

"Your Majesty," I say. Heat rises in my face as unexpected emotion swells within me. When I left Vos Talwyn, I hadn't known whether he would ever smile at me that way again.

"I'm glad to see you're safe," he says, which only makes me feel worse.

While he appears to be unharmed, as did Theyen, he looks battle weary. He's in need of a wash, a comb, and a change of clothes. Dried blood stains his bracers. Has he had a moment of quiet at all today? I'm tempted to take Kou aside and ask him to force King Meilek into taking a hot bath and having a meal.

But right now, the king needs information and level-headed advisors, not a nanny.

He steps back so that he faces everyone in the tent, the smile on his lips fading into something more somber.

"Thank you for coming on such short notice. I'm afraid I bring dire news, which a few of you are already aware of," he says, indicating the Kazan leaders, who pass a look between each other that I don't understand. "The Dead Wood is growing—wildly, swiftly. It's beyond anything I've ever seen."

A flurry of voices rises in alarm. My gaze flies to Theyen. As he doesn't seem surprised, he must have already known and chose to wait for King Meilek to share the news.

"Since when?" asks a woman with brown skin and golden threads in her hair. She's a reiwyn lady from the south near Vos Gillis.

"Since some time before dawn. The falcons began arriving this morning. The trees are devouring everything and everyone in their path. The nearest farms have been evacuated, but it won't be long before they reach villages and towns."

Another wave of panicked voices sweeps through the room before someone asks, "How long do we have?"

"Days. A week, if we can manage to slow them down somehow."

A dull roar fills my ears. This is because of me. By bringing him into my dream last night, I all but told him I had a plan, one I was confident enough about that I would offer him something of an ultimatum. Now, he's chosen to take the offensive rather than wait for me to act against him. He's forcing my hand before I'm ready.

"Sirscha." King Meilek's voice cuts through my thoughts.

My gaze focuses, and I'm taken aback to find everyone watching me. One of his advisors says, "Well? Is it true you can fend off the trees?"

"I . . . yes, but I can't hold off the entire Dead Wood at once." Not by myself.

"Then what good are you?" the advisor snaps, which earns her a cutting look from King Meilek. The woman begins to pace in tight circles, black hair snapping through the air with each turn, but she doesn't say another word.

"Do you know why he's doing this?" one of the Kazan leaders asks me, drawing everyone's attention. "Rumor has it you were in the Nuvali camp last night with the Soulless. Why?"

I raise my chin and meet the Kazan woman's eyes. She's tall and lean, dressed in a fitted tunic with vines sewn into a high collar. A long white braid is coiled into a bun at the nape of her neck. I consider what to say in front of all these people, but I haven't had a chance to discuss what happened with King Meilek. I suppose the simplest answer here is the truth.

"He wanted me to kill the Ember Princess. I refused."

"If that's true, then how did you escape?" she asks, brows arching.

My eyes narrow at the implication. "Because a Kazan clan provided a distraction by attacking the camp. They also provided him a wyvern with which to cross the continent."

She lets out a small, skeptical laugh and turns to King Meilek. "Bringing a soulrender onto your council is brave, Your Majesty."

"Sirscha has my trust," King Meilek says in a manner that doesn't invite argument.

The woman's lip curls. "That doesn't explain why she was with him in the first place."

"I was his prisoner," I say. I don't owe her or anyone else in this tent proof of my loyalties. The only person I have to explain myself to is King Meilek.

"And while you were his prisoner," she says, mocking, "did he say anything about his plans?"

I address King Meilek so that I'm not tempted to tell the woman where she can shove her questions. "Nothing like this. His objective is House Yalaeng. I suppose he's . . . forcing them out of hiding." It sounds like a believable enough reason, and who am I to say it isn't the truth?

"Is there anything else you can tell us that might help, Sirscha?" King Meilek asks.

My chin jerks a little higher when I respond. "He will have returned to Spinner's End to restore his strength. He may be powerful, but he's just like any other shaman who's been away from their familiar for too long." I glance between Theyen and King Meilek, firmly ignoring Kendara in the corner. Her eyes may be covered, but I feel the intensity of her attention. "I thought perhaps confronting him away from the Dead Wood and his source of power would be the wiser choice, but now I think it's best I go while he's still at Spinner's End, before this gets any worse."

The Soulless is waiting for me anyhow. He isn't going anywhere. He has only to perch at the center of his web and await his prey.

King Meilek is silent a moment, and his throat works as he swallows once. Then he nods. Perhaps his thoughts are better suited for when we're alone.

"You said you were his prisoner. How do you mean to stop him now if you couldn't do anything then?" the Kazan woman asks.

"Because I have sunspear armor," I lie, and the shock that flickers across her face is mildly gratifying. "He couldn't touch my soul while I wore it, but he could take other souls hostage and force me to obey him. If I face him at Spinner's End, it'll just be me and him."

She looks me up and down, taking in the dirt stains and wrinkled tunic, the sash that's a little crooked because I hadn't bothered to tie it properly this morning. "And where is this armor?"

"Hidden somewhere safe." I avoid Theyen's narrowed gaze. He's no doubt questioning the veracity of my claim, given that he'd seen me to the Mountain himself and I'd had no such armor with me. But he also doesn't know that I'd discarded all of it when the Soulless attacked Saengo.

"So this is the plan?" an advisor with a round face and wispy beard asks King Meilek while gesturing at me. He slams a palm against the table "We trust this child with defeating a man as ancient as the Dead Wood while the rest of us do nothing but wait?"

Theyen scoffs. "Perhaps *you* mean to do nothing, but we've villages to evacuate and borders to protect in case anyone decides to take advantage of the situation."

The man draws himself up, face turning splotchy with indignation. He sputters a few words, before King Meilek cuts him off.

"Sirscha is the only person on this continent capable of even reaching Spinner's End unscathed," King Meilek says. "And she's right that if we want to avoid more casualties, confronting him while he's isolated is the best choice. Meanwhile, I will return to Evewyn immediately to oversee the relocation efforts. If we can gather some sowers to try and slow down the trees or some earthwenders to carve out a trench and stall them, we might be able to buy Sirscha more time. The shamanborn will remain here to assist in case the Nuvali attack again."

"That should be resolved shortly," Theyen announces, capturing everyone's attention. The bright lanterns strung above cast harsh shadows over their faces. "I've offered the Emperor a deal. There aren't enough soldiers stationed at their western border, certainly not enough to both evacuate whole villages and hold off the Dead Wood, and it will take time they can't afford to move the necessary troops across the entire Empire. So we will take their soldiers there. Gates are the most efficient method of travel. In exchange, the Emperor must sign a new peace treaty."

A tight smile tugs at King Meilek's mouth. I understand his reluctance to believe House Yalaeng would ever agree to work with the Kazan, even to save their own kingdom.

But neither of them knows that the Sun's Heir is dead. And with the recent attack on the Ember Princess, House Yalaeng will be in complete turmoil. An urgent campaign to funnel troops westward—which would take weeks they don't have—in order to defend against a murderous wood is yet another threat on top of everything else. Unless he wishes to see his kingdom torn apart, the Emperor will *have* to agree to Theyen's terms.

They continue to discuss the details a while longer, but I can tell that King Meilek is eager to get moving. When he finally dismisses his advisors and the other leaders, I remain behind, along with Kendara and Theyen.

It's only when his Blades see the last of them out that King Meilek leans over the table, shoulders sagging and head bowed. He rubs a weary hand over his face.

"You need to rest," I say, frowning. "You're no good to anyone if you keel over from exhaustion."

He gives me a dry smile. "I'll be fine. I'll have Kou draw me a bath after this. If nothing else, it'll keep my advisors away for a little while longer."

"It'll also make you stink less," Kendara offers. King Meilek responds with a fond smile. "Have you eaten?" She finally leaves her corner of the tent, reaching out to brush dust off his shoulder. Her hands are weathered, knuckles sharp and palms calloused.

I watch, jaw tight, as she straightens his sash, her fingers running over first the knot and then the length of the ends to ensure they're neat. The envy stings swift and deep. Kendara will return to Evewyn for him, but not for me.

I hate this feeling. I hate that seeing them together only brings into relief how little I mean to her in comparison. Anger and resentment burn up my throat. It's nothing to do with King Meilek—he doesn't deserve to get caught in any of my complicated feelings for her. He's so recently lost his sister, and Kendara has always been more mother to him than mentor. Certainly more than she's been with me.

A hand touches my shoulder. I turn to find Theyen watching me, expression inscrutable.

"If you'd like to leave . . ." he says.

I fix on a smile and shake my head. "How long before you think the Emperor will respond to your offer?"

"The falcon will have reached him by now. If he has any sense, it will be soon."

With Aleng dead, either his advisors will fall in line or they'll seek a new puppet. The Emperor has five other children besides Kyshia, Aleng, and Eren, and any of them could prove a new threat. He should have kept the Ember Princess close, as she's probably the only person he can be certain will have the Empire's best interests at heart.

As Theyen says, if the Emperor has any sense, he'll secure peace with his neighbors before the question of succession starts another war among his children. But if I go to the Mountain now to destroy the Dead Wood, then it might not be enough time to guarantee the Emperor signs that peace treaty. On the other hand, the longer we delay, the more lives are in danger.

"Is Vos Gillis the nearest major city to the Dead Wood? Do you know if they're evacuating?"

"It is, but it's also where the Dead Wood is at its narrowest. The trees haven't stirred much, being so far south. The village in most danger is in the Empire. They have, at the most, four days until the trees reach them."

I consider this. Four days isn't much time, but it's better than nothing.

Theyen tilts his head, his gaze knowing, and says, "You should return to the Mountain and keep Saengo company while she heals. When it's time, I'll come for you."

I shouldn't agree—even if the trees haven't reached a village yet, they're still wildly dangerous.

But Saengo at least will be safe for another few days, and unless we can secure peace for the continent, destroying the Dead Wood now would only give the Empire a clear and straight path to invade Evewyn.

"If the Nuvali attack—"

"We can handle it," he says. "You've got the harder job, I daresay."

Reluctantly, I nod. "But if I'm needed, come for me. I won't use my craft to kill anyone, but I can always scare them a bit."

His mouth twists into a smirk. "I'll bear that in mind."

"Thank you, by the way. I know it's a bother for you to constantly shepherd me across the continent."

He releases a long-suffering sigh. "It is, in fact. I'm not your coachman. So expect your escort to the Dead Wood as the last time I do that for you."

I gently elbow him in the ribs. "It's just so convenient."

Suddenly, his expression shifts, all trace of humor wiped away. "What if it isn't enough?" he asks, frosted lashes fluttering as he briefly closes his eyes. "What if the armor isn't enough to keep out his craft? He'll be in the heart of the Dead Wood, surrounded by thousands of souls feeding him power."

Guilt tugs at my conscience that he doesn't question whether I have the armor at all. Part of me knows that if I tell my friends the truth, they will understand that it's the only way to defeat the Soulless. But why burden them with it? They've already got so much to do, peoples to protect, villages to evacuate, negotiations to conduct.

Learning that I'm not alone has been a long and strange lesson, and I will be forever grateful to them for teaching it to me. But some things I need to carry on my own.

"It's a risk worth taking," I say softly.

"I wish it didn't have to be you," King Meilek says, startling me back a step from Theyen.

"You said it yourself," I say. "I'm the only person who can even get through the Dead Wood to reach him. I'm also the only person he won't kill on sight, and if the armor isn't enough, my craft will be. I won't fail." I smile with as much confidence as I can manage. "Trust me on this."

King Meilek gives me a considering look, weighing my words. "Are you able to use your craft with the armor on?"

"Yes," I say.

Kendara's chin jerks, just the tiniest fraction of movement. After what happened in Mirrim, she knows I'm lying. But because she doesn't call me out on the lie, I forge on.

"The armor only repels attacks. It doesn't inhibit my own."

Before anyone else can question me on the effectiveness of sunspear talismans, I launch into a full account of what happened after Saengo and I left the teahouse with Kyshia. I leave out Kendara's role in Prince Aleng's death, but to my surprise, King Meilek is already aware that it was by her hand—I hadn't expected her to tell him. I suppose that's something.

"I overheard Hlau Theyen's suggestion that you stay on the Mountain with Saengo for now," King Meilek says. He squeezes my shoulder. "I believe in you, Sirscha. You'll get this done."

I nod. Just as I must trust my friends to protect their peoples and restore peace, they must trust me to do my part and defeat the Soulless. They're counting on me. Knowing this gives me the strength to see this through.

But given everything that needs doing, it's unlikely that I will meet King Meilek again before this is over, especially since he's returning to Evewyn. This isn't like when I left Vos

Talwyn with little more than a letter. There is a real chance I won't come back from this. If this is to be the last time we see one another, I need to say goodbye.

"Once the Emperor signs that peace treaty, things will settle down and Evewyn will finally know peace," I say, covering his hand on my shoulder with my own.

He smiles and crosses the tent to retrieve two short swords lying on a desk. "I've no intention of replacing you as my Shadow," he says, handing me the weapons, "so you had best come back alive."

When I step back so that I can bow, he stops me halfway and pulls me into a hug. I stiffen in surprise as his arms circle me. His embrace is strong and sure, and he smells like drakes and sweat. I don't care as I close my eyes and hug him back.

Thank you, I think fiercely. *Thank you for everything.* For nursing my bloodied hands when I was a twelve-year-old nobody trying to prove myself, for trusting me as his Shadow despite my role in his sister's death, and for everything in between . . . *Thank you.*

As he releases me, he says, "It's not too late to just appease him by giving him Princess Kyshia."

I laugh, which earns me a grin. I strap on the swords as I summon up the nerve to turn to Kendara. Even though I'm still unbearably angry with her, I drop into the bow King Meilek hadn't allowed me.

"Thank you for everything you taught me," I say.

Kendara snorts, and for once, I don't resent the reaction.

She has lived a long time, and I can't pretend to understand even half of what she must have seen and done. But I will always value the role she played in my life.

"There are things we need to discuss when this is over," she says, her voice severe. "Don't disgrace me as your mentor by dying."

I smile, cherishing the harsh words, but I don't hug her as I want to. She might knock me off my feet if I try. "I love you, you ill-tempered hag."

Kendara's lips pinch, but she says nothing else. I don't expect her to, but I can tell she still has questions she doesn't want to voice in front of anyone else, not even King Meilek. I wonder if she trusts him the way he trusts her. I wonder if she's ever truly trusted anyone since my mother died protecting Kendara's identity.

Regardless, her questions remain unvoiced. Live or die, our paths have diverged, and I have learned all that I can from her. Now, we can only trust that she trained me well enough to complete my task.

TWENTY-
TWO

"**I**s there some unspoken etiquette about coming and going by gate within an ally's camp?" I ask Theyen as we reach the perimeter of the encampment. "We could have left outside King Meilek's tent. Or inside it for that matter, although I suppose that would be rude."

"What would be rude is if you were to die after all the trouble I went through to save you more than once. I've yet to call in those favors either," he says. "Remember that when you confront the Soulless."

The guilt burrows a little deeper, but I only smile. Then I take his hand, and he pulls me into the gate.

In the oppressive silence, with neither sound nor sight, I thank him as well—for being my friend, for following me into danger more than once, and for helping me even when I neither asked nor deserved it. Theyen might not give his friendship easily, but when he does, it is with his entire self.

I don't know how or why I earned it, but I am humbled by it.

· If I say any of this to him, though, he would probably ask if I'd been possessed.

The darkness recedes as my feet touch solid ground again. We're on the mountain path just outside the temple.

"I'll keep you apprised," Theyen says before he vanishes again into the gate.

Once my stomach settles—I will never get used to traveling that way—I find Saengo asleep in the garden, curled atop a blanket near the pool. With the additional bedding Theyen had brought, we won't have to sleep directly on the ground again. This should be a relief for Saengo, who had whimpered a bit pathetically this morning when she found several bugs tangled in her hair. Her solution had been to jump into the pool and let the waterfall pound against the top of her head.

She stirs when I spread out another blanket beside her before lying down. I rest on my back, my arm pillowed beneath my head, and close my eyes.

"Sirscha," Saengo whispers, her voice barely audible over the rushing of the waterfall. "Tell me what happened."

I do, filling her in on what the meeting was about and what our next steps are. She listens in silence and then reaches out in the dark to grope for my hand. I lace our fingers and squeeze gently.

Four days. That's as much time as we have until the Dead Wood can no longer wait.

As it turns out, I'm only given two days.

Theyen checks in on us the first night, staying only long enough to deposit a sack of clothes and a bamboo basket filled with warm rice in my lap. But on the second night, he arrives immediately after the sun sets. He finds us in the altar room, where Saengo and I are tidying the small space by sweeping the floors and clearing out cobwebs. We've filled the silver tray on the altar with berries, herbs, and freshly washed roots. It's all we could find that might be worth offering.

"Emperor Cedral has agreed to my terms," Theyen says, not even bothering to greet me first. "I will be meeting him outside Mirrim as soon as we're done here to have the papers signed."

I nod and straighten from where I was dragging a damp rag over the base of the altar. I'm relieved and joyful—truly, I am—but I'm also a little disappointed I didn't get one more day. Still, this is what we've been waiting to hear. So long as I do my part and destroy the Dead Wood, there might be true peace on Thiy for the first time since before the Yalaeng Conquest.

"Are you certain it isn't a trap?" I ask. I run my finger along the edge of the altar, satisfied when it comes away clean.

"He agreed to sign after nightfall, and my clanmates have already flown ahead on wyverns. If it's a trap, it would be a poorly laid one."

"It's dangerous for you in the capital," I say. "Even if you're not inside the city walls, it would be easy for them to over-whelm you."

"If we had more time, I would have insisted we meet at the border. As it is, we can't afford to wait for him to travel all the way from Mirrim. This will have to do."

"There are going to be a lot of people unhappy with this alliance," Saengo says. She pauses in her sweeping. The "broom" is really just a branch I stripped and fashioned with thick fronds and grasses at one end. It's rather crude, but I don't think the Mountain will mind.

"There are already a lot of unhappy people," Theyen says. "At least there won't also be a lot of dead ones."

"I pray nothing goes wrong," Saengo says.

Theyen nods. "News of Prince Aleng's death was leaked, and it has led to the discovery of the other deaths House Yalaeng has been keeping quiet. My informant in Luam claims the streets outside the palace and the road into Mirrim have been crowded for days. They're clamoring for answers and action. The last thing the Emperor needs is a village full of dead shamans because he hasn't been able to stop either the Soulless or the Dead Wood. I think he fears the discontent enough that he will make peace where he can."

"Every ruler fears the word 'rebellion,'" I murmur. But in truth, I hope it happens. If I had to guess, Kendara is likely behind the news leaking. Soon, all of House Yalaeng's secrets will be exposed, and the Nuvali will have to decide how to handle that. House Yalaeng needs to be removed from power.

But that isn't something to worry about right now. My concern lies westward, at the heart of a dead forest.

I can't keep stalling. I've a responsibility to my friends. They're doing their part. Now, it's time to do mine.

I toss the rag on the floor beside the altar and offer him a weak smile. "Will you give me ten minutes with Saengo?"

Theyen doesn't answer right away. He regards me, pale eyes searching. "Tell me," he finally says. "If you're so certain you'll succeed, why did you say goodbye to King Meilek and Kendara?"

I try for the usual irreverence between us and roll my eyes. "You know as well as I do that anything could go wrong. Just because I'm confident doesn't mean I'm invulnerable. And if anything happens to me, then Saengo . . ."

He doesn't look convinced, but he says, "Very well. I'll be back in ten minutes."

The moment he's gone, Saengo sets down the broom and wipes her palms on the plain gray robes Theyen had brought us the night before. We pause only to bow before the altar and then we make our way up the mountain path.

There isn't much to say, so we walk in silence. Saengo's flame burns steadily. The rot hasn't receded by much, and I feel her determination even through the fear and nervousness.

Inside the cavern, the moonlight shines brighter than it had the first time the Mountain called me here. Her presence surrounds us. Warm air sifts through our hair and caresses our cheeks, quietly reassuring. We climb the pile of rocks that lead onto the outcropping and listen to the water murmur to the trees. The leaves seem to shiver in response, anticipation vibrating through the stone walls.

"We're ready," Saengo says, clasping our hands between us.

I focus on her candle flame. It's no longer as bright as it once was, but neither is it the sputtering, feeble spark of a few days ago. Saengo rests her forehead to mine, and I breathe in the faint scent of dust and earth, grass and trees.

Then Saengo goes rigid as the Spirit of the Mountain reaches through her to me. I grit my teeth, eyes squeezed shut as the bond between us—already so fragile—is strained near to snapping. The power that floods through nearly splits me in two. Pain sears through my arms, my legs, filling up my chest until I can't think beyond the desperate desire to make it stop.

My back arches, and my legs must have given out because moss cushions my knees. I can't think through the pain, can't see or feel or hear.

If Saengo's soul is a candle flame, then the Spirit of the Mountain is the sun, boundless light and endless heat—scorching, blinding, consuming. I don't realize I'm screaming until warm hands grip my face and Saengo's voice breaks through the haze.

"Sirscha! Sirscha, listen to me."

I force open my lids just enough to glimpse Saengo's face, her eyes bright with tears.

"It's going to be okay," she says. "You can do this. You're strong enough. You're the strongest person I've ever known."

I swallow down another scream and taste blood. It takes all my willpower to focus on Saengo's face, on her palms pressed to my flushed skin. She is my only anchor amid this maelstrom trying to rip me apart.

Then, all at once, the power ebbs. I collapse against her, every muscle in my body burning with exhaustion.

"It's done," Saengo says. "But we have to hurry. You can't stay bonded to the Mountain for very long. It's too much power for your body to handle. You'll burn up."

She helps me stand. I stumble at first and then manage to get my legs and my feet underneath me. When I lift my head to look around, the cavern seems to have transformed. The Mountain's power is a current that flows through every living thing here. Even the wind glimmers like gossamer, strands of moonlight gliding through the air. I sense the roots of the white-barked saplings that tunnel through earth and rock, every leap and surge of the water as it tumbles through the brook.

When the leaves rustle, the Mountain's voice sounds more clearly than I've ever heard her speak. "Go," she urges. "Hurry."

Saengo helps to prop me up by looping my arm around her shoulder as we descend the mossy rocks. Cheerful clusters of red-and-blue-capped mushrooms dot our path, as if leading the way.

"Saengo," I try to say, but she shushes me.

Once we're outside the cave, I force Saengo to wait. I could place a mental window between myself and Saengo when her emotions grew too overwhelming, but that's impossible with the Mountain. Her power is alive, constant, pulsing, raging through my bones and diving into my own magic, wrenching my craft to the fore. It demands to be set loose.

To my surprise, even though it's still dark, I have no trouble seeing the path. Every tree, every blade of grass, every rock and twig and root glimmers with the Mountain's power. She is everywhere and nowhere.

"Saengo," I say again. I nudge her jaw with the slight pressure of my thumb and tug at her collar.

Where the blue veins had been is now smooth, unmarred skin. Nothing remains save for a faint speck of blue at the center of her chest, and once I destroy the Dead Wood, even that will be gone.

"How do you feel?" I ask, relief making the pain more bearable.

"I'm fine. I promise," she says. "In fact, I haven't felt this whole since . . . since before Talon's Teahouse."

I'm grateful she isn't suffering from the Mountain's power. She is only a conduit—a bridge passing one magic to the other.

Smiling, I touch Saengo's pale cheek. "I love you."

Saengo's surprised look instantly tightens into a scowl. "Don't say it like that. You're losing your craft, not your life."

I nod. I don't have the heart to tell her otherwise. "Very well, Lady Phang. Anything you want."

"And don't you forget it."

We're only halfway down the mountain when we meet

Theyen along the path. He's already scowling, so when he spots us, his expression only darkens.

"What were you—" he begins before the state of us fully registers. I'm still leaning heavily on Saengo, although some of the strength has returned to my legs.

"I'm fine," I say, but he's already striding forward and reaching for me.

"What did you do this time?" he demands.

"Wait—" I try to say, but he ignores my protest as he lifts me off my feet. I brace my palm against his chest, wondering if he'd drop me if I struggle. "This isn't necessary."

"Yes, it is," Saengo cuts in firmly.

"Why can I sense your magic?" he asks. He swiftly retraces our steps down the mountain. "I've never been able to do that before."

I sigh and do my best to speak calmly. "I'm ready to return to the Dead Wood."

"Not until you explain."

We reach the temple, where Theyen sets me gently on my feet. I hold up a hand when Saengo tries to support me again. I have to be able to stand on my own.

"Sirscha," he says, impatient.

"I can't explain," I say, wincing. It takes everything I have not to fold under the Mountain's power. "I don't know how much longer I can . . . *contain this*. We have to go. Now."

It must be soon, a voice whispers against my ear like a sigh. Or I'll have burned through my soul, sacrificing my magic and my life, without having accomplished anything at all.

He looks me up and down, lips tight with anger. But when he speaks, his voice is hushed with anguish. "I will not deliver you to your death."

My stomach twists and an ache closes around my throat, but I force a laugh. "Thanks for the confidence."

"This is not funny, Sirscha," he snaps.

"You agreed to do this for me."

"That was before whatever this is," he says, gesturing at me.

"Either we go now, and I destroy the Dead Wood, or you leave me here, and we lose everything."

Theyen glares at me. I glare back. A muscle ticks in his jaw. Finally, he whirls on his heel, stalks away a few paces, and then spins around again, looking thunderous.

"I make the worst decisions when it comes to you!" he shouts.

If there's anything I've learned about friendship through all of this, it's that some will go to lengths unimaginable to many, and considered stupid by others, for their friends. The Bright Sister must have been smiling on me when I became such a friend for Theyen. I *will* repay him someday, whether in this life or the next.

For now, I only say, "Please."

He barks out, "Fine. But whatever you did better work."

"It will."

"Don't worry, Hlau Theyen. It'll be okay," Saengo says with a tight but reassuring smile.

"I'll bring her back," Theyen says to her, looking like he'd rather murder me to save himself the trouble.

She takes my hand and squeezes. "Please be careful."

"Without the Dead Wood, he'll be completely vulnerable. It'll work." Even if I die, so long as the Dead Wood is gone, anyone can handle the Soulless. I won't be needed. "Wait for me."

Saengo nods and releases my hand.

TWENTY-THREE

We make a stop midway across the Empire so that I don't vomit from being in the gate for too long. That happened after he came for me at Spinner's End, and it's not an experience I care to repeat.

The moment we step out of the gate for the second time, gray branches converge on us. Theyen startles and almost pulls me back inside. But I plant my feet and throw up a hand, magic shimmering through the air. The branches disintegrate with barely even a thought.

Slowly, I close my fingers into a fist. Power rises from me like steam—both mine and the Mountain's. Is this what it's like for the Soulless? Every soul within his reach is his to claim without any effort at all? It's frightening and more than a little alluring.

All around us, the trees twitch and turn in constant motion.

The roots writhe beneath earth that ripples and churns like the surface of disturbed water. Overhead, the branches stretch downward, seeking prey, and then jerk away again. Flakes of rotten bark flutter down like ash.

Nearby, a tree groans as the bark splinters open. From within, something barely recognizable as human emerges. Its arms have been crushed against its ribs, and its spine is nearly bent in half. The back of its skull is caved in, and a sheet of matted black hair falls over its face. Since it can't use its arms, the body crawls and slides its way out of the tree until it falls with a wet thud into the dirt.

Theyen curses. "What in the burning inferni is *that*?"

"Where did you bring us?" I ask as a hand with two missing fingers shoves out from another tree, followed by a head with only half a face.

"This is what's left of Sab Hnou," he says.

With this knowledge, I identify scraps of what might have been tent canvas twined around roots. The remains of a building are visible through the seething gray trees. Wooden boards lie splintered and scattered. It must have happened so quickly.

"Then these are what's left of the soldiers who couldn't escape in time."

Theyen's gray skin pales further. With a steadying breath, he turns as yet another tree begins to groan, black sap pouring down the bark as it releases its latest victim in a pile of twitching bone and gristle.

I wouldn't fault Theyen for opening a gate and fleeing.

Instead, he draws his sword. The shadows around us begin to rise, taking on the vague shapes of men with too-long limbs.

"No. You need to go," I say. "I can deal with this on my own."

"How?" he demands as a branch darts forward to rake his cheek. A shadow slices through the wood, but I yank him behind me, anyway.

"I don't really have the best handle on my craft right now," I say, as not just the branch but the whole tree disintegrates into black silt. The lights of souls linger for a breath, hovering like fireflies before they wink out. "I can handle this, but I don't want to hurt you by accident."

Possibly, the only reason I haven't killed him already is because of the modicum of control I discovered while traveling with the Soulless. I've continued practicing these past few nights, but that meager control will soon snap if I don't provide this power a direction and an outlet.

"But they're not . . . They're *people*. They're not trees," he says. The look he gives the bodies dragging themselves toward us is part horror and part pity.

"They're puppets, controlled by the souls trapped here."

His shadows lash out at the encroaching trees while others fan around us like a shield. The bodies claw at the darkness with broken limbs and mindless violence.

"I take it you've dealt with this before," he says, turning so that his back bumps mine.

"More than once."

"That's horrifying."

"Yes, so I'd like to end it. Please leave."

He gives a small disbelieving shake of his head, and a gate opens. "This feels like a bad idea."

"You always say that, but you've an important piece of parchment to sign. I'll be fine."

He sheaths his sword and then turns to face me. "I told Saengo I'd bring you back. Don't make me a liar."

Then he takes a step backward, his eyes not leaving mine as he vanishes into the shadows.

I'm alone with the souls. His shadows slowly dissipate, first losing form and then dissolving like smoke. The trees shiver, bark distended, branches snapping. They are a mass of screaming faces and stinking rot. I've never seen them this way.

While it is wholly unsettling, for the first time since I stepped foot into the Dead Wood with Saengo all those months ago, I am not afraid. The Mountain's power brims within me, desperate to be set loose.

The first body slides through the earth, lips stretched wide behind its hair to reveal a mouth of black and broken teeth. Even though it can no longer quite be called human, its agony is palpable.

Whether it's my heightened awareness or the Mountain's powers, the souls feel more tangible than ever. They are endless, a sea of lights stretching to the horizon, caged by their malice and the Soulless's will.

My fingers flex at my side. Once the Mountain helps me

to unleash the full power of my craft, there will be no going back. I close my eyes and allow myself a moment of stillness. I count my breaths. I listen to the crackle of branches, the slither of the roots, the wet scrape of dead bodies over loose earth. I relish the sensation of air filling my lungs, even if it does stink of decay.

Although I don't need them, my fingers close around the hilts of my swords. The weapons are a reminder of my strength. Well before I awakened my craft, they gave me courage and confidence, carrying my intent in each sharp edge.

I'm ready, I think. The Spirit of the Mountain must hear me, because her magic responds at once, heaving forward, shattering my pitiable idea of control.

I throw my head back, spine arching, every muscle screaming as the Mountain cleaves through me, seizing my magic and scraping every last drop in my soul. Agony razes my limbs. My whole body convulses with it.

The trees nearest me sift away into flakes of ash, leaving only bright specks dwarfed by the glow of my craft. Light fills my vision, emanating from every part of me. I feel like I'm coming apart at the seams. I'm little more than a vessel, too small to contain the power spilling around me into a pool of liquid sunlight. I can't feel the earth beneath my boots or the air in my lungs. I imagine my body unraveling into spools of gold.

For a moment, clarity breaks through the pain—in its purest form, my craft is beautiful. It is pure magic, all the light and life that creates a soul. An entire world cupped within my hands or destroyed with a thought—or restored, as Suri could.

Like a blade, I think, and I unleash all the power within me. My craft ripples outward in golden undulations. The trees instantly still. The waves of my craft grow and stretch, racing farther and farther through the Dead Wood with impossible speed. It is a golden net cast from the grasslands of the north down through the southern tip of the continent—every tree, every soul, snared within my grasp.

My awareness flies through the trees on the wings of my craft. It's almost like soaring on the back of a wyvern, gazing down at an entire city, the impossible spread out beneath me. With the Mountain's guidance, I'm careful to draw back when my craft tries to reach for the souls of the living, those on either side of the Dead Wood still trying in vain to fend off the trees.

There are so many souls, enough to fill cities, possibly even kingdoms. Their voices would drown me if not for the Mountain. She is a constant presence, a hand at my back, propping me up, but with claws that dig and gouge. Her magic burns through my own, too hot and too fast.

When every soul the Dead Wood has ever claimed is within my grasp—every soul the Soulless tethered to his own power—my craft shears through them, a scythe through a field of rice. Each and every soul is cut loose from their moorings.

The air seems to compress around me, as if the very trees are inhaling. Then, the exhale—a great rush of wind, flinging dust into my face, stinging my cheeks and eyes. The branches, the roots, the thick columns of rotting bark—all of it begins to dissolve. Black ash rains down on my head and shoulders. It's as if the night sky is falling down around me.

As I stagger, barely able to lift my head, I see nothing but a barren landscape of dry black earth. The Dead Wood is gone.

I cough, choking on the remains. And still, I don't release the souls from my grip. I can almost make out their voices now, whisper upon whisper waiting for release—begging, demanding, pleading. Ancient fury and infinite sadness.

The power of the Mountain and the power of all these souls shakes through me, and along with them—fear. This will be the last time I feel my craft blazing through me, bright and powerful. Already, the Mountain begins to recede, the depths of my magic reaching its end. A blaze nearly out of fuel.

Now that I am faced with the culmination of my choice, my resolve wavers. Once the Mountain burns through my soul and I am scoured of magic, who will I become? An orphan with no true name and no purpose? The only thing remarkable about me was my craft, and without it . . . I will be nothing once again.

Unless, like the Soulless, while I still have the chance, I bind these souls to mine. Make them my source of magic the way they were for the Soulless. With so much power, I would be ageless and infinite. Impossible to ignore, difficult to kill.

Suri already proved that a soulrender could do great things. I would be Suryali, in truth this time and not just in name.

I would use my power to stabilize, to protect everyone and enforce peace. No more war. No more death.

I'm sacrificing my craft, and possibly my life, to free these souls from the Soulless's torment—don't they owe me that much?

Through the dizzying fog, a voice inside me says, *That would make you no better than the Soulless.* Not quite alive, not quite dead. A monster feeding off the lives of others. Or like Ronin. Peace at the cost of domination.

No, I think. *I would be like Suri. Lauded. Loved. Remembered. But at what cost?*

Hadn't I accepted that I am the only person who can decide my worth? Not my craft, not whether I'm shamanborn, not those who called me Suryali, and not the Soulless.

I was without my craft for far longer than I've had it, and I'll manage fine without it again. I was never nothing.

The pain builds behind my temples, vibrates down my ribs and into my belly. Eyes stinging, I let loose the scream trapped in my throat, and with it, all the souls held in my grasp. My magic burns bright and beautiful and all too quick.

The immense pressure, the heat, and the crushing power release all at once, burned to nothing, like the trees. Dust and ash.

For a moment, peace settles over me. But it doesn't last, and in its wake is a yawning emptiness as bleak as the earth stretching out around me. My bones have been wrung dry. Something wet slides from my nose, slips between my lips, and tastes sharp and warm. I waver on my feet, marveling at how I've been able to remain standing even this long, and then I collapse.

I barely feel it when my cheek strikes the ground. Where Saengo's candle flame had been, there is nothing. The frayed threads of a lost bond. Pressure builds in my chest, and I cough. Blood spatters my chin. Something damp slides from my right ear.

I'm dying. My lungs seize in my chest, strangling my breaths.

But I suppose it's all right. It's a better way to go than most. King Meilek, Theyen, and others can defeat the Soulless without me now. Thiy is safe. Saengo is safe. *Please*, I pray to the Sisters. Let Saengo live a good life and do all the things we'd promised. She will never get her life back, but that doesn't mean she can't still *live*.

Although every part of my body screams in protest, I gingerly roll onto my back so that starlight fills my vision. The moon is clear and bright. This isn't so bad a sight for dying.

Cold spreads through my limbs, chasing away the pain. The darkness deepens around my vision.

As everything goes black, a voice says, "Just like your mother. I knew you'd do something stupidly brave."

TWENTY-FOUR

When I open my eyes, it's to searing sunlight.

The sky is a blue blur, the brightness stabbing my pupils. I try to move and then gasp as pain radiates through my body. The ache in my chest reaches deep beneath my ribs, a wound no medicine can heal. And yet . . . I'm alive.

With a sound that's more whimper than groan, I try to roll onto my side. Then I go still.

Kendara is lying next to me. I blink to focus my vision, wondering if maybe it's a trick of the light or my own delirium, but the sight of her remains. She's on her back, still dressed in the leathers and tunic from the last time I saw her. Her dual swords, which she is rarely without, are strapped at her waist, lightly coated in black dust. She always keeps them looking immaculate. The handkerchief that always covers her eyes is slightly skewed, revealing the edges of burn scars. Her skin, which is darker than mine, has an alarming pallor.

I stare at her for long moments, my mind slow to comprehend. She is quite still. The fear begins as a seed of uncertainty in my stomach and then blooms into vines that wrap around me. Gritting my teeth, I lift one trembling hand. My breaths quicken as my fingers hover beneath her jaw, afraid to touch her or search for a pulse.

Her shoulder spasms. I snatch back my hand and then wince at the sharp stab of pain. Kendara tries to raise her head, but the effort proves too much.

Slowly, I rise onto one elbow. I have to pause for breath before pushing myself into a sitting position. The fear tightens around me, strangling. I have never seen Kendara too weak to move.

"H-How are you here?" I ask. My throat feels raw. "What happened?"

Kendara's head twitches toward my voice. When she tries to lift her hand, I reach out to support her arm, but I'm startled when her fingers seek my face. Holding my breath, I remain frozen as the rough pads of her fingers trace the lines of my face with slow, halting movements—the shape of my mouth, my jaw, the slope of my nose, and my eyes, where the tears gathering against my lashes spill onto her fingertips.

"You look like your mother," Kendara says, her voice thin and hoarse. "I thought you might."

"Kendara." Her name is a broken whisper as I gently adjust her handkerchief over her face.

Before passing out, I might have heard a voice. Given that I was dying, I can't be certain. But I do remember a little of what happened afterward—a yawning darkness and bone-deep chill that had gradually thawed, replaced by a warm glow. It had filled all the places in me that the Mountain had left empty, almost as if returning the light to me . . .

My breath catches. With stiff movements, I bend over her and clasp her hand tightly in mine. For the first time, she doesn't brush away the touch or rebuff my affection. Instead, she smiles.

"You're a light giver," I whisper, horror sweeping through me. "What have you done?"

Kendara's hand is ice cold, her usual bronze skin waxy and pale. Already, what strength she has left is fading, and her hand is limp in mine.

She inhales slowly, as if even breathing is an effort. Her voice is so thin that I have to lower my head to hear her.

Her warm breath washes against my cheek. "Value your own life as much as you value those you're trying to save. Don't throw away the life that both your mothers gave you, fool girl."

A tremor steals over me. Tears spill down my cheeks. The fear closes around my ribs and squeezes. I shake my head.

Kendara—always so strong, able to swing a sword for hours without tiring and scale walls as easily as she can dive from them—goes still. Her hand slides from my grip and doesn't move again.

The grief slams into me before my mind can fully process what's happened. My thoughts are still whirling, grasping for an anchor even as my chest begins to heave. A horrible gasping cry wrenches from my throat. My body folds over, my forehead resting against her shoulder as each sob rips from me, issuing sounds I don't even recognize, sounds I can do nothing to stop.

I don't know how long I remain there, curled over her. The sun beats down on my head. Sweat slides down the back of my neck. My hands rest on Kendara's still chest, waiting for a heartbeat. It's a long while before I can even open my eyes again.

I swallow thickly and then swallow again. It's a little easier the second time, but no less painful.

Get up, I tell myself. *You have to finish this.*

But I can't make my legs obey. There's pain, but there's a bizarre numbness too that makes everything feel distant, like I'm inhabiting someone else's body.

It takes a while longer before I manage to sit up. Kendara would expect me to be strong. She taught me to endure every trial, to meet every challenge. She would want me to set aside my emotions and complete my task. The best way to honor her is to prove she taught me well.

As I make to stand, my gaze falls on the gleaming hilts of Kendara's dual swords. One of them is carved in curling gold filigree, the other silver—Suryali and Nyia, named for the sun and the moon. They're as familiar to me as Kendara, but she never allowed me to touch them.

I remove my shoulder belt with the swords King Meilek had given me. I set them on the ground. Then, chest tight, I carefully unclasp the swords from Kendara's waist. They're surprisingly light but well balanced. My hands tremble, and I fumble with the buckle a few times before securing the belt beneath my sash.

Then, still on my knees, I shuffle backward and bow. My forehead brushes the ground. Black ash clogs my nostrils. It smells of death.

"Thank you for your guidance," I say. Straightening, I wipe my damp cheeks. "I'll come back for you as soon as this is done. Please wait for me."

Wincing, I stand and adjust the swords at my hip. To the east, the remnants of sunflowers litter the earth where the trees tore through them, but in the distance, black gives way to green fields and healthy trees.

Then I turn my gaze westward, toward Spinner's End. The remains of Ronin's soldiers who'd been stationed here lie rotting beneath the sun, and I make a quiet promise to return for them as well.

Straightening my spine, I put one foot in front of the other and tell myself not to look back at Kendara. She'll get a proper burial as soon as I finish with the Soulless.

Although now I don't know what a proper burial would mean to Kendara. Would she want to be put to rest following the funeral rites of the Empire? Or Evewyn's? The ache in my chest intensifies, and I shake away these thoughts. They can wait.

Spinner's End is typically a four-hour walk from Sab Hnou. However, without the danger of the trees, it should be a swifter journey. And yet, the first hour feels like days.

Every step is an effort. The pain that's been overshadowed by my grief is quick to return. My muscles burn. My senses feel muffled and sluggish. My nose and ears have stopped bleeding, but my head spins a little, and the sun doesn't help by scalding the back of my neck.

Even without the trees, the stench of rot remains. If anything ever grows here again, it will take years if not decades for the earth to recover. Or maybe sowers could revive the land—it's said they can make plants grow even in times of drought.

I distract myself with thoughts of what the kingdoms might do with this empty swathe, only occasionally swiping at my cheeks when a tear escapes. I'd never considered a world where Kendara didn't exist somewhere, even if it wasn't with me. She has always existed in my mind as an insurmountable force, resilient and unshakeable, like the Spirit of the Mountain.

How am I going to tell King Meilek?

It suddenly occurs to me that he's lost yet another person he calls family within the span of a few months—and I had a hand in both. The anxiety turns my stomach. I might be sick with it. How can I face him again?

I'll make it up to him, I decide. I will be the best Shadow Evewyn has ever known. I will unearth each and every one of his dissenters, even among the reiwyn, and—

I force myself to halt that line of thought. King Meilek wouldn't want me to serve him out of guilt. That isn't real loyalty or trust. I will simply have to present him with the truth and let him judge me as he sees fit.

I regret every unkind thought I ever had about Kendara, but isn't that the way of things? There's no use feeling bad about it now—it's still true that she had never shown me affection, not in the way I craved it. But I would rather endure Kendara's detachment and her horrendous tasks than this, because exchanging her life for mine is not the demonstration of love I would have ever wanted or asked for.

But this is what she gave me, and all I can do is live with it.

Kendara passed the light of her soul to mine—does that mean she's a part of me now? Should I be able to sense her magic inside me? I slide Nyia free from its sheath. The blade is so smoothly polished that I can make out the reflection of my eyes in the steel, and they're still a vibrant crystalline amber. Should they have gone back to gray now that I'm no longer a shaman? I'm not sure that there's a precedent for this.

Without the obstruction of the trees, Spinner's End appears on the horizon after a couple hours. It is a contradiction of gray stone patched over with white webbing, gracefully swooping roofs, and caved-in towers that were excluded from Ronin's restoration efforts. I squint against the sunlight as I draw nearer, trying to distinguish the tall traceried windows or the jagged remains of a wall along one end of the grounds.

Spinner's End is a relic of an ancient time, as is the person waiting for me there.

Seeing the sprawl of ruins, my footsteps grow stronger and my determination finds new purchase. I can no longer sense souls, but I'm certain he's there. Without the Dead Wood, we are finally on even ground. My body might be the worse for wear after nearly dying, but the Soulless can't be that much better off. So much of his strength came from the souls here. Without them, he will be little more than a shadow. And I am well versed in shadows.

The spines of the bone palisade jut from the earth like ribs. I lift my chin as I pass the remnants of webbing that had once surrounded Spinner's End like a curtain. The scraps of white lie crumpled and tattered, fluttering with the shift of wind. Some of them have gathered around the troll bones, which I gingerly step over as I pass the palisade.

Once, Spinner's End had felt like a spider's web, a lure and a trap. Now, it is a tomb.

Everything is silent. I cross the courtyard, littered with wisps of spider web and stray weapons or buckets from former residents who'd left them there. It's eerie, as if these things are still waiting for their owners to reclaim them.

As I climb the stone steps, I can almost imagine Phaut on my heels, glowering at my back. It plucks at the ache in my chest.

I make my way through once familiar corridors, made foreign by the quiet and a sense of otherworldliness, as if

Spinner's End exists in its own pocket of frozen time. Soon enough, my feet guide me to Ronin's former rooms.

I pass beneath an arched entrance that leads into a closed garden. The flower bushes that once grew here are dead, slumped against one another like corpses and left to decay along with the rest of the castle.

My steps slow, and my boots are silent over the cobblestones. I slide Nyia and Suryali from their sheaths. I don't know how long my strength will hold, but it will have to be enough.

As the path curves around a cluster of trees, the edge of a massive stone throne comes into view along with the hem of dark-gray robes. My pulse quickens.

Squaring my shoulders, I approach. The Soulless is draped over the stone as if he'd fallen asleep and just awakened. His bright amber eyes watch me, his blank expression threading my resolve with unease. The hair around his face has been pulled into a half-knot, the rest of it falling messily around his shoulders. In his right hand, he holds a sword like a scepter, the point of the blade sinking into the earth at his feet.

He looks a bit as he had the first time he appeared in my dreams—weakened and unsteady. His sharp cheekbones emphasize the hollows of his face, which is pale and gaunt. I half expect him to blur at the edges and vanish into vapor, an illusion wrought by the memories here.

But while he remains a very real enemy, his power is gone. I see it in the way he regards me, the blankness behind his eyes.

I lower my swords and pause just out of his reach. He may be vulnerable, but he would also use that to his advantage. I won't be caught off guard.

"How did you do it?" he asks. His voice is a hum on the wind, as if he's already become part of the ruins.

"I made a deal with something more powerful than you." I search inward, but of course, there is nothing—no spark of Saengo's candle, no stirring of my craft beneath my skin, nothing but my own blood and bone.

His eyes narrow, and then a smile slowly stretches his mouth. His shoulders shake with soundless laughter. "The Spirit of the Mountain. How brave. And foolish. No shaman has dared such a feat since Suri, and you survived it."

I shouldn't have survived. I didn't. But that isn't his to know.

"I once tried to make a deal with her," he says.

My brows twitch in surprise. "To avenge your brother?"

"She refused me," he says, without answering my question. "It was just as well. It's no longer a price I would be willing to pay. But you . . ." His smile transforms into a sneer. "Why? You've stripped yourself of everything you could have been. And for what? Why would you reduce yourself to a powerless nothing just to save those who wanted you dead?" He shakes his head in frustration. "I don't understand it. My brother, too, was eager to prove himself to those who didn't deserve his loyalty. *Why?*"

"Because Saengo," I say simply. In truth, I might have done it for Evewyn as well. For King Meilek and Theyen and a peace our kingdoms haven't known for generations. But doing it just for Saengo would have been enough.

There's a complicated look on his face, one I'm too weary to decipher. Perhaps he'd never gotten around to asking his brother the same question. Perhaps he'd simply done what his brother wished, love leading them both to tragic ends.

"Have you considered that maybe your brother wasn't pushing himself and distorting his craft for the Empire? Maybe he did it for you—for a better future for you both. Or maybe he did it only for himself." Because he needed to know he was worth something. Maybe he'd sought glory and validation and all the things I thought I needed to silence the fear inside me. It's foolish, perhaps, but not necessarily wrong.

"I suppose it no longer matters," he murmurs. One pale finger traces the designs on the hilt of his sword. "Whatever the reason, you've chosen House Yalaeng."

"You called me naïve, but for someone who's lived as long as you have, you've a narrow view of the world. It isn't that simple. House Yalaeng will meet their reckoning. But I choose justice, and your way wasn't it."

His head tilts back and he laughs again, soft and humorless. "How quaint."

The Soulless had grown up in a time of war. The Conquest lasted generations until he effectively ended it. It's possible he's never known what true peace is, not well enough for it to become a thing he might want.

"It's not too late." I'm not sure why I bother, but the words spill out of me, anyway. "Return to Evewyn with me. Reveal House Yalaeng's crimes and live to see them paid in full."

"And then what?" he asks, mocking. He slowly rises from his slouch, wincing as if the movement pains him. "Allow your king to execute me?"

I don't know what King Meilek would do, but I imagine it'd have to be something mutually discussed among the continent's leaders. It's very likely they'd want to see him executed or imprisoned—and hasn't he been imprisoned for long enough? He spent the better part of six hundred years in a forced sleep, trapped within his own mind.

I suppose he and Kendara are right—I am soft. Because I understand him. If it were me, I would never allow anyone to return me to a lightless prison.

I would fight to the end. At least that way, I would die on my own terms.

Still, I say, "You will be treated fairly." Perhaps more fairly than he deserves, given how many innocent souls he's taken since his awakening, including those who'd been left here at Spinner's End. They'd been forced to serve him and were then summarily killed when he no longer needed them.

He shakes his head. "I think not." He pushes to his feet, using the sword like a cane for support. "We could have done great things together. We could have shaped the continent to our liking."

"I never wanted that," I say, raising my swords. I only ever wanted to know my own worth. I'm grateful for a family who not only sees it but helps me to see it as well.

Now on his feet, the Soulless straightens to his full height and lifts the sword. "You've won in taking my power, but I simply can't accept an easy death."

"Good." I wouldn't want to kill a man on his knees.

I attack first, swinging one blade and then the other. The Soulless blocks each and then rams his shoulder into mine. I stumble briefly before spinning on my heel and striking with both swords at once, driving him back.

With one foot braced against the throne, he shoves forward again, knocking me sideways. Neither of us are in very good form. His sword is less steady than when we fought last, and mine lack my usual strength. But I draw from whatever reserves I have left, and he must do the same because when he swings his sword again, the blade bites into the throne's arm and shears off a sheaf of stone.

I duck behind the branches, feet dancing to avoid his strikes. As he thrusts for me between the trees, I flip backward, my feet nearly knocking the sword from his grip. He rounds the trees, but I'm ready, using everything in our path to my advantage as I dodge and strike in quick succession. Kendara's voice in my head drives me onward despite the way my muscles burn.

What the Soulless now lacks in precision, he makes up for in ferocity. His sword catches the end of my braid, clipping off a chunk that scatters all over the cobbles. Mine slices his arm, spilling blood down his sleeve. He retaliates with a matching wound along my collar, and the scent of blood fills my nostrils. Even weakened, he is quick and vicious.

But I cannot lose this fight. Every battle before now has been to prepare me for this one. As the Soulless's foot drives into my ribs, I drag the blades of my swords through the rocky earth to keep from falling.

No, not my swords. Kendara's swords. Dual weapons have always been my favorite because even with a shorter reach, they are light and fast. They have always served me best. Kendara's in particular feel as though they were made for me, easy to swing with my already aching arms while sharp and comfortable to maneuver.

One blade follows the other in a perfect dance. The trees are my allies, the uneven cobbles my strength.

I abandon the sword style of Evewyn's armies, first taught to me in the Prince's Company, and shift into Kendara's personal style, which now that I think about it, likely originates in the Empire. It is not a beginner's style, and Kendara only agreed to teach it to me after two years of training with her. It is swift and brutal, elegant but precise, using as few moves as possible to accomplish what it needs.

"Who taught you to fight?" the Soulless asks. He swings with such force that the blade sinks into the bark of a tree. He quickly wrenches it free again, nearly losing a hand to my swords before he darts out of reach. "They must be commended."

"She was Nuvali," I say. She was rude and irreverent and the best sword fighter I've ever known. She deserved to die on her feet with her swords in her hands. "A light giver."

He snorts. "It's been long argued that, aside from our healers, the Order of Light is the most useless."

He dodges again before his blade slices through my sash. How is he still so fast?

"Argued by whom?" I ask. "Warmongers and conquerors?" I wrench off the rest of the fabric and toss it into the dead bushes. I should be able to easily overcome his speed, but my body isn't cooperating.

I can practically hear Saengo's voice in my ear, gently chiding. *"Sirscha. You were basically dead less than a day ago. Don't be so hard on yourself."*

Unfortunately, it doesn't matter whether I've good reason or not. I have to figure out how to get close enough that he can't avoid a blow.

"Precisely, which is why the Temple of Light was so amenable to the Emperor's plans for soulrenders. If proven useful in battle, the Order of Light would become more powerful than any of the others."

"Instead, we became the most feared," I say. I strike out with both swords, but not with any true intention to cut. I need to curb my impatience and study his body language. Kendara always said that when faced with an unfamiliar opponent, the first step is always to learn the way they fight so that you can better anticipate their movements. "But that will change."

"Why?" he asks. "You think killing me will make a difference? A soulrender killing another soulrender that everyone has already deemed impossible to kill? All it will prove is that soulrenders should be feared."

I watch as it happens—he pivots to the side and then bends his knees and strikes. I know in a flash that I won't be able to avoid it. So I clench my teeth and twist, just enough that the sword goes through my shoulder rather than my chest. I hiss as steel tears through blood and muscle, scraping bone. The scent of blood thickens in the musty air.

I drop one sword. The metal strikes the stone with a clang as my fingers close around the Soulless's wrist. Like me, he understands what's happening and that he won't be able to avoid it. He wrenches free, but not before I drive the other sword through his gut. His entire body jerks and then goes very still.

"But I'm not a soulrender anymore," I say through my teeth. Hot blood slides between my fingers and spills over my knuckles.

He staggers backward, face contorting as he pulls himself off the blade. I drop the sword alongside its sister against the cobbles. Then I bite the inside of my cheeks to keep from screaming as I reach for the one still impaled in my shoulder. Before I can think it through, I yank the weapon out.

Fresh blood spills down my tunic. Feet clumsy, I find my discarded sash, wait for the dizziness to pass, and then wind the fabric around my shoulder to try and staunch the flow. The pain is blinding, and my vision goes black for long seconds.

When I blink the courtyard back into focus, the Soulless

has collapsed at the foot of the throne. Both of his hands are pressed to the hole in his stomach.

"You will always be a soulrender," he says thickly. "You will always be what they make of you. Look at us . . . We are not enemies. They made us so." He laughs, a wet, bitter sound. "Together, we could have done so much. Our magic, our souls—they were meant to be shared with one another."

I brace my weight against a tree and shake my head. "I know who I was meant to share my soul with, and she's waiting for me on a mountain."

The Soulless rests his temple against the weathered stone, his breaths quick and uneven. I clutch the tree, willing my strength to hold as I watch his blood saturate his robes. My fingers dig into the bark as his hand slowly unclenches against his wound and his eyes close in exhaustion. I force myself not to look away as his chest goes still and his pale face goes slack.

Then I slowly sink to the earth, too numb to feel much of anything. All that's left is a soul-deep exhaustion.

My breaths come harsh and fast, the only sound in the quiet. If not for the bloody robes, the Soulless looks like he could be sleeping. His face isn't unlike the first time I saw it, behind a prison of webbing, veins vibrantly green like a creature sprung from soil and sunlight. His unkempt hair had wound around his neck like a shawl. He'd been unnervingly beautiful.

"I'm sorry," I whisper to no one. But the words need to be said all the same.

If he'd been given different circumstances, could he have been as great as Suri? If I'd been given different circumstances, could I have become as monstrous as the Soulless?

I ease myself down until my head rests against the cool earth. My shoulder throbs, the pain and exhaustion so consuming that it takes several minutes to realize my whole body is trembling. My eyes burn, so I close them. Something damp slides down my temple.

I'm sorry it had to end this way, but I don't regret it. I did what was necessary—for Saengo, for Thiy, for the souls trapped by his vengeance. But still . . .

"You have not lived in this world long enough to understand what it is to lose everything and everyone that has ever mattered to you."

He'd done terrible things, but he'd endured things just as terrible. The boy he'd been, chasing his brother toward a future neither of them were prepared for, deserved at least a few tears shed for his loss.

"Be at peace," I whisper, for whoever might still be lingering in the ruins of Spinner's End.

TWENTY-FIVE

B y the time sunlight begins to dwindle—perhaps the first full sunset Spinner's End has seen in centuries—I've accepted that I may actually live through this.

Somehow, I find the strength to half-crawl, half-stumble my way to the infirmary. My head spins, so I have to take several breaks to simply grit my teeth and breathe. In truth, I hadn't expected to wake up again after passing out in the garden, not after how much blood I've lost. But it seems the Sisters aren't done with me yet.

My makeshift bandages are soaked through, my movements causing fresh blood to flow and spread down my tunic. Fortunately, the infirmary isn't far and it's well-stocked. A servant with foresight had wrapped the supplies and tools in linen before storing them in the cabinets.

With the promise of seeing Saengo again firmly within

my mind, I fight against the lightheadedness threatening to pull the floor from beneath my feet. Then I somehow manage to find a needle and thread as well as fresh bandages. After an excruciatingly long time, I'm covered in sweat and shaking with pain, but the wounds where the sword entered and exited my shoulder are cleaned, stitched, and wrapped.

Since there's no saving my clothes, I leave them in a bloody heap on the stone floor and wander naked through an enormous larder for anything that hasn't spoiled. Then, chewing on some kind of salt-cured meat, I pull on a servant's tunic I find in a pile of laundry that will never be folded and put away.

My immediate needs met, I make my way with painstaking care to the main courtyard. Groaning, I lower myself to the stone steps where I'd once fought and bested Theyen. That seems like so long ago.

Initially, I'd wondered if I might be able to start making my way back to Kendara, but my minimal efforts have cost me. I'm exhausted and in pain, my skin cold and clammy, and even without a mirror, I'm certain I could pass as some bloody remnant of the Dead Wood. I must be a little delirious because the thought makes me want to laugh.

That's how King Meilek and his soldiers find me sometime later, sprawled across the stone steps and half-conscious. I'm only aware of gloved hands and sturdy arms as someone lifts me, a low familiar voice murmuring soothing words when I moan from the spike of pain.

"Search the castle," says that same voice, which my murky brain finally connects to King Meilek. Then he gently tucks my head against his neck and the cushion of his thick cape.

I'm so tired that I don't fight it. I've done my part. I've completed my task. I've proven myself. The rest can be left to kings and princesses and royal advisors. For the first time in my life—even if only for this brief moment—I'm relieved to be merely a girl with no true name.

"You did well, Sirscha," King Meilek says, voice quiet but rough with emotion. "She would be proud of you."

The view from the southern tower hasn't changed.

Ships speckle the sea, carrying goods or passengers from Byrth to Vos Gillis and beyond. The water is awash in gold and pink, deepening to violet as the stars begin to appear. The air smells sharp and brisk, but the wind is warm, sweeping sea spray over the lip of the roof where I sit. The tiles beneath my palms are crusted with salt.

"Sirscha!"

I lean over the ledge and peer down. Far below, gazing up at me with a look of long suffering, is Theyen. Smiling, I flip neatly over the roof's edge, finding purchase in old bricks and the jut of a window frame. As I descend, I wave through the window at two soldiers playing a game of cards by the light of several candle stubs.

They wave back, well used to the peculiarities of their King's Shadow.

"You're early," I say as I drop to the ground beside Theyen. I brush the brick dust and salt off my palms and then adjust Nyia and Suryali in their sheaths on my back. I roll my shoulder, wincing a little when it twinges. King Meilek found a stitcher to attend to it, but the wound still pains me on occasion. Even in death, the Soulless is determined not to be forgotten.

"And I see you're still keen on hobbies that might kill you," he says. Together, we seek out the path that will return us to the city walls.

"I was just watching the ships. How was the meeting?"

"King Meilek had a few amendments, but he has agreed to most on the proposed list. Invitations will go out next week."

I nod. Thanks to Kendara, with House Yalaeng's secrets exposed, whispers of revolt within the Empire have reached even the walls of Vos Talwyn's Grand Palace. Lest anyone in Evewyn draw inspiration in such whispers, King Meilek's most pressing responsibility—aside from his continuing efforts to reintegrate the shamanborn—is to secure the throne by marrying and producing an heir.

"Good," I say. "A royal marriage will lift everyone's spirits." Of course, that depends on who King Meilek ultimately chooses, but that's a concern for another day.

As we approach the plain metal gate leading back into the city, the sentinels stationed on the wall above announce our arrival. Once inside, I arrange for a falcon to be sent to the palace. As his Shadow, I must always apprise King Meilek of when I leave the kingdom.

With that task complete, Theyen opens a gate and escorts me through. No matter how many times I've done this with him, I still can't get used to it.

We make two stops as we cross the continent. First, the courtyard of Spinner's End to ensure it's remained abandoned. Even thieves would probably hesitate to pillage what had been the seat of the Spider King's domain, but it's always better to be certain.

Fortunately, Spinner's End is as barren as when I left it three weeks ago, but it's especially eerie in the dark. This is a haunted place, filled with the ghosts of memory and tragedy, and I don't know if I want it torn down or rebuilt.

No one has quite decided what to do with it yet, so the great swathe of blackened earth will remain unclaimed until some Scholar digs out the old maps and determines where the three kingdoms' borders once stood. As for the Soulless, with the source of his power gone, his body was able to be burned, and his ashes were scattered as an offering to the Spirit of the Mountain.

Kendara, though, was returned to the Temple of Light. King Meilek and I discussed burying her in Evewyn, but ultimately decided we would be doing so only to appease our own grief. Kendara was Nuvali, but since we didn't know which kingdom she called home, we returned her to the place of her birth. Princess Kyshia gave her ashes a place of honor within the Light Temple tombs.

The next stop is midway through the Empire, somewhere in the midst of a sunflower field west of Luam. Theyen gives me pitying looks as I try to retain the contents of my lunch. Then, hoping the farmer who owns this land won't mind, I snap the thick stem of a single sunflower and we continue on.

At last, we emerge before the entrance of the cave on the Mountain. As I take deep breaths to calm my deprived senses, Theyen makes another derisive sound.

"I'll wait here," he says. "Be quick. Princess Kyshia is expecting us shortly."

"Right," I say, shaking out my arms and legs. While Theyen still protests being my coachman, he doesn't mind stopping at the Mountain to see Saengo when we have meetings in Mirrim. We're to discuss how to make peace with the remaining shadowblessed clans along the Kazahyn border who aren't allied with the Fireborn Queens.

Inside the cavern, a warm breeze sweeps over me, rustling the branches and shaking the leaves in welcome. As water tumbles over stone, I can almost hear a voice murmur hello.

Saengo sits on the outcropping, legs dangling over a spray of saplings. An open book rests in her lap, and a lantern perches at her side. She looks up at the sound of my footsteps, her face brightening.

"Sirscha!" She sets aside her book and drops from the ledge, landing nimbly among the stones. Then she hops over the brook, and she's beside me, throwing her arms around my shoulders. She smells of moonlight and moss.

"How are you getting on?" I ask, glancing over her shoulder.

Because her soul is now bound to the Spirit of the Mountain, she has to return here every week, for at least a few days at a time. She's seemingly made the most of it. She's furnished the cavern with a bed, a desk filled with parchment and ink, an armoire, and a bookcase stuffed to bursting with books and scrolls. The rest of her week is spent either at Falcons Ridge with her family or in Vos Talwyn with me. If King Meilek can spare me, I stay with her when I can.

It isn't an ideal arrangement, but Saengo is happy and alive, which is more than either of us expected to have.

"Perfectly well," she answers. She leads me to the brook, where a wrought iron bench rests along the stony bank beside a white-barked sapling.

A gentle breeze tugs at my braid, playful and warm. It feels like a hello.

"Saengo, tell me your father isn't making you go over ledgers while you're here," I say, spying the bounty of scrolls and papers piled atop her desk.

Taking a seat on the bench, she clasps her hands primly in her lap and says, "He isn't making me do anything. I asked to help. And it's much easier to focus on work when my only companion is a mountain."

"Is she good company then?" I ask, settling beside her. The iron bench is warm, the heat seeping through my clothes.

"We have interesting conversations to be sure. She thinks that once we've been bonded for longer, I might be able to stay away for greater periods of time. Maybe even a week or two."

Beaming, I say, "That's wonderful! It'll challenge us to plan excursions that are particularly efficient. *Without* Theyen's help, because if I ask him again, he might actually toss me into a gate and leave me there."

"I somehow doubt that."

"That's because he's decent to you. But we should start making a list of all the places to visit." It's a marvel that we can even do this, that we can plan a future together.

Another breeze whispers against my cheek before sweeping through the sapling. Its leaves rustle, like happy laughter. I turn my face to the sunlight streaming in from the opening overhead and close my eyes, smiling back.

"Sirscha?"

There's an odd note to her voice, and I open my eyes to regard her. "Hmm?"

Her head tilts. "Can you still hear the Mountain?"

"Not in words," I say, trailing my fingers against the warm iron. "But I get . . . impressions, I suppose." When Saengo's only response is to arch her brows, I ask, "Is that not normal?"

The trees shake again, leaves fluttering in quiet susurrations. Saengo is still, listening.

"She's speaking to you, isn't she?" I ask, trying to discern words from the shifting wind and the splashing brook. I can *almost* hear it, a voice that isn't quite a voice.

"She says . . . only lightwenders should be able to hear her voice."

I blink at her, uncertain how to take this news. Does that mean I'm still a shaman? When Kendara traded her life for mine, had she reignited the spark of my craft? I never thought to question whether some ember of my magic might yet remain, so I hadn't considered trying to bond with another familiar to test it.

A leaf shakes loose from the sapling, spinning lazily downward until it cascades down my forearm, like a caress. I catch the leaf between my thumb and forefinger. Sadness brushes against my senses—loss, like this leaf that will never again be bound to its branch, but there is hope as well, a new bud to take its place.

She's trying to tell me something, and I think I understand. I will never be as powerful as I once was, certainly not enough to rip a human soul. But I can accept that, and perhaps one day, when I'm ready, when my grief has diminished to a dull ache and I've grown comfortable with the path I've taken, I will bond with a new familiar and rediscover my magic without fear or expectation. It's a future I'm excited to wait for.

ACKNOWLEDGMENTS

I began the first draft of *Forest of Souls* in 2014. It feels rather poetic that ten years later, in 2024, I'm saying goodbye to this world. It's bittersweet, but I am ready and comforted to know that I'm leaving these characters in the capable hands of readers.

I owe eternal gratitude to a host of amazing people, without whom Sirscha's story would not exist:

Suzie Townsend, always an anchor in tumultuous waters.

Ashley Hearn, whose love and enthusiasm for Sirscha and Saengo's friendship were vital to uncovering the heart of their journey.

Lauren Knowles, who is the embodiment of patience and grace, and to whom I owe so many apologies for how long it took to finish this book.

Lauren Cepero, Laura Benton, and the whole Page Street team who've left indelible marks not only on these books but also on me. Thank you for being the very best home Sirscha could have found and for always making me feel welcome at every stage of the process. Also, thank you to Charlie Bowater for painting the covers of my dreams.

The readers who never stopped waiting for the conclusion to Sirscha's story: You'll never know how much that means to me, or how it kept me motivated during a difficult time.

My Fellowship—Lyn, Patricia, Audrey, Myra, Imaan, and Em—who makes every day better: You guys don't know how grateful I am for you.

My family, for indulging my love of reading and writing and never yelling at me every time I blithely signed up for another monthly book subscription my mom would then have to cancel. Sorry, Mom.

And, of course, you, dear reader, for opening this book and spending time in its pages. Thank you, thank you, and I hope to see you again in our next adventure!

ABOUT THE AUTHOR

Lori M. Lee is the award winning author of young adult and middle grade novels. Her books include *Forest of Souls*, *Broken Web*, *Pahua and the Soul Stealer*, *Gates of Thread and Stone* and more. She's also a contributor to the anthologies *A Thousand Beginnings and Endings* and *Color Outside the Lines*. She considers herself a unicorn aficionado, enjoys bingeing anime and Asian dramas, and loves to write about magic, manipulation, and family.